Easier
Dead
Than
Drawn

Easier Dead Than Drawn

A PAINT BY MURDER
MYSTERY

Bailee Abbott

LEVEL
BEST BOOKS

Author Photo Credit: Kathryn Long

First edition

ISBN: 978-1-68512-633-9

Cover art by Level Best Designs

This book was professionally typeset on Reedsy.
Find out more at reedsy.com

To wall muralist, Ruston Baker, who inspired me to write this story. 1958 - 2023

Praise for the Paint by Murder Mysteries

For #1 – *A BRUSH WITH MURDER*:

"Plenty of local color blends with romance, an intrepid detective, and a tricky mystery."—*Kirkus Reviews*

"Bailee Abbott paints a charming lakeside town filled with colorful suspects and an unexpected protagonist in artist Chloe in her new novel *A Brush with Murder*."—Sherry Harris, Agatha Award-nominated author of the Sarah Winston Garage Sale mysteries

For #2 – *KILL THEM WITH CANVAS*:

"The Abbington sisters continue to display a talent for art and murder…with pleasant characters and a light romantic touch."—*Kirkus Reviews*

"Beautifully constructed and original 'whodunnit'."—*Midwest Book Review*

Chapter One

"**M**ove it a couple of feet to the left!" Miles Terrell waved his arms like a cop directing traffic while the crew in motorboats glided the floating amphitheater to a position he would accept. Sweat trickled down their foreheads, even though the May temperature was barely in the sixties, and a cool breeze rippled across the lake water to give some relief. One crew member heaved his chest and drew out a lengthy sigh as he lifted his hat and raked fingers through his hair.

Reaching in my pocket, I pulled out a baggie containing the quinoa muffin Mom had insisted I take with me this morning as I hurried out. She'd frowned and scolded that breakfast was important to everyone's nutrition. I sighed. Moms never changed, even when their children reached adulthood.

I glanced over at Izzie, who wrinkled her face as she bit into her muffin. "Better not throw that away. Moms possess psychic powers. She knows our every move."

Izzie rolled her eyes and wiped a brown curl from her face. "Chloe Abbington, who are you trying to fool? Besides, as long as Dad loves her quinoa recipes, I think we're fine."

"Or does he?" I wiggled my finger in her face. "Sometimes I think he knows how we feel and puts on this act to cover up. Anyway, Mom's motive is to keep her family healthy. Nothing wrong with that. Hey!" I snapped my fingers and pointed. "From the look on his face, I think Miles and the crew finally got it right."

Miles formed a plump-cheeked grin. With two thumbs up, he gestured to the men and shouted. In unison, the boat crew fist-bumped a victory

1

salute. Several hopped off shore and in the water with their equipment to anchor the amphitheater while the rest revved up engines and motored across Chautauqua Lake to dock their boats on the opposite shore.

Besides Izzie and me, a crowd of people had gathered. They either grouped together on the ground or took up the empty spaces on park benches. They sipped coffee and munched on breakfast while holding up their cell phones to take snapshots and videos of the unusual spectacle. After all, the return of the floating amphitheater to Whisper Cove was a big deal.

Several years ago, our town had lost the attraction to Mayville, a small lakeside town north of here. The town treasurer's report stated our account was bleeding money to pay for keeping the theater in Whisper Cove, and soon we'd be in the red. No one understood how that could happen, but the town council believed the treasurer's prediction. Of course, the sad part was that, along with the theater, we lost the music concerts to entertain us and the money visitors would spend.

Now, thanks to Miles, we could celebrate victory. He had assured the council his proposal would turn a profit. The marketing plan he presented had wooed the members, and the bid to return the amphitheater to Whisper Cove had been set in motion. Of course, offering to invest a generous portion of his own money in the project helped sway votes. As for the business community, plenty of merchants were happy and excited, anticipating how events would bring back those fans who loved to peruse the shops and spend their cash. Unfortunately, not everyone felt the same way. The town meetings resounded with complaints. The theater's return meant an increase in noise and traffic, something many in our peaceful community didn't want.

"Can't please everyone," I mumbled.

"What was that?" Izzie wrinkled her brow as she stared at me.

"I was thinking about how the town is so divided. Not everyone is pleased with this." I pointed at the amphitheater.

"It'll get worse, I'm afraid. Did you hear some folks are organizing a protest walk? I know Rita Morgan is one of them. When we ran into each other at For Sweet's Sake the other morning, I tried to start a conversation, but she glared at me and walked out of the shop without a word."

"I guess my suggestion to hire Lana to paint the mural hasn't helped win friends or, as in Rita's case, keep all the ones we have," I said.

Lana Easton and I had a long history. We'd met while living in Paris to study art. We'd roomed together in a small apartment near the artists' district of Montmartre for two years. When we returned to the states, we got together at least twice a week. Of course, those twice-a-week meetings dwindled to once a month as soon as the exclusive circle of talented artists in Manhattan, the ones who were treated like royalty in the art community, lured her away while I remained an unknown, working at an art supply store and struggling to get my work showcased in one of the posh art galleries. Eventually, I moved home to Whisper Cove and became a partner with Izzie in the paint party business. We hadn't spoken since last summer when I called to say I was moving and to give her my new address, until I recently contacted her about the mural painting gig.

"Doesn't matter. Lana is such a talent. Her mural paintings are in every part of the world, on buildings, in palaces, and museums even. We're lucky to have her. Rita should know that. She's an artist too." Izzie plucked a wildflower from the ground and sniffed the pedals.

"Which is why she's upset. I thought she would blow her top when the town council announced Lana got the job. Rita was desperate to paint the mural."

"Her ticket to fame, or some other nonsense she keeps spouting." Izzie shook her head.

"I don't blame her. I just wish she'd come to accept the decision and then work on something that makes her happy." I stood and brushed off the pine needles stuck to my jeans. "You ready? Lana texted she and Nick should be arriving at the house by noon."

Nick Poling was Lana's significant other. She hadn't gone into the details of their relationship, only that they'd been dating a while, and he would be tagging along on this trip.

The sun peeked from behind an otherwise mostly cloudy sky. I glimpsed the lake water that sparkled with the rays of light. In the distance, a kayak bobbed in rhythm with the waves caused by a small speedboat racing by. Whisper Cove was the perfect place to live, if you loved any kind of water sports. Boating, swimming, skiing, and fishing kept residents and vacationers entertained during the warmer months. When winter brought the snow to western New York, folks traveled to places like Ellicottville, the home of several ski resorts. While the temperatures dropped and the snow fell, shop owners here in town shortened their hours. It was like Whisper Cove hibernated, waiting for the first spring bloom when it would awaken for another busy season.

It was a short walk from the park to home. Our town had one main road. Whisper Cove Boulevard ran north to south, where it ended at the ferry dock. The ferry, a favorite attraction for tourists as well as locals, took cars and passengers back and forth across the lake from Whisper Cove to Stow. A turn left at the last intersection of the boulevard put you on our street, Sail Shore Drive. If, instead, you traveled to the right, that led to Artisan Alley.

Our shop, a cute bungalow painted canary yellow with a huge picture window in the front and situated on the corner, was followed by a string of craft businesses that skirted Chautauqua Lake. With clever names like Go Fly a Kite, Light Your Scent, and The Healing Touch, customers couldn't help being curious enough to take a peek inside and maybe buy a souvenir or two.

We passed Millie's Diner on the corner. Out front, a billboard sign listed today's specials. When the light changed, we turned onto our street.

"Let's not bring up the protesters, okay?" I stared anxiously at Izzie.

Lana had what I called artistic sensitivity. She didn't take well to criticism, and, at times, Izzie could be a little too honest with her comments. Her heart was in the right place. I knew my sister better than anyone. We were only a year apart. On the plus side, her behavior had improved in recent months. Mom persuaded her to take yoga classes to relax and find her Zen mood, or whatever it was called. I had no clue. Contrary to Izzie's type-A personality with her over-planning and obsessive stressing over the tiniest detail, I was the impulsive, fly-by-the-seat-of-your-pants kind of woman. If I failed at something, I brushed it off and moved on. Or at least the majority of the time I did.

Even our appearances were the opposite. She had the runway model build and the most beautiful long and wavy brown hair. I styled my black hair in a straight, short bob, and my petite, curvy body looked almost clumsy and awkward next to hers.

"Why would I bring up the protesters? We want Lana to feel confident and think she has the town's total support." Izzie bit her lip. "Besides, she'll find out soon enough when they parade in front of the park and shout whatever people like that do. Right?"

I sighed. "I guess she will." I traveled the sidewalk to our front porch. With any luck, the protesters would lose interest in their cause. Otherwise, I worried how their behavior could provoke even more trouble.

"You know, I think that wedding invitation has put a downer in your mood. Where's the upbeat sister I've gotten used to?"

I shrugged and threw open the door. Ross had been my roommate and boyfriend while I lived in New York. My patience had withered as he spent more and more time at work, practicing law and less time on our relationship. I could understand his job was important, but filling his downtime with the guys to play poker, attending basketball and football games, and less with me wasn't acceptable. I'd broken off the relationship when I returned home. Of course, he tried to fix our problems by coming to Whisper Cove. Even so, I just couldn't see us working.

Now, he was getting married. Something I hadn't considered would happen, and I was knocked off balance. At least I had time to consider whether to RSVP yes or no. I gave him credit for calling ahead and asking if I'd be okay with the invitation. His fiancée seemed fine with the idea, which meant she had lots of confidence in their relationship. Put in her situation, I didn't know if I could be that generous.

"Don't be ridiculous. I'm fine with him getting married. In fact, I'm relieved. Having him show up here unexpectedly again would be too much." I marched upstairs.

Izzie kept pace. "You shouldn't feel like it was your fault. Relationships are hard and complicated and—"

"Izzie." I swiveled on the top step, almost causing her to fall backward. My voice edged, but with one deep breath, I grew calm. "Please don't. Talking about him or our relationship is not what I need to focus on right now."

"You're absolutely right. I'm sorry. I just worry about you and…" Her eyes teared.

I grabbed her arms, then pulled her up the last two steps before planting a kiss on her cheek. "Thank you. Now, let's shower and change before Lana arrives."

"Right again. A shower to wash off all this pine pollen and sweat will do the trick," Izzie followed me down the hall.

I settled into a chair across from Lana who sat next to Nick on the family room sofa. Izzie was helping Mom in the kitchen with lunch preparation.

"Did you have a nice trip? I hope the construction work outside of town didn't cause you any problems." I stroked Max's fur while he slept in my lap. My canine buddy always gave me comfort and kept me calm. He was doing that right now, just by being here. My gaze strayed for a moment to study Lana's boyfriend. His jaw muscles twitched as if he felt tense, and also rather distant as he kept his eyes on anything but me or Lana. His broad shoulders and tall, athletic frame towered over Lana's small figure. The thick dark hair, chiseled face, and piercing blue eyes would easily attract women. Yet, the two of them didn't act like a couple who were in love.

Lana teetered her hand. "Not too much. Just one detour, then we were back on the main route." She rubbed the front of her neck. "Nick, why don't you go to the kitchen and get me a refill? My throat feels like sandpaper." Holding out her tea glass, she lifted the corners of her mouth into a stiff smile.

"Not a problem." He smacked his thighs, grabbed the glass, and stood. Without another word, he headed to the hallway.

I bit down on my lip. "Is everything okay? You seem kind of…uneasy." Even though it had been a year and a half since we'd last been together, I was shocked at how worn out she looked. The normal pink glow of her face had paled to a pasty white. The shiny, thick hair she'd been so proud of appeared dull and limp. I would even bet she'd lost several pounds. Not a good look for her already thin frame. How long had she been this way, I wondered.

She covered her mouth to stifle a yawn. "Tired, I guess. The project in Finland took longer than planned because of the lousy weather. We just got back last night. No time to rest."

"I see." I paused, giving my next words some thought. I hated to pry into what wasn't my business. "How long have you been seeing Nick? He seems nice." *Not* the question I wanted to ask.

She and Nick acted like they were ready to put on gloves and spar, and that made me feel uncomfortable. We used to talk openly about everything, but that was when we were close.

"Give me a second. I want to say this right." She tapped her lip. "How about almost ten months, but it feels like ten years?" A grin surfaced, and she laughed. "Just kidding. What about you, Chloe? Someone special in your life?"

Before I could answer, Nick returned with two glasses of iced tea, followed by Izzie and Mom who carried bowls of chips and salsa and a tray of sandwiches.

"If it didn't look like rain was coming any minute, I'd suggest taking our food out to the patio." Mom's auburn red tresses were woven into a thick braid that hung over one shoulder. A denim jacket covered her turquoise shirt and matched her faded jeans. Kate Abbington was a throwback to the sixties. The only details missing that would've made the look complete were a headband and hippy beads.

"We're fine in here, Mom. Thanks for making this. Izzie and I will fix dinner this evening. How about tacos?" I put Max on the floor and took the tray out of Mom's hands then set it on the coffee table.

She waved her arm. "Don't worry about that. Your dad is bringing home a pasta dish from the Blue Whale. He and a couple of friends are eating lunch there," Mom snatched her bag from the hall coat rack. "Meanwhile, I'm going to pop next door and chat with Joanna. You kids have fun!"

I grinned. Joe Abbington catered to his wife's every need. It was as if he read her mind and knew exactly what she wanted. They were the perfect match. Even if he was inches shorter than Mom's willowy height, and his dark hair contrasted with her auburn locks and fair skin, their personalities clicked.

"Nick, would you call Audrey and see how far from Whisper Cove she and Tate are? They should be at the hotel by now. I don't understand why they haven't contacted me." Lana removed the top bun of her sandwich and picked at the almond and grape chicken salad.

"Sure thing. Excuse me, ladies." Without giving her a glance, he walked out of the room.

I chomped on a generous bite of my sandwich and shifted my gaze from Lana to Izzie, who raised her brows and shrugged.

"Are Audrey and Tate part of your team?" Izzie took over the conversation.

Lana dabbed her lips with a napkin. "Yes. Audrey is my assistant. Interning for me brought her to the States. Not your typical Parisian snob, thank goodness. What really sold me is how talented an artist she is, probably more talented than anyone I've known, especially at that young age. But don't tell her I said so." Lana chuckled. "No room for inflated egos on my payroll. As for Tate, he's my tech guy. He creates computer grids for my projects. Those keep me from making huge mistakes that would waste valuable time. He's pure genius."

"Does Nick work on anything? I mean, I wasn't sure if..." Izzie blushed.

"You mean besides being my boyfriend?" Lana winked. "It's okay. Don't be embarrassed. Nick's actually quite good at keeping my website up to date. He videotapes me as I work. Believe it or not, I get millions of viewers on YouTube. People love to watch how murals are created."

"That is so cool. I'll have to check them out." Izzie tapped the keys on her phone. After a few seconds, she looked my way. "We should do something like that. You know, maybe film one of our events to show how much fun our guests are having. Who knows? It could help us get more business."

"It totally would." The healthy glow on Lana's face returned for a moment, and a smile brightened her eyes. "I'll get Nick to help you set that up. Maybe he can film one of your events while we're in town." Lana set her plate aside, the sandwich barely touched.

"Great! Thank you." Izzie squeezed her napkin. Nothing excited her more than discussing ways to promote the shop. Of course, her new friend Brody could make her heart race, too.

Nick walked into the family room and sat back down. "They just arrived in town. We should go over to the hotel and meet them, don't you think?" Glancing at Lana's plate, he picked up the sandwich and finished it in three bites.

Lana stood and stepped closer to give me a hug. "I'm so glad to be here and spend time with you. It's been too long," she whispered.

"Me too. Hey, I almost forgot. In two weeks, the town has this thing it does at the end of May. A big event held at the casino. There's dancing, of course, and gambling to raise money for charity, and so much food. The town council agreed to invite you all as our guests of honor. I hope you'll stick around and come." I prayed I didn't sound too anxious.

"Sure! Sounds like fun." She tapped her watch. "We really should go and meet the others. I need to check into our room and take a long nap."

"Absolutely." I squeezed her arm. "We can meet up tomorrow and show you where the mural is going to be placed. Miles Terrell—he's the producer, manager, and financier of everything that has to do with the amphitheater—he'll be there. He's always there, actually." I stopped and took a step back. "Anyway, call me in the morning when you get up. We'll discuss details then."

I waved goodbye at the doorway as they headed to their car then turned to face Izzie. "Well, that wasn't too bad."

"You mean besides the awkwardness between Lana and Nick? Yeah, I guess. I still don't understand why they didn't agree to stay here instead of the hotel. I mean, the hotel is nice, but come on." Izzie swiveled with arms outstretched and palms up. "This is like paradise in comparison."

"You heard her." I carried plates to the kitchen while Izzie followed with the tray and bowls. "She wants to be close by Audrey and Tate to discuss the project whenever she needs to."

"If you say so." She pulled her phone out of one pocket and wiggled it. "A call or text seems just as easy. Plus, the hotel is like, what? Five minutes away."

"Hey, it's not our decision. Now, are we heading to the shop?" We had a paint party scheduled for this evening. A tour bus of seniors chose our business as one of their stops. They were visiting the National Comedy Center in Jamestown this afternoon and wanted to top off their day painting and sipping wine.

"Willow offered to set up, and she's already finished the step-by-step sketches for instruction. If she needs help, she'll call. We have an hour to relax a bit and change before heading over."

"The guest list—"

Izzie interrupted. "I checked our website while at the park. Every seat is filled. I even called our contact for the tour group while I was helping Mom in the kitchen and made sure the group would be at the event on time. Anything else?" She raised her chin.

I pointed. "What about the flyer for our summer events? Will we have them in time for the winery gig?"

She anchored her fists on her hips. "Wow. Talk about switching roles. Worrying about those details is my thing. The flyer mockup is at the printer's. I dropped it off last week, or did you forget?"

I loaded the dishwasher and sighed. "Sorry. Guess I've been too distracted thinking about this mural painting." My suggestion to the council to hire Lana had me worried enough. Seeing my friend in that worn-out state this afternoon certainly didn't help to calm me.

Izzie rubbed my arm and chuckled. "Look, I worry enough for the both of us, so you don't have to. Right? Now, I'm going upstairs to shower, then call Brody. He's supposed to come down tomorrow with Rex."

Brody Lawson came into our lives last fall when his dog Rex ran away. We'd found the frightened pooch hiding in a storage shed next to the ferry. Max had been thrilled to have a full-time play pal, but as good situations sometimes come to an end, Brody showed up, and Rex left with his owner. In the perfect plot twist, all worked out because Brody and Izzie became an item. Ever since, Max saw Rex at least twice a week, whenever Brody came to visit.

I filled Max's bowl and whistled. In seconds, the white ball of fur skidded into the kitchen with tail wagging. He bounced up and down, trying to reach my hands. I laughed and set the dish next to him. At once, he buried his face in the mound of kibble. "I swear I don't understand how your twelve-pound body can consume so much food and not gain an ounce."

Leaving him to his meal, I turned to stare out of the kitchen window. Drops of rain pinged as they hit the glass. Izzie was right. My friends reunion didn't go as I expected, but after what had happened in New York, how could meeting face-to-face again be easy? Lana had mostly shut me out and found new people to hang out with. I'd felt like an old car traded in for a new and shinier model.

I shifted to lean against the counter. None of that mattered because I was on her side. Always. Deep down, underneath all that fame and time she spent with the art world's elite, was the same shy girl I'd met a few years ago in Paris. The one who had friended me when I'd been a stranger in a strange place. We'd forged a strong bond that I couldn't or wouldn't break just because some snobby artists snatched her from my life.

Still, I had to admit the truth. Being lured away by snobby artists wasn't the real issue that tore us apart. She'd done something much worse to destroy my trust, but I didn't like to think about it because remembering made me hurt all over again. I had to remind myself the incident wasn't the act of the Lana I'd known. I guessed fame could do that. Change you in ways that weren't so nice.

And now? What worried me now was seeing her worn down and obviously unhappy. Almost a ghost of herself. My instinct told me she needed help. What that help consisted of, I didn't know, but I was determined to find out.

Chapter Two

Willow arranged the three canvases on the wall. Each one showed stages of the painting for our next event at Tasty Spirits winery. She always suggested ideas that made our events better. Before responding to Izzie's job ad and arriving in Whisper Cove, she'd worked with kids on all sorts of art projects. During the interview, Izzie recognized her talent at once and hired her on the spot. Being only twenty-one, Willow was a natural, having had no formal training. The innocence of her dimpled pixie face contrasted with the pink and green spiked hair and several piercings that signified her tough attitude. No one would ever guess she came from one of New York's wealthiest families. Refusing to be a part of what she called her greedy capitalist parents, she rebelled and severed ties with them, both physically and financially.

"What do you think?" She hopped down from the ladder.

Izzie studied the images, then finally smiled. "Perfect, as usual."

"Great." She slapped large sticky notes to each canvas. They listed how-to instructions for guests to follow, in case they got behind in their painting and the three of us were busy helping others.

With fists anchored to my hips, I took a deep breath. Monday morning and the start to a new week filled me with hope. I glanced around the shop. For many decades this building was a two-room cottage, rented out to vacationers. When a clever entrepreneur had the brilliant idea to turn Artisan Alley into a shopping experience with various craft shops, all the rentals were remodeled and transformed into businesses. As expected, the genius idea became a financial success, and those craft shops added to the tourist attractions in Whisper Cove. Even locals enjoyed shopping here on a regular basis.

However, I had to give Izzie credit for the layout and design to make this the perfect paint party shop. Three rows of tables set up with easel stands and cupholders provided enough stations to seat thirty customers. At the far end of the room was a small platform stage. A huge projector screen hung on the wall to give everyone a clear view of the drawing progress during our instruction. Painted canvases decorated the walls with images of various subjects we switched out at least once a week to showcase our guests' work. Themes for the holidays were favorite choices. Pumpkins at Halloween, snowmen at Christmas, and fireworks on the fourth were only a few displayed. Izzie had planned down to the tiniest detail. We had hair dryers dangling from hooks for guests to dry their canvases before leaving. Nothing worse than staining your car upholstery with paint.

"When are we meeting Lana at the park?" Izzie added more bookmarks and brush sets to the counter display.

I entered the event scheduled for late August named Gone with the Wind and its description into the computer. Gwen Finch, who owned the shop next door, would be teaming up with us by showing guests how to make a kite while we instructed them to paint one. Whenever we could, each of the craft shop owners helped the others to promote business. It was a win-win opportunity for all of us. Even Claire sometimes brought goodies from For Sweet's Sake, and Bob from Bob's Barbecue Pit offered to sell guests delicious sandwiches from his barbecue business, along with providing free beverages. His Fizzy Orange was an original family recipe. Last autumn, he sold a pumpkin version. Both were total hits with patrons.

"Hmm. She said around three would be good." I typed the last word and pressed *save*. "Finished. We have forty-eight events to cover June through August. I shared the file on Google Docs so you can check for anything I missed." We'd built up the business so much in less than a year. Our reputation had grown, spread especially by word of mouth and of course through lots of advertising. We were averaging three and often four events a week. Plus, Izzie's idea to sell art products, along with the touristy items we painted ourselves, helped keep us afloat. Then, there were the occasional portraits Izzie was commissioned to paint. She sank almost every dollar from those sales back into our business.

"I'm sure the schedule is fine. Willow, would you stay and cover the shop for an hour or so while we're gone? I'd like to be there when Chloe asks Lana if she's willing to team up to do a mixed event."

"Sure. I want to work ahead on details for the next party theme. I have some ideas." Willow folded the step ladder and carried it to the storage room.

Izzie nibbled on her thumbnail and stared at me. "Do you think she'll agree? I mean, you know her. The idea of thirty or so guests watching her paint the mural won't freak her out, will it?"

I scoffed. "Hardly. She told me once that when she painted her murals, dozens, probably hundreds of people, stopped to watch her. Even asked for her autograph."

"Yeah, I figured as much, but you're the one who said she doesn't seem like her old self."

The door chime tinkled as someone entered the shop. Rita Morgan dug in her shoulder bag to pull out a wallet while a scowl furrowed lines on her face.

"Hi, Rita." I tried for a cheerful lilt.

"Chloe," she grumbled. Setting her bag on the closest chair, she lifted her gaze to the counter where Izzie sat on a stool. "Izzie."

"Good morning. What can we do for you, Rita?" Izzie greeted like a proper hostess.

"Well, for starters, you can rewind time and not invite your friend to come and paint the mural." This was directed at me with as much bad-tempered attitude as she could manage.

"Rita, I'm sorry, but Lana is one of the best muralists in the world. We are lucky to have her paint ours. You have to agree," I said.

"No, I don't think I do, but what's done is done. Now, the reason I came in has nothing to do with the mural. I need three tubes of magenta and two white, please." She waved her wallet.

Izzie pulled open a drawer, picked out the items, and then bagged the paint purchase.

After the exchange, Rita stuffed her items and wallet in her bag. "Speaking of the mural, as you know, most folks in Whisper Cove aren't happy about the amphitheater returning. In fact, the signup list keeps growing for our protest march. You'll see." She wagged her finger. "Trouble is coming to town. In my opinion, that mural and the theater are cursed, and your world-famous friend along with them. You can count on it." She gave her chin a firm nod and marched outside.

"There she goes again." Izzie groaned. "Talking about curses, remember how manic she was last Halloween? Panicked about the ghost of Abigail Bellows coming to destroy us all?"

"I'm more worried about the growing protest march she mentioned. What if enough people petition to have the theater removed?" I drummed my fingers on the counter.

The town council members wanted to keep the peace, and I could count at least a half dozen times when they were swayed by public opinion. Of course, Miles would put up a fight. He'd invested a great deal of money in acquiring the theater.

"I don't think that would get anywhere. Miles is a clever and powerful businessman. He'll work his way around any protest or petition. He has all the schemes up his sleeve, kind of like a con man who manages to stay just this side of legal. Trust me. I know. My parents are exactly like that." Willow came from the storage room and stood next to Izzie.

"She's right." Izzie patted Willow on the shoulder.

"Fine. I'll stop worrying, but I'm keeping my eyes open for trouble. Nothing worse than getting caught off guard." I blew out a puff of air.

"Now that we've got that settled, let's finish up hanging a new set of canvases on the walls and changing the window display," Izzie added. "What do you think? Spring flowers and some of those lake paintings we did last summer would look cute."

We spent the next few hours redecorating and organizing until the clock inched closer to three. Leaving Willow in charge, we grabbed the laptop, notepads, and pens, then headed outside.

Making a quick stop at home, I grabbed Max and placed him in the back seat of Izzie's Land Rover. After a quick drive up Whisper Cove Boulevard, we pulled into the lot next to the park entrance. Max squirmed to work his way out of my arms. He'd spotted Brody and Rex getting out of his car. In seconds, both dogs collided and sniffed to greet each other as I held tight to Max's leash.

"Hi, Brody," I said. His winning smile and dimples, along with those ocean-blue eyes, only touched the surface. Underneath that attractive exterior, Izzie had found a kind, generous soul she could connect with. I was truly happy for her.

"Hey, little sister." Brody grinned while embracing Izzie and planting a kiss on her lips.

He gave me the nickname because of how much shorter I was than Izzie, even though I was a year older than her. Of course, his six-foot-something towering height didn't help me argue the point.

"Wait until you see the amphitheater and the wall being used to paint the mural." Izzie leaned over to scratch the top of Rex's head. "It's freestanding, which is really cool because it can be moved anywhere. Oh, and it's made of polystyrene, that faux wood material, so it will weather well, even though Miles plans to store it indoors during the winter. Of course, it's not painted yet, but the theme is fantastic. Lana's idea is to paint musicians playing guitars and with these music notes floating all around them and—"

I laughed. "I think he gets the idea. I see Lana and Nick standing by the amphitheater. Let's go." I tugged on Max's leash and led the way into the park.

Nick held a camcorder in one hand and panned the area. Another man, a bit thinner and shorter than Nick, stood close by. He held what looked like a graphic drawing tablet. He was making quick strokes with a stylus and seemed totally focused on the task. A woman sat on one of the picnic tables, with her arms braced behind her. Her long red hair lifted off her shoulders and moved as the breeze coming off the lake grew stronger. She stared out at the water, not at all engaging with the others.

"That must be her crew." Izzie stopped alongside me.

"We should greet them. After all, we'll be working together…sort of." I scrunched my nose and shrugged.

I wasn't sure if Lana would want us to help. Heck, I didn't know whether or not she'd agree to us merging for a mixed event. What I'd told Izzie was pure speculation. Maybe Lana had changed so much I couldn't know how she felt about anything.

"Chloe." Lana hurried to approach, grabbed my hand, and squeezed tight. "I have to tell you I'm getting more excited about this project by the second. Thank you for suggesting me to do the job."

I blinked. Maybe a night of solid sleep was all she needed. Whatever the reason for her enthusiasm, I was relieved. "I'm glad you're glad. So, what do you think of the amphitheater?"

"Such a clever idea, using the lake as a venue. Not very many towns can claim they have a floating stage to host concerts. I wonder how the acoustics are. Wish I could stick around for one of the performances." She rattled on without taking a breath.

Definitely energetic. "Never know what can happen to change your plans. You want to introduce us to your team?" I gestured with one hand as Izzie approached, alone.

Brody stood at a distance, near a thicket of pines, while Rex sniffed the area.

"What am I thinking? Let's do that." She turned and waved. "Tate! Audrey!"

Tate jogged over to us while Audrey hopped off the table and walked ten or twenty steps behind him.

"Chloe, Izzie, this is Tate Gordy, the guru of IT."

Tate waved his free hand and fixed his gaze on me and winked. "I've heard a lot about you." Then he turned to stare at Izzie. "You must be Izzie. I've seen your profile and photo on LinkedIn. You've painted portraits of some powerful and famous people. I'm impressed."

Izzie's brow lifted. "I don't do that as often as I used to. The shop keeps me busy these days." She extended a hand to shake his. "But thank you. It's nice to be recognized."

Brody approached, tugging at Rex's leash.

"Guys, this is my boyfriend, Brody." Izzie pointed at each of the mural team members as she announced their names.

Brody blushed. "Glad to meet you."

When Audrey approached, Lana leaned her head to the side. "This is my assistant and intern, Audrey Laurent. Audrey, I want you to meet my very close friend, Chloe Abbington, her sister, Izzie, and this handsome guy is Brody. We'll probably be seeing a lot of them in the next couple of weeks, so, be nice." She laughed.

I sensed Audrey didn't get the joke or wasn't appreciative of Lana's words. Instead, she turned to us and cleared her throat. "Glad to meet you all, but I should get to work. Wouldn't want to disappoint my boss." Her smile was stiff, and the edginess in her voice was obvious. Her English was impeccable and with no apparent accent to hint she was French.

Lana ignored her and continued on with the conversation. "Tate, why don't you show them what you're doing on that tablet?"

"I love those graphic art devices. Does this one add color to your drawings?" Izzie walked to stand alongside Tate and peeked over his shoulder.

My attention followed Audrey as she returned to the picnic table and sat next to a stack of books. Picking up one of them, she leafed through the pages.

"Catalogs. I asked her to search for a list of equipment items and compare prices. I don't think Audrey cares for the job. She's eager to paint murals, but she needs to learn patience. Right now, she has very little of that or modesty. Her inflated ego is her Achilles heel. Once we get past those hurdles, she'll learn quickly." Lana snapped her fingers. "Be back in a second." She hurried closer to the park entrance where the wall structure for the mural stood.

"After I draw the images on the tablet, I upload them to my laptop. See these lines going vertically and horizontally?" Tate pointed to the screen as Izzie squinted to look. "When I'm through, I'll have a grid that can be used to scale. Each inch represents a foot or more, depending on the size of the wall surface Lana paints, and that will help her know exactly where to sketch each detail. It's fascinating, really. Computer technology is making great progress." He beamed while rolling back on his heels. "I love my job."

Izzie laughed. "I can see you do."

"What about a projector? Those are useful in painting murals, aren't they?" I stepped closer to study the tablet image.

"That's what I like to use when I paint larger surfaces like those on buildings. This project is smaller so the grid works well. All I have to do is follow the lines." Lana held up the tape measure in her hand. "Exactly twenty-two feet and eight inches in height. Eleven feet three inches wide."

"The mural wall structure?" I hiked a thumb over my shoulder.

"We have to be accurate. Mr. Terrell gave me measurements of twenty-three by eleven. I figured that was rounded off."

Tate tapped the tablet against his leg. "The issue with using a projector is it skews the image at the edges. So, you have to get down from the lift or ladder, stand back to get a more accurate view, then go back to the mural to sketch."

Lana sighed. "It's the artist's preference that counts, Tate. You know that."

"Absolutely." Tate's face reddened. In seconds, he excused himself.

Max whined and tugged at his leash.

I pointed at Max. "Excuse me for a minute, Lana." I led him down the path toward the lake and amphitheater. By the look of it, the work crew had returned from a break. Miles pointed his arms in all directions, as if shouting orders to them. Several yards away, Nick stood with his camcorder, filming the scene, then slowly panned to view the lake where boats pulled skiers across the water. After a minute or two, he shifted back to Miles and one of the workers. They seemed to be deep in conversation.

"How can their conversation be useful to Lana's website, Max?" I shrugged my shoulders.

Max sniffed at a bush before lifting his leg. With a low growl, he jumped in a pointless attempt to reach a squirrel that scampered up a tree with its bushy tail twitching in protest.

"Yeah, well, I'm curious even if you're not." I pulled him back along the path. Nick had disappeared, and there was nothing more to observe.

By the time we returned, I spotted Izzie and Brody sitting on the lawn with Rex nestled between them. "Where's Lana?"

Izzie pointed to the amphitheater where Lana and Nick stood facing each other. "Major relationship problems is my guess. From what I could overhear, Lana had snapped at Audrey, something about doing her job and how mishandling the supplies costs her time and money. As you can see, Audrey doesn't seem happy. She's keeping a safe distance from Lana. Meanwhile, Nick is trying to diffuse the situation. I don't think it's working."

I scratched behind my ear. Playing mediator might not be the best choice, but how often did I listen to reason? "Here. Watch him." I handed Izzie Max's leash and moved quickly toward Lana before I changed my mind.

"Why don't you butt out and let me handle her? I'm in charge. Not you," Lana snapped. The creases in her face deepened.

"You're impossible sometimes, you know?" Nick raked his fingers through his hair. "I can't deal with you right now." He stormed off.

"Everything okay?" I told myself to tread lightly. "Can I help?"

Lana sniffed and heaved her chest as she breathed in and out. "I'm fine. We're fine." She turned to face me, and a nervous laugh erupted. "What a lousy way to make an impression, right? Miles will probably think he's made the biggest mistake ever in hiring me. Hell. *You* probably do, too."

"Not at all. I'm sure you're suffering jet lag from that trip to Finland. After a couple more nights of solid rest, you'll feel better. Besides…" I pointed at Audrey and Nick, who was patting her on the shoulder. "No harm done, right?"

"Yeah, no harm." She frowned. "What is *that*?"

I turned to follow her gaze and hitched my breath. Like a white picket fence had come to life, posters bobbed up and down just above the hedge of shrubs bordering the park. I cringed at the sight as I pictured dozens of people gathering and lining up on the sidewalk. Sure enough, they cleared the shrub covering and marched into view. Some of them I recognized. Frank Benworthy, owner of the local B&B, led the group. Rita's bright orange hair made her easy to pick out. Behind her was Penny Swenson, with that poofy bun of her platinum blonde hair bobbing, waving a larger-than-life poster. Seeing her was a surprise. She managed the Alley's aromatherapy shop and swore more than once that to take sides on any issue was suicide for an owner's business. I guessed this was the exception. The group now marched in a circle, chanting phrases like "go home" and "move the theater" while the sound of their voices grew louder by the minute.

I chewed on my lip and turned to Lana. "Yeah, about that." Under my breath, a curse or two slipped out. The protesters didn't waste time in demonstrating. This jump to action gave me no opportunity to prepare Lana for the population of our residents who didn't support the theater or her part in it.

"As you can guess, not everyone in Whisper Cove is happy about the, um, new attraction," I fumbled for a second. "But that group is so tiny. Maybe less than one percent of our population. Most residents are happy...thrilled even, confident the theater and concerts will bring tons of business." My voice dwindled as I braced myself for some kind of outburst, but it never came.

"I see. Well, that's nothing new." She shrugged. "You should've seen the mob gathered around this wall I was painting in Nice. The client owns a business that manufactures ladies' garments. He wanted to advertise his apparel with a couple of models wearing the unmentionables. He figured the mural would make a bigger impact. And it did. Most of the men loved it. The women? Not so much." She waved an arm toward the sidewalk. "That doesn't bother me. I'm not going to let a few protesters scare me off."

I sighed. Then, peering over her shoulder, I let out a gasp. "That's good to hear, but looks like not everyone is taking the situation well."

With a fierce, steely-eyed glare, Miles marched across the lawn toward the protesters.

Chapter Three

I tossed the ball across the lawn. Max sprang into fetch mode, running as fast as those eight-inch-long legs could manage. Snapping his jaw, he bit down on his catch and circled back around toward me. "I've never seen Miles lose his temper like that." I shuddered, grateful yesterday's spectacle had passed without any casualties.

The Tuesday afternoon sun broke through the mostly cloud-covered sky. We'd finished at the shop and closed up early since the road crew came a couple of hours earlier than expected to fix the potholes on Artisan Alley. Their vehicles blocked the way, and, with only a trickle of customers, most of the merchants locked their doors and left. Fortunately, we didn't have an event scheduled today.

"What happened to the smooth, persuasive sales pitch he likes to use? I don't get it." Izzie chewed on a blade of sweetgrass. "Maybe he's going through a male midlife crisis. He looks to be about that age."

"I doubt that's it." I jiggled the ball and tossed it again. "I think this theater project has been too much for him. The protesters were his breaking point."

The squawk of geese flying overhead startled Max. He dropped the ball and ran in their direction, jumping up and down like a pogo stick, trying to reach higher with each attempt. He barked at the intrusion for several minutes until the last of the birds disappeared as they traveled north. Plopping in the grass, he panted, exhausted but appearing satisfied with his effort.

"Good thing Nick persuaded him to back off before anyone threw a punch," Izzie said.

"Well, Frank calling the sheriff's office didn't help. You heard him. He accused Miles of threatening him. For a second, I thought Deputy Daniels would arrest Miles." I stood and whistled for Max.

The lawnmower whirred and then hummed into silence. Dad stood at the opposite side of the yard. He wiped his brow with a towel and pushed the mower toward the garage.

"I wonder what's going on with Miles and Frank. I've heard them arguing at town meetings more than once," Izzie said.

"Nothing friendly between them at all. Oh well, should we head over to the park? I want to make sure Lana has everything she needs. I'll drive this time."

"We already delivered the paints she asked for, and everything else we could think of, but yeah, I'm curious to see if she's made any progress. I mean, after yesterday…" Izzie lifted her shoulders.

"She's fine. Not much can rattle her. You'll see." That tiny hint of doubt trickled through me. Attempting to convince myself seemed more likely the reason I spoke up, but Izzie didn't comment.

I put Max inside the house before heading to the driveway. I started up my used but functional Mazda. Not one to spend a ton of cash on certain things like car repairs, I decided to make a trade-in. Jake Marino, the owner of Whisper Cove's car repair, found me a dependable and reasonably priced vehicle. And this one had AC that worked.

Izzie hopped into the passenger seat, sipping her drink through a straw. "Want some?" She held out the cup.

"No thanks. I've got another idea." I rounded the corner to follow Whisper Cove Boulevard. "Let me make a quick stop before going to the park." I pulled to the curb in front of Claire's shop. In minutes, I returned with a bag of donuts and a hazelnut iced coffee for me. "In case they need something sweet for an energy pick-me-up."

Reaching our destination, I pulled into an open spot. The park was filled with visitors. Some walked their dogs along the trails, others sat on benches having a picnic meal, and a number of them gathered on the shore to view the lake and sailboats gliding across the water. Workers chatted and laughed as they packed up their equipment, ready to quit for the day. In contrast, Lana and her team were busy on the mural project. She had explained how taking advantage of good weather and daylight was important because tomorrow could bring rain and a loss of progress. She'd promised Miles the job would be finished in two weeks, which made him happy since the concert season began the first week of June. Everything needed to be ready to go, or else he'd lose money. Not something Miles accepted easily.

As we entered the park and made our way to the wall structure, the tension I'd built released in one breath. Lana stood next to Nick, laughing as he made a comment. She appeared relaxed and happy. Tate set up a ladder in front of the wall, then stood back. He called for Lana, who answered with a wave. Grabbing a canvas bag from Audrey, she hefted the strap over her shoulder, then directed her steps to the ladder.

As she spotted us, Lana cupped the sides of her mouth. "Hey, you two. Come over and take a look. I'm ready to begin sketching."

Tate tilted his laptop our way to view more easily. The sketch was amazingly detailed. The grid lines divided the image into squares that mathematically would be configured to work on the larger surface of the mural. I'd seen enough videos muralists had posted to show their process, but to view it in person excited me.

Tate explained the need to coat the wood surface with primer to make the painted images stick. Grid lines had already been lightly drawn on the mural wall. Now, Lana prepared to sketch the image going into the first square at the bottom. By using a can of spray paint to outline images on the bottom portion of the wall surface and an extendable pole to reach the top area, the process went amazingly fast. Nearly finished, she stepped several rungs up the ladder and extended the pole to paint one of the upper corners.

"She'll use the lift when we get it set up later this afternoon. That will move things along. Problem with the ladder is she has to keep getting off to move it to the left or right to work on another section." Tate checked his phone as it beeped. "Great. Looks like she won't need to use the ladder for much longer. The guys will be here in a few minutes with the lift."

"The weather forecast looks promising too. I'm sure—" I clutched my throat and gasped as a scream cut off my words and pierced the air.

Running toward her at once, both Nick and Tate broke Lana's fall as the ladder collapsed. With cautious steps, they helped her to the bench close by.

She rubbed her ankle and winced. "I'm fine, you guys. You can stop fussing." She scowled and brushed Nick's hand off her shoulder.

I grabbed a bottled water from my bag and approached. She took it from me and gulped down almost half.

"Thanks." She took a last swig before setting the bottle down. "I'm okay, really."

"You sure?" I frowned and bit down on my thumbnail. "I can call our family doctor, or we can drive you to the hospital emergency. Your ankle looks okay, but you never know."

"Not at all necessary. See?" She flexed her ankle then stood to walk a few steps. "Back on my feet and ready to go." She laughed but shot Tate a glance layered in disappointment and irritation.

"I'm sorry, Lana. The ladder looked fine when I checked it earlier. Even climbed it myself to make sure." Tate hurried his words.

I walked in front of the mural structure and knelt to examine the ladder. A jagged crack had damaged one leg, nearly splitting it in two. An accident waiting to happen, I guessed, but relief eased through me. My quick assumption that someone had tampered with the ladder was silly. Tate wouldn't tamper with it. He'd never want Lana to have an accident. She was his friend and employer, the one who paid his salary. I slowly retraced my steps.

By now, Izzie had joined the group. She handed Lana an ice pack. A few hiccups erupted before she could speak. "Glad you're okay. I mean, what if you'd broken your ankle and couldn't finish the job? Of course, your ankle is what's most important."

"I'm always prepared for whatever happens. If I couldn't work, which isn't the case right now, but if I couldn't, Audrey would take over until I was up and running again. She's an excellent pupil and talented. I'm confident she'd do a great job." Lana pressed the ice pack to her ankle.

Hearing Audrey's name mentioned, I scanned the area and spotted her picking up the tools that had spilled when Lana fell. Placing them in the canvas bag, she then walked to the workstation set up behind the mural wall. She hadn't hurried to help Lana like the others. Perhaps she struggled to forget the lecture Lana had given her yesterday, embarrassed that everyone heard and angry for feeling unappreciated. I understood those feelings. I'd been in that kind of situation once or twice. She'd want to prove Lana wrong. She knew how to do her job and do it well. Cleaning up the mess after Lana's fall rather than fawning over her injury was a wise move.

As I peered at the lake behind Audrey, I saw movement. Someone was partially hidden behind a thick tree trunk. A flowered, ankle-length dress billowed with the wind, showing pink, orange, and purple blotches of color. All at once, she backed up then hurried across the lakeshore. I grimaced. Rita. How long had she been watching us? And why? Several ideas and motives came to mind as I drew conclusions. I kept in mind that my thoughts were pure speculation and not helping me figure out whodunnit.

"Hey, Chloe. I was just explaining our mixed event idea to Lana," Izzie called out to break my train of thought.

"Sounds like we'd be doing each other a favor." Lana handed the ice pack to Nick and stood, putting pressure on her leg. She walked back and forth several feet in front of us then stopped to face me. "How about next Saturday? The sketch will be finished, and I should be well into painting the mural. Tate can explain his role in this. Oh! We'll supply paper grids to hand out. Your class can work on one of the images from the mural and use the grid lines to guide them. Sound good?"

"Creative minds thinking alike." I chuckled.

Someone shouted behind us. I turned as a group of men pushed the lift across the lawn until it stood in front of the wall structure. One of them worked the gears to raise and lower the platform as Tate stood by to supervise. I gasped. Right behind them, Miles approached. The grim expression creasing his brow was telling.

"Oh boy," Izzie muttered as she stood close. "What if Frank filed charges against him for attempting assault?"

"I'm sure he didn't do that," I whispered.

"If he had, I bet the entire group of protesters would back up Frank's side of the story. Who are the authorities going to believe? Or a judge?" Izzie waved. "Hi, Miles. Beautiful evening for a walk."

Miles grumbled under his breath then, facing Lana, turned on his usual charm. "I heard from one of the work crew you took a tumble off the ladder. I hope you're not injured."

"I'm fine, Miles. In fact, the lift just arrived, so we're getting back to work." Lana leveled her gaze at him.

"Wonderful. I'm relieved to hear that because we wouldn't want to fall behind on our schedule, would we?" He cleared his throat and tugged on his collar.

Lana rolled her tongue and kept quiet.

I knew that move. Once, when the landlord had tried to cheat us on the rent, she'd used the same tell and kept her cool. She told me later how she would silently count to ten, higher if she needed more time to calm down, then speak. Whatever she had to say now would have some sort of underlying sarcasm.

"You know, Miles, I was just saying how wonderful it is to be working for such an intelligent and successful businessman." She linked her arm through his. "You've certainly shown me how this project has come about so smoothly, and without a single hitch. Congratulations."

I coughed, covering up what almost came out, and watched Miles's face turn a bright shade of red. *Smoothly* and *without a hitch* definitely didn't describe this project, and he knew it.

"Well, just stay on schedule, Miss Easton." He slid his arm free, pivoted on his heel, then took long strides toward the parking area.

I studied Lana. Even after the glib comment to soften the tense mood, she clenched her jaw. First, the ladder accident, and now Miles pressuring her with his reminder to keep working and stay on schedule. All this and her noticeably troubled relationship with Nick were too much. While painting, distractions always ruined my efforts, but a time clock and deadlines weren't usually issues for me like they were for Lana.

"Nick, why don't you and Tate head back to the hotel? And leave the camcorder here. I want to check some of the footage you took today. Besides,

I'd like to load some of my tools and supplies on the lift, then finish painting the sky background in the top corner. Audrey, you should stay behind for a few minutes. I have something else for you to do," Lana said.

Tate frowned. "Are you sure? I can stay and help you. Check to see everything with the lift is working properly."

Lana sniffed. "Stop. I can work the lift just fine. Go to the hotel and relax, Tate. You being uptight and nervous isn't helping."

Tate stuffed his hands in his pockets and stepped back.

"Say! I have an idea. How about we all meet at Duckies around nine?" If I had any chance of diffusing the tension among them, I needed to act now. "It's a new spot, kind of an upscale bar with a dance floor and always a great band playing. You can blow off steam, relax, and meet some of the friendly locals who aren't protesters. What do you say?" I spoke to all four of them but kept my gaze fixed on Lana.

"Sure." Lana's lips curved into a smile. "Thanks, Chloe."

"Then it's settled." I pointed a finger at her. "Now, I'm not giving you a chance to bail, so I'll come back here around eight-thirty or a little after to pick you up." I turned to Nick. "Maybe you three can drive straight to Duckies from the hotel, or walk if you like. You're only a block away from the place."

"I'll drive separately. I want to invite Brody, but he won't get off work until nine," Izzie said.

"Great. Maybe give Willow a call to see if she wants to come. Might as well make it a party."

Lana laughed. "Sisters. It's like you read each other's thoughts and work together."

"Definitely saves time," Izzie quipped.

We parted ways and headed out of the park, except for Audrey and Lana, who carried her tool bag to the lift.

"Does she ever relax?" Izzie walked next to me.

"Someone as successful as Lana probably didn't get to where she is by relaxing. That's my guess." I unlocked the car doors.

"Kind of sad, actually," Izzie said.

"It is, but that's the degree of sacrifice she's chosen to make." I fired up the engine and steered toward home. For a moment, I wondered if I had chosen that level of commitment, would I still be living in Manhattan, pursuing my dream to conquer the art world? There was still time, I told myself. I could take a different course one day. I glanced at Izzie and shook my head. Or maybe not.

I cursed under my breath as I stole a second to look at the dashboard. Eight-forty. I swerved around the corner. I'd planned to be at the park by eight thirty, but made a quick stop at Bob's Barbecue Pit for a Fizzy Orange drink. I hoped Lana would be too busy working on the mural to notice. Dusk was quickly turning to the darkness of night. "She'd notice. Of course she'd notice. It's almost dark, Chloe. She's probably packed up her gear by now." I groaned.

Tires screeched as I came to a stop and parked alongside the curb. In a no parking zone, of course. Grabbing my keys, I exited the car and hurried across the sidewalk and down the path, forgetting the bottle of Fizzy Orange sitting in the cupholder. My shoe stubbed an uncovered tree root, and I nearly stumbled. "Seriously?" I stopped for a second or two and took a deep breath, then continued toward the hedged entrance to the park. I tensed. The sharp trill of a nightingale had broken the silence. Silly how I overreacted, but as if to make a point, a high-pitched scream pierced the air from just beyond the hedges. I jumped back a few steps, and this time, landed on the ground. My shoe popped off and flew to the side. My mind raced, charged with details and quick assumptions. I crawled to grab the shoe, not bothering to put it back on. Standing once more, I limped to reach the hedge and beyond that, the mural. "Lana!"

I skirted around the hedge opening and to the left, where the wall structure stood. My breath caught as I clutched my throat and dropped the shoe. My heartbeat skipped but slowed in rhythm. I froze for what seemed like minutes, but was really only an instant. The pounding of footsteps drew my gaze toward the lake. The dark silhouette of someone tall receded into the night as it reached the far end of the park. I blinked, then snapped my head back to the ground in front of me.

Lana lay still in front of the mural, eyes closed, head bleeding, and her neck bent unnaturally to one side. A painful cry choked my throat as I clutched my chest. Each detail of her was intense, too vivid, too real. I twisted around and bent at the waist. The queasiness unsettled and churned my insides. Within seconds, I heaved the contents of my stomach. While struggling to get a grip, I turned back and knelt next to her. I put my fingers to her neck but felt nothing. I sat back on my rear and pulled out my phone, trembling as I tried to punch numbers. My voice shook as I spoke into the phone. "Yes, I'll stay on the line." I lowered my head to stare at Lana. As if the gesture was the only way left to help, I took her hand in mine, squeezed tightly, and wept.

Chapter Four

I let go of Lana's hand and stood. The sirens had stopped. I gazed first at the lake where I'd seen the person running along the shore and repeated the details of the scene in my head to keep from losing them. Fear and tension and panic of being a foot away from Lana's body contended with my thoughts. Footsteps pounded and shouts from across the park grew louder. I hurried to scan the area around the base of the mural wall. I knelt down to examine several prints. They were large, which told me they couldn't be Lana's. I frowned. Something about them bothered me, but I had no time to consider what that meant.

I glanced up as several medics approached. They rushed forward and knelt down to examine Lana. Crossing my arms tightly over my chest didn't stop the cold running through me. This couldn't happen. Lana couldn't be dead. In the next instant, two more medics arrived with a gurney. I couldn't trust my questionable state of mind, but their actions appeared to move in rather choppy still shots, like dominoes in slow motion, tipping over and into the next in line. I wished they'd move faster.

Someone short with sparse hair arrived and carried on a discussion with the medics. The coroner. I recognized him from the other cases he'd worked on, where I unfortunately got caught in the middle of last year. I moved a bit closer and shuddered to hear comments like "broken neck" and "deep gash." One of the medics pointed at the lift, and the coroner shook his head and spoke into his recorder as he walked away.

Lana's limp form was hefted onto the gurney. The medics retraced their steps toward the emergency vehicle. I turned to stare at the medic near me and dropped my gaze to his steady hand that only moments ago had examined Lana. As he packed his bag, he avoided my gaze. Was he indifferent or uncomfortable? I couldn't imagine doing his job. I wanted to ask what he thought about Lana's death but knew he most likely couldn't or wouldn't answer.

The rustle of leaves and heavy footsteps broke my concentration. I faced the park entrance and spotted a man wearing a Yankees cap and sweats. As he drew closer, the weathered, tan skin of his face and the stern expression evident from his tight lips and set jaw became more defined. Hunter had described his appearance perfectly. Detective Calvin Winsell. He'd taken over all the cases in the Chautauqua area since Hunter had been commissioned to work with a department in a neighboring county. As Hunter worded it, Winsell was strict, the always-go-by-the-book detective with dry humor that ventured into insults if he was in a bad mood, and that did not help my already traumatized condition. I chewed on my bottom lip as he stopped and spoke to one of the medics who then pointed my way.

Turning, Winston stared at me, and his eyes narrowed. At once, he closed the space between us.

"You found the victim and called nine-one-one?"

I could only manage a nod.

Not taking his gaze away from me, he pulled off his cap. Tucked inside was a notepad. His fingers raked through a tangle of brown curls until a pen emerged. "Your name?" He planted the cap back on his head.

"Ah, Chloe Abbington. I was planning—"

"Address? Any relationship with the victim?" He scribbled furiously without glancing up at me.

The chill I felt earlier thawed slowly. I tried not to show my irritation by becoming defensive, but emotions were running at full tilt. "The *victim* is Lana Easton. And yes, we have, *had* a relationship. She is...she was a close friend." The last few words came out in a breathy whisper. "I live on Sail Shore Drive with my parents and sister Izzie. She and I own the Paint with a View shop on Artisan Alley. Lana was hired to paint the mural for the amphitheater, you see. She, that is, we were helping her and her team set up

32

and we..." My heart was beating too fast.

"Did you see or hear anything before you found the, that is, Miss Easton?"

"I heard a scream. That's when I ran." I pointed at the hedged entrance. "From that direction. I saw a man, at least I think it was a man, running toward the lake and away from here. Or at least I think he or she ran from here. I, I don't know for sure." I shook my head. I couldn't do this.

He tapped his pen on the notepad, and his brow wrinkled. "Let's keep this to what you do know for sure. Give yourself some time to think about the rest. You saw someone running along the lake. That much, you know. Tall? Heavy or thin? Wide strides and traveling fast? Or going at a slow jog? Those details are important to an investigation."

"Yes, of course. I just need..." I heaved my chest. How could Lana be dead?

"Maybe we should let Miss Abbington take a moment." The tall medic who'd examined Lana smiled and handed me a bottle of water. "Hi. I'm Justin. Why don't you sit down?"

"Yes. Of course." The detective cleared his throat and grumbled some other words while nodding at me and then pointedly at Justin. "No doubt, a bit of a shock finding a friend that way." His brow squirreled up as if he was asking rather than stating the obvious.

I practically collapsed on the park bench near me and chugged water instead of commenting. Yes, I would need a moment and then some.

"Chloe! Are you alright?" Izzie breathed heavily as she nearly collided with Winsell. She pulled me from the bench, wrapped her arms around my shoulders, and squeezed.

Willow and Brody, followed by Mom and Dad, hurried to catch up. As each one crowded around me, I peeked through the opening in the circle of family and friends to see Detective Winsell. His jaw stiffened, and in the next second, he yanked down on the brim of his Yankees cap, visibly irritated at the interruption.

"How did you know to come?" I shifted my attention.

"Brody and I were leaving the house when Willow called to say she'd heard someone had been hurt at the park," Izzie started. "All I could think of was you. If any..." She stroked my back and let go of a breathy whimper. "I'm glad you're okay." Releasing me, she glanced around. "Is Lana...?"

"Excuse me, folks." Winsell interrupted and waved his arm. "My name's Detective Winsell and this is a crime scene. If you'll step back from the area while my team collects evidence, I'd greatly appreciate it."

Crime scene. Those words left me both worried and somewhat puzzled. "Detective Winsell, couldn't this have been an accident? Lana was working on the mural, and the lift is right there. If she climbed—"

Winsell held out his palm. "I appreciate your theory, Miss Abbington, but until I have done a thorough investigation, I can't rule out foul play."

Mom came from behind me and linked my arm with hers. "Why don't we take you home, sweetie? You look exhausted. I'm sure the detective can wait and follow up with his questions, tomorrow." She leveled her gaze at Winsell.

"I suppose that will do. Once I have a chance to look over the evidence report, I may have something new to ask," he said.

I shook my head. "No. I want to stay." Clutching the sides of my jacket, I sucked in air.

Mom sighed but dropped the matter, even though she remained at my side.

"Excellent. Thank you, Miss Abbington. Now, can you tell me more about this person you saw running away? No guesses, just what you're sure of."

I squinted. "The person was tall, for sure. He was taking long strides and moving fast. He, or she, didn't look back, so I couldn't make out a face. Plus, dusk was coming, and the light wasn't the best." He didn't want me to guess, but my instinct told me the jogger was male. I pointed. "I noticed footprints next to the mural. Too large to belong to a woman, I think. At least they don't belong to Lana. Her feet are small. And some of the prints seem to be stained blue. Cerulean, if I'm being accurate. Maybe from the paint can near Lana that is tipped over." At once, I cringed as Winsell stopped writing and silenced me with those piercing eyes that didn't blink.

One of the medics approached and interrupted. "Thought you should know, there are footprints trailing from here toward the lake. Athletic, grooved pattern on the bottom, size twelve or thirteen. You want the team to search farther down the shore path?"

Winsell scratched behind one ear and sucked on his tongue. "That would be wise. Good work, Dennings." He glimpsed me for a split second. "And make sure to check those prints underneath the mural wall. See if they match the others and show any blue…" He studied me with brows raised. "Cerulean is dark blue. Correct?"

"Yes," I said.

He returned his gaze to Dennings. "See if the prints have any dark blue paint stains." He scribbled on his notepad then, looking at me, added, "Did you touch anything?"

"What?" I frowned.

"The body? That paint can? Anything that might have your prints."

"Oh, of course. I checked Lana's pulse." I shuddered, not wanting to replay the scene in my head. "Nothing else." I forced myself to face the mural wall as if to remind me that what happened really did. Someone from the investigative team had set up equipment to light the area since darkness set in. The lift had been lowered and cleared. I guessed Lana's tool bag had been confiscated. The crime team members moved about and, with gloved hands, were bagging anything that could be evidence. My stomach grew squeamish while one team member picked up the blue scarf Lana had worn today, lying where it must've come loose and fallen off, and then a rock that had a blood-red stain on one side.

Izzie and Brody walked alongside Mom and me, while Willow and Dad trailed behind. I could hear most of their conversation. Willow was relaying her account of things to Dad.

"I knew something was up when Rita Morgan ran into Duckies with her arms waving at the group sitting at a table next to ours. You know how loud she can be when she's hysterical."

"Yes, she often lets her emotions get out of hand," Dad said. "Go on."

"Well, anyway, she rambled on about an ambulance with sirens blaring and how it stopped in front of the park. I admit, I got almost as hysterical as Rita, thinking the worst."

"Are you warm enough, Chloe?" Mom asked. "You're shaking." She hugged me and rubbed my arm with vigorous strokes.

"No, I'm fine. It's just...I can't believe she's gone." I refused to say the "D" word. Or the "M" word. I knew Winsell was right, but that didn't mean I wanted to believe it. I didn't want to think someone would murder Lana. I squeezed my eyes shut for an instant. Or make a guess who could have.

As we neared the street, a crowd came into view. They hovered together, whispering behind cupped hands while others pointed at the EMT vehicle only yards away. I recognized Rita and Penny among them. Trailing from behind, Frank Benworthy joined the gathering, wearing a hoodie tucked snugly around his neck. He shoved both hands deep inside his pockets and hopped up and down a few times, as if the cool evening air chilled him.

I mirrored his move and slid my hands underneath the covering of my jacket, attempting to dissolve any leftover fear and worry in me. That totally wasn't working. My breath hitched as I recalled Rita's words at the shop the other day. *Trouble is coming to town. In my opinion, that mural and the theater are cursed, and your world-famous friend along with them.* It looked like Rita's prediction had become a reality.

Izzie squeezed my hand and gave me an unwavering smile. "On our drive over, I called Hunter. He's more than an hour away, but he's on the road now. I told him to meet us at the house."

"Good. Thanks, Izzie." My thoughts were slowly catching up to the moment, and like a web of threads, they connected the tragic event this evening to how Lana's death would affect everyone. I gasped and came to a stop. Pulling my hand out of Izzie's grasp, I held it against my throat and stared at her. "Nick."

As if saying his name was a command, Nick ran down the sidewalk toward us, followed by Tate and Audrey. He shouted Lana's name. For an instant, while bathed in light from the street lamp, the wild-eyed fear on his face revealed he wasn't really expecting an answer.

I patted both Mom's and Izzie's hands. "Let me tell him."

"Sweetie," Mom said.

"Chloe, maybe you should—" Izzie chimed in.

"No, I can tell him. I think he should hear it from me." I left them to stop

Nick before he reached the park entrance. I attempted to smile, or at least keep the outside of me from revealing the emotional turmoil erupting my insides like an earthquake.

Nick reached me. We stood toe to toe. With a moan slipping out of his downturned mouth, he gripped my arms. "I heard people at the bar talking. I asked the bartender if he'd seen you and Lana. He, he told me there'd been an accident at the park." He let go of one arm and raked fingers through his hair. The tufted mess matched that wild-eyed fear.

Tate and Audrey had stopped to speak with someone in the crowd. From the reaction on Audrey's face, I guessed she and Tate had learned the tragic news.

I shifted my attention back to Nick and cradled his hand in mine. "Nick," I whispered. The air in my lungs seemed to dissipate. I lifted my chest and forced a breath. "Lana…"

Back inside the park, Winsell shouted orders at his team members; his voice resonated deep and stern. In seconds, the EMT vehicle's engine rumbled. I dug my nails into the palms of my hands. "Lana had an accident. It looks like she fell and hit her head on a rock, or maybe…" *Just what you're sure of.* Winsell's words came to me. "Nick, I'm so sorry, but Lana is dead."

Chapter Five

Nick stared, not so much at me as through me. He didn't attempt any movement, not even to utter a response.

I squeezed the hand I'd been cradling. "Nick? Did you hear what I said?"

As if my voice brought his mind back from someplace else, he blinked, followed by a slight nod of his chin. It seemed to be all he could manage.

"Maybe you should sit down." I tugged his hand. "There's a bench on the other side of the hedges." I waved my arm at Tate who glanced this way and mouthed the words "come here." I guess courage could always use a helping hand.

As if she'd sensed my urgency, and before Tate could react, Izzie rushed over to take Nick's other hand. Giving her chin an encouraging lift, she smiled at me and helped lead Nick to the park bench.

"Miss Abbington!" Winsell's footsteps pounded across the path to meet us. "Good. You're still here. I have a few more questions. First, would you give me a description of your evening before you arrived at the park and found the, er, Miss Easton?"

I shrugged. "I left the shop after putting a few items away."

"Anyone with you at the shop?" He scribbled in his pad.

"No. Izzie and Willow had gone home." I tensed. All alone meant no one to confirm my story. "Wait. I stopped at Bob's Barbecue Pit for a drink, right before I came here."

"Right." After a few more scribbles he looked up. "Anything else?"

"Ah, not that I can think of."

Winsell's brow inched up as he turned to gaze at Nick. "And who are you?" He lifted his head to catch sight of Tate and Audrey who'd arrived to stand behind the bench. "And you?"

I bit my lip. There was no way to avoid adding more to what already was overwhelming Nick. I'd learned my lesson last summer when Fiona Gimble was murdered with a paint knife behind our shop, and then in the fall, Viola Finnwinkle drowned in Chautauqua Lake. In my amateur sleuthing attempts to solve the murders and clear the Abbington name, I found lying or, as in this case, omitting facts never ends well.

"This is Nick Poling. He is...that is, he and Lana were in a relationship." I gestured behind me. "Tate Gordy and Audrey Laurent are Lana's employees."

Winsell barely gave them a glance. His focus was entirely on Nick. "Boyfriend. Yes, well, we should talk."

He seemed to have forgotten the questions he had for me, or maybe he'd lost interest. Poor Nick, I thought. I also had learned that during their investigations, detectives gravitated to those typical murder scenarios and suspects. Boyfriend being one of them. My heart broke. Nick had loved Lana, or at least seemed devoted to her. Whatever Lana asked him to do— and from what I'd seen in the short time I'd spent with them, she certainly asked a lot—Nick would do so without protest or argument. Was that it? Did he tire of being treated merely like a go-fer rather than her boyfriend, fetching whatever Lana demanded? Is that how he viewed his role in her life? I gave my head a firm shake. I was making assumptions, something Hunter had warned me could lead to taking the wrong path in solving a crime. Besides, until Detective Winsell found the evidence to prove otherwise, I could assume Lana's death was an unfortunate accident. And that's what I should do.

A sharp voice broke through my mental discourse, and I frowned. Nick's face had turned a deep shade of red, and his eyes glared. Winsell's questioning must not be going over well.

"I told you. Lana wanted to stay at the park to finish up some work, and she told Audrey to stay behind. So, I went back to the hotel with Tate. It's a short walk. We got there by five-thirty." He waved an arm at the mural team.

"Tell him."

Audrey spoke first. "I saw Nick and Tate walking out of the park. That was a little after five. Then, I helped Lana view the video footage. We discussed some changes to the design, and I left about twenty to thirty minutes later. When I got to the hotel, it was around five-forty. I noticed Tate and Nick sitting in the bar having drinks. They waved at me to come and join them. I stayed for a few minutes to chat, but I was kind of tired. So then, I went straight to my room. After a shower, I took a nap, then headed to the dining room for a bite to eat. That was at six-thirty. I know because I checked my watch to see how much time I had to kill before going back out.

"I was back in my room, probably close to seven. I wanted to finish a novel I'd been reading and add notes to my work journal. It's something Lana wanted me to keep, log what I learned, how much time I spent on each task. Things like that."

Glancing away for a moment, she shuffled her feet then turned back to face Winsell. "Anyway, it must have been at least twenty after eight when Tate showed up at my hotel room." She shifted her gaze to Tate and shrugged. "Is that about right, you think?"

Tate scratched behind one ear. "I'd say more like eight-forty. We were planning to meet up with Lana and friends at Duckies around nine. Anyway, I knocked on Nick's door first. He said he'd meet us downstairs in a few minutes."

Winsell pointed at Tate. "And your account of events after returning to the hotel?"

"Well, after Nick and I sat at the bar having drinks, I went to my room. That would've been close to six. I spent a couple of hours updating Lana's website and the tutorial feature she wanted to add. It's for viewers who're interested in learning about her process, you see. And, of course, working on my program took up some time." Tate tapped on his phone, then leaned forward to show Winsell the screen. "It's still in the beginning stages, but I'm hoping video game companies will like it enough to buy." He licked his lips. "After that, I took a shower, got dressed, and by then, it was time to meet Nick and Audrey."

Winsell scribbled in his notepad. "And you, Mr. Poling? What did you do to occupy your time after having drinks with Mr. Gordy until meeting with your coworkers in the hotel lobby? Naptime? Shower? Dinner? Watch some TV?"

I squirmed in my seat as Nick's brows inched together, furrowing the creases across his forehead. None of his defensive remarks or tone of voice earlier had intimidated Winsell who seemed determined to put the pressure on. Yep. The detective might be painting a picture of the classic scenario: angry or jealous boyfriend kills girlfriend in a fit of rage.

"Let's say all of the above." Nick groaned.

"More specific, please." Winsell tapped his pen.

"Fine." He scratched the stubble that darkened his jaw. "After drinks with Tate at the bar—two Tom Collins and a shot of brandy—I went to my room and took a shower. I ordered room service. A steak, medium rare, baked potato, salad with no tomatoes—I hate tomatoes—and a beer, Guinness Stout. I don't much care for domestic beers. After eating, I turned on the television to watch the evening news. Crime is up, and the stock market is down. Big surprise. By then, it was close to seven-thirty. I sat on the balcony to smoke my pipe. Black cherry tobacco is my favorite. I must've dozed off because the alarm I'd set on my watch for eight woke me. I cleaned out my pipe, got dressed, and it was about then that Tate knocked on my door. Does that satisfy you?" Nick's lips curled, but his chin quivered like he was about to cry.

I felt I could at any second. Cry loud, body-quaking sobs because Lana was dead.

"Sorry. I'm…just, sorry." Nick lowered his gaze.

Winsell tipped his chin. "Quite all right. Yes. Yes, that will do. Thank you." His gaze bounced from Audrey to Tate and back to Nick. "So, what I'm hearing is that each of you were alone from the time you got back to the hotel and had drinks until you met in the hotel lobby a little after eight-thirty. Except for the time Miss O'Connell had her bite to eat in the hotel dining room, which we're assuming would've been for approximately a half hour, give or take a few minutes." He looked up. "Would you agree?"

I pressed my lips. The uncomfortable look on both Nick's and Audrey's faces surfaced as they must've caught on to what Winsell implied. I know I did. Tate's expression, on the other hand, appeared unchanged. I guessed he had no clue or didn't care, but Winsell's unstated message was damning. Having no solid alibi at the time of Lana's unfortunate death meant any one of them could be added to the detective's suspect list.

"Unless you have something else to tell me?" Winsell tilted his head.

I held my breath, waiting for someone, any of them, to speak. Awkward. I could imagine the marathon of thoughts going on inside their heads. They'd be desperate to conjure up anyone who could vouch for them, placing them somewhere other than here with Lana in her final moment.

Winsell flipped the cover on his notepad closed, then hid the pen inside the curled mess of hair. "Well, then. I'll be in touch. The three of you will be staying in town at the hotel." It wasn't a question. He lifted the corners of his mouth with a tepid smile at each of us, retraced his steps, and disappeared behind the hedges.

Audrey looked as though she'd faint when she grabbed onto the arm of the bench to steady herself.

Nick shifted his body from side to side as if deciding whether to stand or remain seated.

"Guess maybe we should head to the hotel?" Tate spoke up. "I mean, considering."

He didn't need to elaborate, but I needed to make sure Tate wouldn't try. I quickly switched topics. "Tate's right. You should go and get some sleep. Maybe we could meet tomorrow? I'll treat you to lunch at Millie's Diner. Then we can discuss what to do next."

"What do you mean by discussing what we should do next?" Audrey frowned.

"How can you even think about anything past what happened to Lana?" Nick's voice croaked.

I blinked. Maybe I hadn't put my words right. "Okay. I didn't mean, that is, I thought—I'm only suggesting something normal to do. Like lunch and discussing what to do next or whatever you'd like to talk about." I expelled the air constricting my lungs.

"Great idea," Tate said. "How about it? Nick? Audrey? We have to eat, and Chloe's being generous enough to pay. I, for one, can't pass up a free meal. Not on the salary I get." His smile flattened as if he suddenly remembered who paid that salary.

"Look." I took a chance and didn't skirt around the issue. Besides that, I was desperate for a boost in morale and a break from my troubled thoughts. "I know it may be insensitive right now to talk about this, but you came here to do a job. That mural needs to be finished. I'm sure the town council and Miles will want you to continue with the project. Miles is desperate for it to be done before the grand opening concert at the amphitheater next month." I braced my shoulders, ready for arguments, shouts of protest, or even name-calling.

"She's right. Besides, Lana would want us to be professional and go on with the project." Nick stood. "I can't think of a better way to honor her memory. Especially if Audrey finishes painting the mural."

I couldn't say I was surprised, not after witnessing how attentive he was with Lana. Perhaps chivalry wasn't dead, after all.

"I'm sorry you all lost a good friend and boss." Izzie hugged my shoulder. "But we promise to try and show you as much support and hospitality as we can manage."

"Thank you," Audrey said. "We'll see you tomorrow." She waved then linked her arm with Tate's while Nick caught up to her other side. Their steps led them toward the hotel, as the dark soon swallowed up their images.

"Come on, shortcake. We should get back to the house." Dad took my hand.

My eyes widened, and I checked my watch. "Hunter." I'd completely forgotten he was coming.

"Don't worry. It's only been a little over an hour. I bet he's just approaching Whisper Cove," Izzie said.

The EMT vehicle rumbled past us at a crawl, weaving around the crowd of onlookers as it reached the street. No flashing red lights or screaming siren, or buzzing conversation, only silence. I squeezed my eyes shut. A solemn moment if there ever was one.

"Come on." Dad tugged my arm. "There's nothing more to do here."

I sat in the passenger seat of my car while Dad drove. I buried myself inside my head to sort through all the details of Lana's death while Dad tapped the steering wheel, keeping beat to music resonating from the car stereo. The medic's comments played back. Broken neck, gash to the back of her head, probably caused by the rock when she fell...or was pushed. I fingered the hem of my jacket. Lana was experienced at working on a lift. Surefooted, careful, not the kind of person to lose her balance and fall. And what about the footprints near the mural? Or the jogger running away from the scene? *Only what you know for sure.* Okay, maybe running away, or *maybe* it was an innocent evening run...except for those footprints with paint stains, athletic shoe prints, size twelve or thirteen. I rubbed my temples. I glimpsed Dad and attempted to speak, my jaw opening and closing, as I worked on a decision. I shifted in my seat. "I can't help thinking...if only I'd arrived earlier, even twenty minutes earlier, she might be alive." My voice fell at the end.

"Hey. Hey there." Dad squeezed my hand. "Chloe, you shouldn't, you *can't* let yourself think that way." He pulled into our drive and killed the engine, then grabbed me in a tight hug. "What if you'd been hurt? If it's true Lana was murdered, and you arrived before the killer fled the scene..." He tightened his grip on me. "Let's not do this. Okay? You're safe, and we're together. You, me, your mom, Izzie. We've got each other. Let's just cherish that for the moment."

I rubbed my cheek against the soft leather of his jacket. All those memories I had of years spent with Lana raced to the forefront, reminding me that even though a lot of time had passed, it hadn't stolen my feelings for her and our friendship. Time had only put it to sleep for a while.

Tires crunched. I removed my face from Dad's jacket. My heart warmed as I viewed a familiar car in the side mirror. I opened my door and bolted out onto the pavement. In seconds, the tall, muscular frame of Hunter stepped out and took hurried strides toward me.

Dad came around the side of my car and held out his hand to shake Hunter's.

"Hello, young man. Glad you came. It's been a hell of an evening."

Hunter gave his chin a curt nod. "Winsell called me with the details." His gaze settled on me, and his brown eyes softened. In one swift move, he wrapped both arms around my waist and pulled me close. "I'm so *very* relieved to find you okay." His breath tickled my ear.

"Me too." I sighed, reassured by the sound of his voice and the firm embrace. My head rested against his chest, the quick thump of his heartbeat resonated in my ear. As if my mind caught up to what he'd said, I twisted to loosen his hold and stared. "Why would Winsell call you about Lana? Isn't he handling your cases?" I shivered as worry crept inside. With any luck, the feeling was unwarranted.

"Why don't we all go inside, and I'll make us some hot chocolate?" Mom stepped closer to us.

Hunter seemed not to hear her comment, or he ignored it. "The coroner suggested Lana's death may have been a homicide." He peeked over my shoulder. "Would you excuse us for a moment?"

"Of course. We'll be in the kitchen making that hot chocolate." She took Dad's hand,

Hunter waited until their footsteps faded, then he squeezed my hands while gazing down at me. "Look, I'm telling you this in confidence. Promise you'll keep what I have to say to yourself."

I frowned. "You know I will, since you asked. Go on."

"The coroner has determined time of death was between eight and eight-thirty. Also, he discovered large bruises on Lana's upper arm and wrist, which may or may not be relevant to the case, but it's concerning. And her neck was broken, most likely from hitting her head on the rock when she landed. Of course he'll follow procedure to run more tests, and Winsell will do his job to thoroughly investigate, but…I'm sorry, Chloe. With all the evidence at hand, those shoe prints, someone running away from the scene, and now the bruises, Winsell seems to agree with the coroner. At least for the time being, he's looking at Lana's death as a homicide. Be prepared for more questioning. I know Winsell. You being at the scene makes you one of his prime suspects."

Chapter Six

I refilled Mom's coffee mug and handed it to her before skirting around the table. I sat in my seat next to Izzie. Breakfast time was pretty much a family ritual, except for mornings when everyone was in a hurry, running late to work, or whatever was on their agenda for the day. This morning, none of us were in that big of a rush to get somewhere, and it was obvious why. The shock of Lana's death, only hours ago, left us all stunned. As for myself, I tossed most of the night, managing no more than two or three hours of sleep, I guessed.

"Most of the evening is a blur. I'm not sure what I saw or imagined I saw." I poured syrup over my wheat cakes. Detective Winsell had messed with my head and made me doubtful. After hearing Hunter's news last night and having to keep it a secret, even from Izzie and our parents, I was a mess. I didn't do well with secrets, especially the kind that targeted me as a murder suspect. Still, I'd made a promise to Hunter, and I couldn't handle the thought of worrying Mom, Dad, and Izzie more than they already were doing.

"Come on, Chloe. There has to be some tiny detail you are sure of." Izzie coaxed with a smile.

I puckered my forehead to concentrate, quietly picturing the moment I entered the park. "Like I told Winsell, the person running away from the mural, or whatever direction he or she came from, was tall and moved like an athlete." I paused. More details fell into place. I widened my eyes. "Very agile. The person jumped over a metal grill and whipped around a bench without so much as a break in speed."

46

"There! See? You're remembering lots more." Izzie squeezed my arm. "Maybe the runaway is a professional athlete."

"Living in Whisper Cove?" I frowned.

"Or on vacation?" Izzie lifted her brow.

"And maybe that person just happened to be taking a jog through the park at the time and has nothing to do with Lana's death." Dad leaned his head to one side.

"Is that your way of reminding me to be careful of what I say?" I sighed. "Okay, we won't jump to conclusions. Guessing can hurt innocent people." Not to mention, Winsell probably wouldn't take it well if he thought we were interfering in his case. I drummed my fingers on the table. What would Lana do if she were me in this situation? Give up? Take a backseat and not look for answers? Not if she were suspected of murder. I shook my head as I glimpsed Izzie. "We can still snoop on the sly, right? Lana deserves that much."

"Absolutely." Izzie held out a palm to high-five me.

"Be careful, girls." Mom pointed at each of us. "Trouble doesn't seem to have a problem finding you. We know that from past history."

The warning conjured up memories of last year and the murders. Izzie and I had some close calls with our involvement, and Hunter had lectured me plenty of times. "Don't worry, Mom. We'll play it safe. Won't we, Izzie?"

Izzie dabbed her lips then pushed away from the table. The twitch in the corner of one eye didn't go unnoticed by me. "Of course. Safety first. Isn't that a girl scout motto? Anyway, trouble is not something I want in my future. I have Brody, Chloe and I have our paint business to run, and there's summer to keep all of us busy. Why would I want complications in my life?"

"You're rambling." I covered my comment with a deliberate cough.

"Okay then, I'm heading upstairs to freshen up before heading to the shop." Izzie blushed as she hurried to load her plate and silverware in the dishwasher.

"I'm right behind you." My gaze flickered to Dad, then Mom. At once, I tensed. Their expressions told me they weren't falling for Izzie's reasons why we would stay out of trouble. I wasn't hanging around to answer any more questions or make more promises I'd find difficult to keep.

"Love you, guys. We'll be home to help with dinner. Tacos, right?" My voice trailed behind me as I called over my shoulder while hurrying down the hall and sprinting up the stairs.

I stepped into Izzie's room. She was slipping into a pair of skinny jeans. Sitting on the edge of her bed, I groaned. "That didn't end well."

"Mom and Dad will be fine. They're acting like all parents do and with justification, wouldn't you say?" Izzie tugged at the mock turtle neck sweater until her head popped through. She blew air to remove the long strands of hair covering her face.

"Yes. I know." I twisted and tucked one leg under my rear. "But we can't stop, right? I've been making a mental list of who could've caused Lana's death." I refused to say murdered. Even though Winsell thought her death was most likely that, I was uncomfortable accepting the idea. Not until there was proof or a plausible motive in hand. Besides, Lana could've gotten those bruises anywhere.

"Like your mysterious athletic runaway with no name?" Izzie sat next to me. "How about a suspect with a name? We must have one or two of those to add to the list."

"We do. How about Rita? She was jealous of Lana getting the job."

"Rita? I agree she's a bit dramatic, always panicking about something, but murder?" Izzie shook her head.

"Okay, but I'm keeping her on my list. At least until she comes up with an alibi."

"Who else? My mind is drawing a blank." Izzie stood and walked to the mirror. She ran a brush through her hair, then pulled it back into a ponytail.

I squirmed in my seat. I didn't like thinking of him in that way. "What about Nick?"

Izzie gasped and dropped the brush. "But he's...*was* Lana's boyfriend."

"Exactly. You saw the way they acted together at the house and at the park. The tension between them was fierce. What if Nick pushed Lana? Maybe they had an argument, things got out of control, and it just happened." My voice trailed off into a whisper.

The frown wrinkling Izzie's brow deepened. "Oh, wow. Not easy to picture that scene." She snapped her fingers. "While we're considering jealousy as a motive, what about Audrey? Lana treated her badly, from what I could tell. She dished out menial tasks, and I never heard her give much praise. If Audrey has talent, which I'm guessing she does, she could be a suspect."

"Yep. I agree. So, we have the runaway, Rita, Nick, and Audrey on the list. Anyone else?" I tapped my chin with one finger.

"How about any resident of Whisper Cove who is dead set against the amphitheater coming to town and crazy enough to take it out on the muralist?" Izzie threw up her arms. "I know. That's a stretch. Seems like we've got nothing until we learn more about Lana's death. No clues, no true motives, nothing."

I dug at the palm of my hand with one fingernail. I'd promised Hunter to keep quiet, but this was Izzie. If we planned to snoop together, she should know everything. "About that. Hunter told me a few things last night." I relayed the coroner's report and Winsell's decision and how I was a suspect. "He swore me to secrecy, so please, don't tell anyone else, especially Mom and Dad."

"Wow." She paced the room. "Holy wow. That's big." Her eyes widened. "Oh, Chloe. You're a suspect?"

"Yeah, that's why we should do our own snooping." I sank deeper into my seat. Winsell wasn't about to give up anything he learned about the case. To him, we'd be two nuisances getting in his way. Far worse than Hunter had acted when it came to protecting his investigations.

"Winsell won't like it." Izzie wagged her finger.

"*Winsell* has me on his suspect list of people to investigate. That gives me a reason to find answers. I have to defend myself, don't I?"

Izzie kept quiet. Reaching for her bag and jacket, she then headed to the hallway.

I followed. She knew I was right. If I didn't fight to prove my innocence, I could end up behind bars. An idea hit me as I landed in the foyer. "Let's stop by Spill the Beans on our way to the shop. I want to grab another coffee."

Izzie buttoned her jacket, keeping her gaze on me. "Didn't you already have four or six cups?"

I snorted and reached for the doorknob. "Hardly. At least no more than three. Besides, stopping there will give us the opportunity to hear what everyone is saying about Lana's death." Spill the Beans was the center of town gossip. Folks stopped by in the morning and stayed until the news talk became boring, or they left quickly when there was nothing juicy to dish.

"Hmm. You have a point." Izzie directed her steps toward the driveway and her jeep.

I gave the tangerine cement swan sitting in the yard a pat on the head. Mom had painted it to match the porch swing. No one could claim this family didn't have a colorful flair when it came to decorating. This spring, she'd decided to give the mailbox a coat of tangerine as well, despite Dad's protest. I had to agree with him. Too much flair would be gauche. At least the mail carrier didn't have a problem spotting our box, even during a winter blizzard.

We rode into town and parked across the street in the ferry dock parking lot. I spotted Dewey Sawyer mopping the deck and smiled. After last fall and the catastrophic events that put him in the middle of trouble, I worried he'd quit the ferry and never return. Thankfully, that didn't happen. Dewey appeared happier than he'd ever been.

The coffee shop sat on the corner of Whisper Cove Boulevard and Sail Shore Drive. With the dozen breakfast barstools and five tables spaced tightly together, seating was limited. It was a cozy and warm atmosphere, which customers liked. Framed photos filled the walls, ones of Tom Pritchard, the owner, and his ancestors who'd opened the business during the twenties, right before the great depression hit. Tom bragged how his great, great grandfather held on and managed to survive when many businesses didn't. There were also a few snapshots of famous people who'd stopped in for coffee, like comedian Lucille Ball, which made sense since she was from nearby Jamestown.

I slid onto a leather barstool while Izzie walked over to a table to speak with a couple of locals. "Hi, Tom. I'd like two large coffees, both with cream, please."

"Sure thing, Chloe." Tom pointed behind me. "Got quite the crowd today. Nothing like trouble to get the gossip stirring."

"I agree." I swiveled my stool to study the people around me. Certainly, the noisy buzz of conversation filled the air, along with animated expressions, mostly excited. I felt a twinge of sadness to realize someone's tragedy could make people act in unsympathetic ways, not thinking how cruel they sounded to others.

"Here you go. Two coffees. I marked Izzie's with her name. I know she likes extra cream." As his face flushed with a bright shade of red, he turned to clear his throat. "That'll be six dollars."

I pressed my lips together to keep a serious face and not embarrass Tom. He'd had a crush on Izzie since high school, but never let her know. I certainly knew. In fact, everyone who took notice of the way he acted around Izzie knew. No secret there. I handed him the money. "Keep the change."

"How is your sister doing, anyway?" Tom glimpsed me without coming in full eye contact. He wiped the counter to occupy the moment.

"She's great. Business is great. Her life is…great." I avoided any mention of Brody. I didn't want to be the first to break the bad news, in case he hadn't already heard. Instead, I switched topics. "So, what is everyone saying? About Lana's death, I mean."

Tom shrugged. "Mostly talk about Frank Benworthy being a suspect."

"Oh?" My voice hitched, and I leaned into the counter. "Why Frank?"

Tom scratched behind one ear and whispered. "Guess you haven't heard. The detective and his team found one of those posters from the march lying on the ground. Bill Evans told me the detective questioned some of the protesters and found out the poster belonged to Frank." He shook his head. "Gotta feel sorry for the guy. I really like Frank."

I rubbed the hem of my jacket while letting the news sink in. "Yeah, me too. Still, I don't get it. How does his poster connect him to Lana's death?" I still couldn't get myself to say the word murder.

"You know that paint can and shoe prints with the same blue paint found at the scene?"

"Yeah, so?" My stomach churned.

"According to one of the detective's team members—he's some kind of expert in this sort of thing. Anyway, he claims Frank's poster has smudged fingerprints with the same color of paint. Circa. Sari. Shoot. I forget the word."

I gulped. "Cerulean blue." We'd provided the can of it for Lana to paint the mural. The same can of paint that spilled over next to Lana's body.

I slid open the box of paper plates with the cutter. We'd been in the storage room for the better part of an hour, unpacking this morning's supply delivery, mostly materials for paint events, like plates, paper towels, and cups. "Aren't we supposed to get a new delivery of canvases today? Without them, we might not have enough for the winery event."

"Let me check." Izzie swiped her phone screen and finally gave a nod. "Tracking says the shipment will arrive late this afternoon or evening. So, we're good."

I swiped my hand across a sweaty brow. "How'd it get so hot in here? We have AC."

Izzie nibbled on a fingernail. "I turned the temp up. We have to cut corners somewhere. Utilities and rent are digging into our profits way too much."

I recognized the worried expression. Izzie always worried about the business, even when things were going great. "You're right. We should do what we can. However, the calendar is full. We have at least three or four events booked each week for the next several months and some weeks with five. Lots of guests have already registered. Gotta celebrate that news, right?" I lifted my chin.

A nervous chuckle escaped, and she smiled. "Absolutely. I say we head over to Duckies this evening for drinks and dancing. The band, Soundwave, is playing." Izzie twirled around. "Maybe you can get Hunter to come. I'll call Brody. I think he's off work this evening."

The sudden change in mood brightened my spirits too. All the talk about Frank being a possible killer had spooked me and rattled my confidence in judging someone's character. Like Tom, I thought Frank was a good person.

Kind, generous, always looking out for the town's welfare. "Great suggestion, Izzie. I'll call Hunter before I meet with Lana's team at Millie's Diner. You sure you don't want to come?"

"Too much to do in the shop. Besides, you can tell me what they say when you get back." Izzie stacked paper towel rolls on the shelf, then straightened the row of paint tubes.

I sat on the bench and sighed. "Hard to believe Frank would hurt anyone." I couldn't help talking about him. "Right?"

Izzie turned. "Well, after what I heard people at Spill the Beans had to say, I'm not sure. He's always been the most critical of the amphitheater returning to Whisper Cove, but to practically threaten Miles about it?" She shook her head. "Doesn't look good for him. Plus, it's obvious his bed and breakfast will suffer. All the noisy concerts. How do you promote your business by claiming a stay at the B&B will be relaxing and peaceful? Concert noise, traffic flooding the town, crowds of people. Nope. Detective Winsell has plenty of reasons to suspect Frank Benworthy."

"Yeah. I guess." Despite all of those reasons Izzie talked about, I felt sorry for Frank. If Winsell was as professional and detailed about his cases as Hunter proved to be, he would not jump to any conclusion. Frank wasn't the only one with some kind of motive. I had to believe that.

The front door chimes jingled. "Hey? Where are you guys? I saw the light on and came in to say hi." Footsteps clicked on the wood floorboards as someone crossed the front room. "You should really keep your door locked if no one's out front."

I peered through the doorway to get a better view of the round, cheery face framed by blonde curls. Megan's generous curves bounced along with her quick gate. A bright smile greeted me as she waved. "Hi, Megan. Watch you don't trip over the mess of boxes. We're in the middle of unpacking."

"Megs!" Izzie squealed and wrapped her arms around her best friend's shoulders.

"Happy to see me?" Megan's words muffled from under the folds of Izzie's sweater. She pulled away and frowned. "You may change your mind after hearing what I have to say."

"What?" Izzie tilted her head. "Why? Are you in trouble? I'll help any way I can."

I walked to the front and grabbed three bottles of Bob's Fizzy Orange from the mini-fridge. Returning, I handed one to each of them. "We're both here for you. No matter what."

Megan Hunt was a fellow shop owner on the alley. Sadly, she'd gone through a lot of challenges in the past year. Being scammed and blackmailed led to nearly losing her shop, Light Your Scent, where she sold her specially made candles. Even worse, Megan couldn't keep up the rent on her condo. Ashamed and feeling like a failure, she moved home to live with her parents. I pointed out to her that living at home wasn't failure. In fact, lots of young people our age found it financially necessary at some point. Izzie and I were doing our best to save up for a place of our own. With the paint shop expenses and inflation making everything costly, we realized that might take a while.

Megan pulled one of the crates over to sit near us. "You remember when I told you several months ago about the business opportunity I got with that huge company to sell my candles?"

Izzie and I nodded.

"And how I might have to spend time in New York City for consultations and promotions?" Megan leaned in. Her jaw worked back and forth for a few seconds. "Does the offer you made to help cover my shop when I'm away still stand? Mom's surgery got put off because of her blood pressure. She's going in for the knee replacement next week." A huge sigh released. "Look. I know it's bad timing, with Lana's death and all that trouble to get the mural painting finished before the first concert. And I'm so sorry about your friend, Chloe. Talk is spreading like the fury of a spring tornado with all kinds of rumors. Did you know Frank Benworthy filed a complaint with the town council about the amphitheater's return? Insisting all those concerts will disrupt the town and bottleneck traffic. He was fuming when the council decided last Friday his case was unfounded. Sure gives that detective even more reason to focus on Frank in his investigation, doesn't it? Anyway, if you don't feel up to taking on running my shop, I can hire someone part-time to take over when I'm gone."

"Absolutely not. We said we'd help, and that still stands. Right, Chloe?" Izzie sent a look that pleaded with me to agree.

I frowned. "Wait. Back up a sec. What's this about Frank?" Checkmark the box next to reasons why the B&B owner would look guilty in Winsell's eyes. Heck. Even I was beginning to doubt my opinion of Frank's innocence. The runaway stranger at the crime scene who could've easily been him, the protests, the poster with cerulean blue paint, and now this thing with the town council. All of those details added up to one very likely suspect of foul play. But why take it out on Lana? That didn't make sense. Maybe she was the unfortunate victim who'd been in the wrong place at the wrong time.

"I know. Awful, isn't it?" Megan winced. "That poor man. If he gets arrested for murder..." Her eyes widened. "Sorry. I meant *if* Lana was murdered. Of course, her death could've been a tragic accident. I shouldn't— sorry." She grabbed my hand and squeezed. "I'm making it worse, aren't I? Rumors are like poison. I should know."

"That's okay." I patted her hand. "Some rumors turn out to be fact." I had to clear my head and concentrate on something else other than Hunter's news that Winsell strongly leaned toward classifying Lana's death a homicide. "Say. It's almost noon." I stood. "I hate to leave this party of three, but I have a lunch date."

"Oh!" Megan sprang out of her chair. "I'm sorry. I won't keep you. I've got lots of errands to take care of before heading back to the shop. You need anything dropped off at the post office? I'm on my way there."

"Nope. We're good." Izzie gave Megan a peck on the cheek. "Give us a heads up when you're making that trip to New York. Chloe and I can take turns covering your shop."

Megan thanked us and hurried to the front.

I studied the back of her as she reached for the door. The information she'd shared about Frank surged through my brain and left me unsettled. I didn't want to single him out. Plenty of people could've wanted to ruin the amphitheater's opening. I turned to Izzie. "I should go."

Izzie chewed on her bottom lip. "Okay. I recognize that look."

"What look?" I blinked.

Her finger circled. "The deep frown that almost swallows your face. You're planning something. What's up?"

I shrugged. "I'm anxious to talk with Nick and his team mates."

"You mean to question them. I get it. We can't give Frank all of our attention."

"We do think alike." I grinned.

"We're sisters."

I almost stated the obvious, which was that blood relations didn't always think the same, but in this case, she was right. "Okay. I'm off." I grabbed my bag and jacket. "If Willow comes in early, why don't you join us for lunch?"

She waved an arm. "I'll stay to get work done. You can handle Nick and the others."

I headed out the door and jogged to my car. Pulling to an abrupt stop, I squinted and bent down to examine the rear bumper. A visible dent puckered the left corner. A few colorful words came to mind but remained unspoken as I straightened and turned around to see that no one was close by. The dent wasn't there this morning. At least, I was pretty sure it wasn't. I circled around the car, slowly to check for any other signs of damage to my slightly used but new-to-me vehicle. When I stopped in front of the windshield, I grumbled under my breath. A note stuck under the wiper fluttered in the wind. I plucked it free and unfolded the pink paper to read a message.

"Sorry, sweetie. I confused my brake and gas pedals and tapped your bumper. I'll pay for the damage, even though it's hardly more than a scratch. Love always, Aunt Constance." My voice inched higher and tighter on the last few words. Crumbling the note, I tossed it on the passenger seat while climbing inside to take the wheel.

Aunt Constance was married to Dad's only brother, our Uncle David. He passed away a couple of years ago. Constance grieved in her own way, mostly keeping her sadness hidden underneath an endless supply of smiles and hugs, surrounding herself with friends, and engaging in hours of group activities, like her former job as president of the Chautauqua Sisterhood chapter. She loved life to the fullest and took bold chances, like opening a craft shop on Artisan Alley after her daughter Spencer left town for a better job offer. Dad complained she spent the family inheritance like there was no end to it. I understood why it upset him. After all, we didn't always have money. That came later, after Granddad Abbington passed away. Mom and Dad were grateful, but never lost sight of the way things had been before.

However, Aunt Constance never gave that detail a thought. She definitely had flair and a personality that attracted lots of attention. Despite her faults, Izzie and I loved Aunt Constance dearly and didn't know what we'd do without her in our lives. Even when she dinged my slightly used Mazda that I'd owned for less than three months. I shook my head, and with a smile teasing my lips, I motored down the road to find a parking spot in front of Millie's Diner.

Approaching the front entrance, I spotted Tate and Nick seated at a booth. Audrey wasn't with them. I waved at Millie, then skirted around tables to reach the booths lined along the wall. The succulent smell of today's special—roast beef sandwiches with onion rings—wafted through the air to tease my appetite. Behind me, the squeaky voice of Stevie, one of Millie's servers, reeled off the choice of desserts for customers. I groaned while mentally adding a slice of apple pie to my lunch order.

"Hi, guys. Where's Audrey?" I slid into the booth next to Nick.

"She's dealing with a migraine and staying in her hotel room. They hit her pretty hard," Nick explained.

Tate gave Nick a pointed stare before turning to smile at me. "Yeah, it's a shame. Anyway, how about we order? I'm starving."

I got the hint that discussing Audrey's migraines was not welcome. "Well, if there's anything Izzie and I can do to help, let me know." I tapped the menu. "Millie's roast beef sandwiches are the best. She slow bakes the meat, and the spice recipe she uses is a family secret. No one can pry the ingredients from her lips. Trust me. I've tried." I laughed. My planned strategy was to satisfy their appetites before probing them with the serious talk. Of course, I would make it a point to corner Audrey later to ask about her relationship with Lana. Whether the migraine was faked and Audrey's way of bailing out of lunch, or the absence was legit, I couldn't be sure. Either way, her name was at the top of my suspect list. Right now, I'd focus on Nick and Tate. Pointing at each of them, I added, "Drinks for everybody? The raspberry iced tea is freshly made every morning." With a wave, I motioned Stevie to our table.

"Thanks, Chloe." Nick folded his arms and rested them on the table. "Treating us to lunch is really nice of you, but I have to tell you something." His gaze shifted for a second to Tate, who was shaking his head.

I volleyed my attention between the two of them. "What's going on?"

Nick leaned in. "The reason for Audrey's migraine has more to do with a certain resident of Whisper Cove than anything else. How well do you know Rita Morgan?"

I grumbled under my breath. "Let me guess. Rita's squawking about taking over the mural painting. Right?" The heat rose to my face. Rita didn't have any right or vote in the matter. Only the town council and Miles had the power to decide who finished the mural. I took deep breaths to calm myself. Besides feeling angry about Rita's behavior, I was depressed about Lana's death and how Rita now seemed to be making everything about herself. I didn't want to steer my mind toward rash assumptions. However, Rita certainly pushed to the front of the line as to who gained from Lana's death.

Nick hitched his breath. "More like accosted her, right in the hotel lobby, pushing to know who'd take over painting the mural and how it was her right to be chosen. Of course Audrey's upset. Lana's death has put her on edge, and she's feeling insecure. I'm worried she might fall into one of her depressed states. It's happened before."

"Nick, you shouldn't be telling Chloe." Tate frowned. "Not your place, you know."

"Chloe might as well know what she's dealing with, if Audrey stays to paint the mural." Nick leaned back. "Personally, I think we should cut our losses and leave town."

My mouth flapped as I tried to respond. What just happened? "Look. Don't make any decisions yet. Let me talk to Audrey. And I'll deal with Rita and persuade her to apologize. She may be high-strung and too outspoken, but I know how to reason with her. Trust me." I forced my lips to curl into a smile. "Now, how about those roast beef sandwiches?"

I took a long sip of water to wash down the sour taste in my mouth. What started out a few days ago to be a reunion between two friends and plans to celebrate the amphitheater's homecoming with a colorful mural had quickly spiraled into a Shakespearean tragedy. Rita's outburst and Nick's threat to leave town only added another dismal scene.

Chapter Seven

"Doesn't matter what Nick decides, or Audrey, or Tate. Until Lana's case is closed, Detective Winsell won't let them go anywhere," Izzie argued as I shoved supplies for our event in boxes. Since my lunch date with Nick and Tate and the news that surprised me, I'd spent the better part of yesterday stewing. After a good night's sleep, I woke this morning determined to let the matter rest. Winsell could handle it. Now, Izzie had me worried again.

I pointed my finger at her. "You're right. I hadn't thought of that reason because Nick got me so flustered with the way he talked about packing up and leaving us." I straightened one of the painted canvases that hung slightly crooked on the wall, then grabbed several rolls of paper towels and shoved them in a box to carry out to my car. My stomach rolled. The leftover spicy taste of Millie's roast beef mixed with the news from Nick during lunch didn't sit well with my digestion.

"Wait. I'll follow you out. Willow, are you coming?" Izzie shouted just as our assistant stepped out of the storage room, carrying mini canvases for the paint party at Tasty Spirits winery.

"Everything will turn out okay." The words coming from Izzie's mouth garbled as she spoke with the shop key clamped between her lips while balancing a box stacked full of program brochures listing our future events in her arms.

I pulled the door open and held it while Izzie and Willow stepped outside. "Absolutely okay, as soon as I have that talk with Rita. Seriously, what was she thinking? I mean, yeah, she's all about drama, but confronting Audrey in that way was beyond drama." Lunch with Nick and Tate had settled into an awkward affair. I had wanted to probe more about the depressed side of Audrey that Nick had mentioned but instead stuck to safer topics like the New York city life and all the places I missed going to. That alone took up the time. At least nothing more was said about leaving town.

Once the cars were loaded up with supplies, we took Route eighty-six out of town for our two-hour drive to Keuka Lake. Quite a trek for one event, but Izzie negotiated a sweet deal with Sal Vincent, the owner of Tasty Spirits, which included an impressive performance fee for us and his promise to promote Paint with a View by distributing our event brochures to customers and spreading the word to other winery owners. No doubt, Izzie was a force of nature when it came to business.

Keuka Lake was one of the Finger Lakes and the perfect destination for wine lovers to tour any or all of the dozen vineyards surrounding it. What I loved, though, were the scenic images that inspired me to paint. Mom and Dad spent plenty of time visiting the area to host artist workshops for seniors, one of their favorite pastimes in giving back to the community. They'd suggested contacting Sal after he expressed interest in scheduling an event.

As our destination neared, I turned off the AC and cracked open a window to let in the fresh air. Spring had finally bloomed and exploded with pine tree and floral aromas that tickled my senses. The car speaker erupted with a phone call, and Izzie's name appeared on the dashboard display. I punched the button to answer as a chuckle escaped my lips. "What's the matter? Missing me already?"

"Ha. Funny you. No, Willow and I were just talking about Rita and your uncomfortable conversation with Nick. Do you think there could be another reason why he wants to leave town so soon? I mean, other than the issue with Audrey."

I tapped my fingers on the steering wheel. "Like if Lana's death wasn't an accidental fall but rather murder, and Nick is feeling guilty? I don't know." I paused. Nick's reaction when he learned of Lana's death looked like genuine shock and dismay. At least, in my eyes, it did. Yet, as Winsell pointed out,

Nick couldn't account for all of his time that evening. He claimed to be in his hotel room alone for more than an hour. Audrey and Tate had the same issue. Yet, Nick had acted so in love with Lana, doting on her every need. I couldn't make up my mind what to think about him. "I guess we should keep an eye on all three of them. Nick, Audrey, and Tate. Like you said, Izzie, they won't be going anywhere until Winsell closes the case."

"Of course, I hope Nick had nothing to do with Lana's fall, but if you were guilty of murder, wouldn't you want to get as far away from the authorities as possible and quickly? I sure would."

"Let's save this conversation for later. I see the exit. And we're right on schedule. Tasty Spirits, here we come!" I gave my mood a shot of optimism, banishing all thoughts about murder and suspects for the moment. The sun shone, and the lake water sparkled. A late afternoon, painting while sipping wine? Nothing could make me happier.

A warm breeze eased through the open windows of Tasty Spirits, and the pleasant tinkling of wind chimes filled the room. Dark walnut fixtures contrasted with the shiny steel counters and brightly colored light fixtures. Sal, the owner, stood with arms crossed over his barrel chest. He narrowed his gaze while appraising the setup of our equipment with a nod. He'd helped us by carrying in boxes of supplies, connecting the projector, and unfolding easels. His eyes sparkled along with his smile, evidently excited to see so many customers flocking into his establishment. A display of wines lined the counter. Sal didn't miss a beat as he greeted the guests and boasted how Tasty Spirits carried the best wine in the Finger Lakes region, adding that all bottles were available to purchase at a special price today, just for them. I had to admire his business savvy.

I finished placing art supplies at each table while Izzie and Willow set up the projector. The step-by-step images Willow had drawn were situated on easel stands for guests to easily view when they needed some assistance with their paintings. With hands on hips, I perused the winery, doing a mental checklist of every detail and item for our event. The only thing left was for the owner to set out charcuterie boards on the sidebar.

I tapped my watch, and the display showed we had minutes before class would begin. By my headcount, all the paint party guests had arrived. The tingling feeling I'd get before every event surged through me. Excitement, nerves, whatever caused that feeling would disappear as soon as we started our introductions. I grew to love this business as much as Izzie did, which was fortunate since making it big as an artist in New York hadn't worked out the way I planned.

"I think we should get started." Izzie leaned close and murmured under her breath. "Sal is already talking about booking us for another party. We might have to hire more assistants in the near future."

My brow inched upward. "How about we get through this day first before that happens. Hmm?"

"Yeah, you're right. Typical me getting carried away." Izzie's voice sobered.

"It's showtime," Willow said as she stood alongside us.

After filling their plates with items from the charcuterie board and making their wine selections, everyone had settled into their chairs. Soon, the chatter in the room quieted as guests focused their attention on us.

Izzie tapped her wine glass with a brush and smiled. "Welcome, everyone. My name is Izzie Abbington, and this is my sister Chloe and our assistant Willow. We're so excited to bring our paint party business to Keuka Lake and Tasty Spirits Winery. We hope you enjoy the experience as much as we do."

"And if you plan a trip to Whisper Cove, please stop by our shop, Paint with a View, to chat, or maybe to reserve a spot for one of our events. You'll find a list of what's coming up on your brochure," I added.

"Before we dive in to paint our canvases, notice the drawings with written notes staged along the wall. Those are to help you with each step of painting in case you need it," Willow chimed in.

"Okay then, everyone take a look at the brushes in front of you." I held up mine.

While Izzie carried on to explain, my attention wandered elsewhere. Through the front window, I spotted a familiar vehicle pull into the parking lot. As it passed out of sight, I grew anxious to leave the room and follow, but of course, I couldn't. Instead, I brought my thoughts back to the event, where they should be. Putting on a cheerful face and ignoring the worry inching its way up inside me, I circulated the room to help the guests while Izzie gave instructions and drew the first lines of a lake scene on her canvas that projected onto the screen above.

By the time we'd gotten halfway through our instruction, the paintings of Keuka Lake with colorful sailboats were taking shape. Izzie called for a five-minute break so guests could refill their glasses and plates.

I took the opportunity at hand and tugged at Izzie's sleeve. "I'm going outside for some fresh air. Be back in a few." Before she had a chance to respond, I grabbed my water bottle and hurried to the exit door. If my hunch was right, I'd spotted Miles Terrell's yellow convertible. A classic Mustang. I'd not seen many of those on the road around here. The important question in my mind was how much of a coincidence would it be for him to show up at the winery at the same time as us? It could be the paranoia taking control of my thoughts, but I didn't buy into that sort of coincidence.

Tipping the bottle, I swigged on water and shifted my gaze back and forth across the lot. The neon yellow convertible stood out alongside a drab grey sedan. The vanity plate with the name MILES VIP1 confirmed my hunch. I tapped the bottle with one finger, giving myself a few seconds to decide whether to pursue the matter. A quick glance through the window showed Izzie and Willow laughing while guests busied themselves at the sidebar pouring wine and choosing from the assortment of cheeses, meats, and condiments. A few more minutes away from the activities wouldn't hurt. I sprinted across the lot to reach a row of grapevines bordering several tables that looked out over the lake. Bright red umbrellas provided shade for those patrons who chose to take their wine and meals outside.

Hiding behind the curtain of vines, I peered through an opening. Miles sat at one of the tables, facing toward me. Another man sat across from him. Dark hair with a slight waviness and those broad shoulders caused me to gasp. "Nick," I whispered under my breath. Why the two of them would be together, having a meal at Tasty Spirits, I couldn't guess. Other than the amphitheater mural, what did they have in common? Maybe Nick was renegotiating the contract Lana had signed. That thought puzzled me. Nick had firmly suggested he, Audrey, and Tate would leave Whisper Cove, that matters with Rita's outburst and Audrey's emotional reaction were making it difficult to stay. However, why else would he and Miles meet?

As if to help answer my questions, Miles suddenly sprang up from his chair. He tossed an envelope on the table. Shaking a finger at Nick, his face reddened with a rush of anger. "This better be the last I hear of this." The raised voice and his words carried across the lawn. I winced at the sound and shrunk into the cover of vines as he stormed away.

Within seconds, Nick stood. Glancing side to side, he then gathered the envelope and tucked it inside his jacket pocket. Turning, he walked toward me and my shelter of vines.

I held my breath, hoping he wouldn't look in my direction. As he passed, I could see his face clearly. Tears welled in his eyes. Before they could spill on to his cheeks, he swiped them away with the back of one hand. Lifting his chin, he grimaced in anger and hurried his steps. I watched as he stopped by the grey sedan and slid into the driver's seat. By now, the yellow Mustang was turning out onto the road. Nick trailed a safe distance behind.

Mulling over what I'd just witnessed, I walked slowly back to the winery. As I reached for the door, another figure caught my eye. I twisted around to get a full view and gasped for a second time. The rumpled coat covered the slouched form of Detective Winsell. He jogged stiffly to his car and got behind the wheel. The engine rumbled to life, and the vehicle peeled out of the parking lot.

"Well, what do you know?" With a sigh, I pulled the door open to step inside. Discovering more questions than answers weren't helping to solve Lana's death. Yet, here I was, those questions popping into my head, one after another. Not to mention, the suspect list wasn't growing any smaller. Nick somehow had made Miles angry. And what was in that envelope? I had to find out.

I wove past tables and easels to reach Izzie and Willow. "Hey, guys. Do I have a story for you."

Izzie tilted her head. "I don't know. Do you?"

"It was a rhetorical statement, Izzie." I smiled kindly, then went on to give them details of what happened. "As if seeing Miles and Nick wasn't surprising enough, Detective Winsell popping up sure did."

"Now, the question is, who was he following?" Willow tapped her pointer stick against her leg. "I say his plan was to tail us, but when he spotted Nick and Miles, he found their meeting more interesting."

"Huh. Good point. All he had to do was check our schedule to know we'd be here. Not so with the meeting between Miles and Nick, I bet." None of this made me feel better. Winsell followed us, and more importantly, followed me. I couldn't blame him. Time and place put me at the crime scene. However, what could he think was my motive? I came up with zilch, which left me exasperated.

"Okay, ladies. We need to discuss the comings and goings of Winsell later. We have a paint event to finish." Izzie tapped on her microphone and redirected the guests to their seats.

I took over instructing the last details of the project while Izzie and Willow circulated the room to help those who needed it. With concentrated effort, I kept my mind on the task at hand, but tiny bits of conversation and the images of Miles' angry face, Nick's tears, and Winsell's rumpled coat crept into my mind every minute or so. No doubt, I'd be consumed with the mystery of Lana's death until the case was solved. Just as Winsell would be determined to keep me in his detective radar.

Rain pinged on the windshield as I pulled into a parking spot. Leaving our cargo of supplies in the trunk, I shielded my head with my oversized handbag and sprinted to the shop. Inside, Izzie and Willow shrugged off their raingear and folded umbrellas, which of course I forgot to bring with me this morning. Preoccupation with anything and everything murder related forced me to forget practical things like checking the weather forecast. I grumbled while brushing raindrops off my bag.

"I'd say that our event was a success. Sal gave me the names of three winery owners who are interested in booking us." Izzie clasped her hands and sighed. "Isn't life great?" Her eyes widened as she looked at me. "I mean when murder isn't hanging over our heads, and you're not being accused of your friend's death. That's what I meant."

A weak smile formed my lips. "The paint event *was* a success. That's what counts."

Izzie squeezed my arm. "First things first. We need to track down who killed Lana, if someone really did. Winsell might be making the wrong call on this one. Detectives don't always get it right, do they? Anyway, we'll do our bit of snooping and come up with our own answers. Agreed?" The hope conveyed by raising her chin accompanied the enthusiasm in her voice.

"Agreed." I gave her a hug and dismissed my moment of despair for the moment.

At once, Willow jumped in to wrap arms around us both. "Everything will turn out fine. You're innocent, and my gut tells me Winsell knows it. He's playing his role. That's all."

I chuckled. "You mean the grumpy old detective role with a suspicious eye? Thanks, guys. All this positivity gives me hope." Chances were, the old me would've got on the phone to call Ross and ask for legal advice to prepare for that just-in-case moment. However, the newly engaged Ross would be busy juggling law and wedding plans. I refused to bother him with my problems.

The wind chimes hanging from the door tinkled, and Rita stepped inside. She shook her umbrella, leaving a puddle on the floor. "That rain is brutal. Wouldn't be surprised if a tornado stormed through town." She smoothed the top of her hair, which stuck out in a tangled swirly mass.

"Rita! What a coincidence. Your name came up in conversation at lunch today." I bit down on my lip. Here was my opportunity to question her about the incident with Audrey.

"Oh? Well, that's nice." Rita hummed a tune while going through our selection of paints, brushes, and hand-crafted bookmarks.

My brow inched north, and I turned to Izzie, who shrugged. The Rita I knew would fire off a dozen questions, wanting to know the details. After all, her appetite for gossip was fierce. She'd gobble it up. I sidled up to stand closer to her and straightened a basket of paint tools on the counter. "I suppose you heard the town council has to make a decision about who'll finish the mural painting."

Rita stilled. Slowly, she moved to pick out two tubes of paint and three bookmarks. Turning, she pursed her lips, then let them ease into a smile. "I'm sure they'll make the right choice. I spoke to one of the council members. You know James Quill? He hinted that I have a very good chance of being picked."

I skirted the counter and stood next to the register. "Would you like to buy those?" I pointed at the items in her hand.

She pulled out her wallet. "He said they are looking for someone qualified. I handed him my resume and asked him to take it to the council meeting."

"I guess that's what you told Audrey yesterday, right? Nick says you practically accosted her in the hotel lobby, insisting you should be chosen to finish the mural, not her." I searched her face for any reaction, like guilt or embarrassment. Instead, her face reddened and cheeks puffed out.

"She's lying. I only mentioned how I was being considered and then wished her the best of luck." Rita snatched the bag of purchases from my hand. "And I don't appreciate people talking behind my back, accusing me of what never happened. Good day." Rita yanked open the door and disappeared, only to return five seconds later. She grabbed her soaked umbrella. With a final shake she thrust it like a sword. "You ladies are lucky I do so much business with you. Really, to think how I'm always telling people what a fun shop this is." She snorted. "Unappreciative. That's what young people are. Unappreciative."

I winced as the door slammed shut. "Well, we sure got a reaction, didn't we?"

"Yeah, maybe a little too over the top?" Bracing her arms, Izzie lifted to sit on the counter.

Willow sat on the barstool and next to Izzie. "Gotta admit, if Rita ends up getting the mural job, Winsell might take a closer look at how much she had to gain from Lana's death. Big motive for murder."

"Speaking of our infamous detective," Izzie whispered and jabbed me in the arm before pointing to the window.

"Fantastic." I let out a groan as Winsell entered the shop. Would this day, with all its problems, ever end?

He stood quietly in the doorway. As if it were a practiced ritual, he removed his soaked coat, folded it in half, and draped it over his arm. "Ladies." He grinned. "It's a beautiful evening. All this rain leaves everything smelling fresh, don't you think?"

I laid one finger against my chin. "What brings you to our shop, Detective?" As if I didn't know or already suspect.

"Here to sign up for one of our events? We have a Paint Your Pet Red White and Blue event around the fourth. Do you own a pet? Dog? Cat? Maybe a python or moray eel?" Izzie curled her lips into an impish grin.

I stabbed her in the side and whispered out of the corner of my mouth. "Izzie, behave."

"Ouch." She rubbed the afflicted area and stepped aside. "Just kidding."

Winsell chuckled with a head shake and pulled an available chair closer to sit. "Moray eel. Don't know anybody who keeps one, but I'll be sure to check into that. I'm actually here to ask Chloe a few questions." He leveled his gaze at me.

Not even a tiny sign of humor in those eyes. My chest deflated as I exhaled to ease the tension. "Okay. Would you like something to drink? We have bottled water and Bob's Fizzy Orange." I navigated to the mini fridge while a mental list of questions he might ask checked off in my head. Well, I had a few of my own.

"Water would be nice. Thank you." Winsell settled into the chair.

Izzie stepped forward. "I have a question. How can you be sure Lana's death was a murder? I mean, plenty of people slip and fall and have accidents, don't they? Especially off of a skinny board like that lift has. One missed step, and you're on your way down." She scratched her brow. "I'm just saying it's possible."

I groaned. Now, it wouldn't take much for Winsell to guess who told us about his decision to call the case a homicide. Poor Hunter. I handed the detective the bottle of water. "So, what would you like to know?" I sat across from him at the nearest guest table, careful not to knock over the easel.

"First, I can't be one hundred percent sure it's murder, but the evidence is leaning that way. My process is to dig for evidence until I am sure." He waved his arm. "You have a beautiful shop. I envy artistic talent. From what I've heard around town, the business is very popular. Lots of compliments. Congratulations, ladies."

I chewed my bottom lip, waiting for the lethal punchline. This had nothing to do with Lana. "Thank you. We're proud of what we do."

"I was surprised to learn you'd moved here from New York City and interrupted the career path you were working on. Speaking of New York, didn't you and Lana room together at some point?" He tipped the bottle to take a swig without breaking eye contact.

The direction of the conversation veered down a new path and became a bit clearer, but not enough for me to guess why. I swallowed. "Izzie asked for my help in opening the shop."

"That's right. We support each other in any way we can." Izzie squeezed my shoulder a bit too hard.

"Thanks, Izzie." I eased out of her grasp. "Besides, I needed a break from the big city life, and I missed my parents, Izzie, and friends. You understand."

Winsell finished the water and set the empty bottle on the floor. "Yes, of course. About your relationship with Miss Easton. Had it always been pleasant? Did you have arguments, for instance?"

I frowned. "All friends have arguments at times."

"Any serious ones?" He leaned forward, placing both palms on his knees.

"I don't understand what you're asking." I squirmed in my seat.

"Any that would ruin your friendship or greatly damage it?"

"I, ah, guess there were moments, but nothing to ruin what we had." My face heated, and I glimpsed Izzie who shook her head.

Winsell stood and unfolded his coat. Giving it a couple of shakes, as if that would smooth out the wrinkles, he sighed. "I've had cases where friends become enemies. Often, the situations didn't end well. I'm glad you and Miss Easton were able to settle any differences you had. It's a shame you didn't have any more time, though." He reached for the door, then paused to turn. "How long would you say it had been since the two of you spoke? I mean, before Miss Easton came to Whisper Cove?"

I blinked. "I'm not…months, I guess. Moving didn't help. Busy lives and all that." My voice faded.

"Yes, busy lives can make us become distant. Well, I should be off. Lots to do on the case. I'll be sure to let Hunter know you said hello when I see him." He tipped his hat and walked out.

"That was intense," Willow said.

"Intense and awkward. What the heck was all that about friendships not ending well?" Izzie rolled her eyes.

"Yeah, I'm not sure." I stood and pulled the phone from my pocket. "Look, I think I'm gonna pass on Duckies this evening. I'm exhausted. Besides, I need to call Hunter and warn him that Winsell knows he spilled news about the homicide decision." I avoided staring at Izzie. No point in blaming her or getting angry. Besides, Hunter knew what he was doing by telling me.

"Oh boy. Tell him I'm sorry. It was all my fault. Me and my big, flappy mouth. Okay?" Izzie hiccupped.

"It's not a big deal, Izzie." I patted her shoulder before heading to the storage room. My heart was pounding like I'd jogged around Chautauqua Lake. Twice. The something I had worried about earlier today, the something Winsell might know about me, just became clearer. It wasn't a good sign, either. The phone clicked.

"Hunter. Hi. We really need to talk. Winsell was here at the shop a few minutes ago." I plopped down on a crate of supplies and gave him a blow-by-blow account of the visit.

"I was getting ready to call you about that." He sighed. "Why didn't you tell me you and Lana had a falling out over some painting she stole from you and used it to paint a mural?"

I grimaced. "She didn't *steal* the painting. I gave it to her as a gift." The last thing I needed was Hunter accusing me of hiding parts of my life and me having to defend myself. "The problem was she didn't ask me if it was okay to use the images in one of her murals. I had no idea until I found the article and a photo in the newspaper." I sniffed. "The whole incident felt like she'd betrayed me. Betrayed our friendship. Anyway, I confronted her.

She apologized, even offered to give me part of her commission. As if that would make up for it." I left out the part how Lana never gave me credit for the work. She'd wanted to impress her artist friends, the crowd I never would belong to or have any desire to belong to. "Sometimes, the thirst to become famous will destroy you," I mumbled.

"Are you talking about Lana?"

I heaved my chest. "She wanted to become famous, and I think choosing the moral low ground once in a while became that slippery slope. I wanted no part of that. But…how can I put this without looking like a pushover? Lana helped me out when we lived in Paris. I was this newbie tourist who couldn't find her way around, and it showed. Lana saved me from trouble more than once." My breath caught. "She was a good friend who made a bad choice. That's all. I loved her like a sister, and I wasn't about to dump that friendship in the trash over a silly painting."

"You're a compassionate and loyal person, Chloe Abbington. No wonder I love you so much." Hunter's voice softened.

"Love, huh?" I grinned. "Well, since you said it first, I love you too. Now, how much does Winsell know?"

"Everything. Or at least all of what you told me. However, that isn't the worst part."

"How can it be worse?" I sprang to my feet.

"It sounds outrageous even to me, but Winsell is contemplating how you may have lured Lana here to murder her and get revenge."

Chapter Eight

I stirred creamer in my coffee and returned to the table. Aromas of turkey bacon and cinnamon hotcakes wafted from the warming tray on the stovetop. Staring at my plate stacked with too many hotcakes and at least eight slices of bacon, I rolled my eyes. Stress eating was really a thing. At least for me, it was. With knife and fork, I furiously cut the cakes into pieces.

"I can't believe a seasoned detective who I thought was practical and reasonable could come up with such a ridiculous theory." I bit down on a slice of bacon and chewed while waving my fork in the air. "Me murdering Lana over some stupid painting? Me jealous of her career?" I speared a bite of hotcake. "What kind of assumption is that? He doesn't know me." I hitched my breath. "He doesn't know me at all."

"Of course, he doesn't, sweetie." Mom squeezed my shoulder as she leaned down, the end of her braid tickling my neck. "The truth always comes out in the end. He'll soon toss that theory of his into the lake and move on. You'll see." She moved to the other side and sat next to Dad.

"What I'd like to know is who told him about that story? Someone close to you or Lana that knew what happened between you two is my guess." Izzie tapped her lip. "Like Nick or Audrey or Tate?"

"I was thinking the same thing." I hadn't told anyone in Whisper Cove about what happened. Not even Izzie or our parents. Not even Hunter, which now I realized was a mistake. Any details that connected me to Lana, ones that made me look like a suspect, were obviously relevant in a detective's mind. But the accusation hurt. I could never hurt anyone, especially not a friend or family member. I shivered and took a generous swig of hot coffee. And murder was unthinkable. "Whoever could've told has to be desperate."

"You're right, the killer would be desperate, wanting to pull Winsell's attention away from himself or herself and onto you. Makes sense," Izzie said.

"How about we pull our attention away from this topic and talk about the council meeting we attended last night?" Mom glanced at Dad. "You want to tell them?"

Dad laid down his fork and leaned back. "Seems the members have made their decision. Audrey will replace Lana to finish the mural. Miles gave quite a speech, praising her talents."

I frowned. "He hasn't even seen her paint. How would he know what talent she has?" Come to think of it, I didn't know either. Still, Lana would've never hired Audrey if she wasn't talented. I was sure of that much.

"Money, Chloe. With Miles it's always about money, and the town council seemed to agree last night. Hiring a new artist would be more costly, Miles argued. Claimed he'd already checked into it before coming to his decision," Dad added.

Something was missing in that story. Miles was the kind of businessman who always came out way ahead, ending up with a little something extra. Or... My mind kept circling back to the meeting between him and Nick at the winery. The envelope Miles had thrown on the table and those words he'd spoken with an angry face. *This better be the last I hear of this.* What did he mean, and what was in that envelope? I tapped the side of my mug. Could it be a bribe? Blackmail? Miles guarded his reputation like it was Fort Knox with its precious gold. I glanced at Dad.

"Then, if it's about money, did Miles bargain to change the amount paid to Audrey? She's not a famous muralist like Lana."

Dad shook his head. "Not Miles. That's what I puzzled over. The council members were the ones who insisted on lowering the amount. They used the same reasoning as you."

Mom chuckled. "You should've heard the gasps when Miles announced he would pay the difference so Audrey and the team received the same amount as previously negotiated."

"But then it got even better." Dad pointed. "Miles agreed to add a thousand-dollar bonus, if Audrey finished the mural early."

I blinked. This wasn't what I expected to hear. I kept replaying yesterday's scene at Tasty Spirits. Something suspicious went on between those two men. Forking the last bite of hotcake, I pushed my empty plate to the side.

"Are you kidding me?" Izzie's voice squeaked. "Miles dishing out bonuses is not normal. He's as greedy as Scrooge, even worse. I don't get it."

Mom shrugged. "Everyone heard him."

I stood and carried my plate to the sink. "Izzie, I'm gonna take Max for his morning walk before heading to the shop."

"Sure. It'll probably be a slow morning anyway." She eyed me as she shoved her plate and utensils in the dishwasher. "You okay?" she whispered.

The volume of my voice matched hers. "I'm fine. Just having too many thoughts about this case. And questions. So many questions." I shifted my gaze to study Mom and Dad for a second. "I need to get on my laptop and search Audrey's name. We can talk later."

Izzie's gaze lingered, but then she swiveled on her heel. "So, what are you two up to this morning?"

Mom smiled. "We're making a trip into Jamestown. It's Friday and the start of a new exhibit at the National Comedy Center."

"The trip is only partly for pleasure. We're commissioned to sketch and paint a scene of the exhibit for the center to use as publicity." Dad sighed. "Our gift to them."

"It's for a good cause, Joe." Mom patted his arm. "Besides, we don't really need the money, do we?"

I grinned. Of course they didn't, but that work ethic and the expression "easy come, easy go" would always be a part of Joe Abbington. I whistled for Max and grabbed the leash. Walking down the hall, I heard Izzie.

"Hey, did I show you the photos I took when Brody and I visited Jamestown last week? We're going back in August for the Lucille Ball Festival. You two should come with us."

Max followed me as I climbed the stairs to my bedroom. Mom and Dad had enough to worry about without knowing their daughters were full-time snoops determined to find a killer. Audrey getting the mural job reminded me of my earlier conversation with Izzie. Audrey's motives were pretty strong. Her strained relationship with Lana, the way Lana assigned her menial tasks, the demeaning way she sometimes spoke to her? How about the opportunity to paint a mural that would give her reputation as an artist a huge boost? Was that enough reason, though, to murder Lana? I had to know more about their history together.

I lifted Max onto the bed and opened my laptop. "Let's see what we can find."

Max uttered a subtle woof.

The search led to a sparse amount of info, mainly business and education details. According to her profile on LinkedIn, Audrey had graduated with an art degree from Les Beaux-Arts of Paris. Under job experience, she'd listed working at some art school for youths as an assistant three years ago, nothing after, until she snagged the internship with Lana. I leaned back, resting against the headboard. My fingers curled around Max to scratch his fur while I thought about what Lana had told me. Audrey was very talented, and that's why she'd agreed to intern her. Did Audrey seek out Lana for the job? Or was someone or something else involved? I moaned. "And does that even matter?"

I straightened and once again searched for any social media site that she might belong to. A Facebook account gave me nothing. In fact, she hadn't posted any news since last year and almost nothing before that. "Not a fan of social media, are you, Audrey?" I chewed on my lip, then scrolled down the screen. The name Laurent popped up several times. I clicked on a few of them, but as far as I could tell, nothing connected to Audrey. I powered off the laptop and set it to the side. It was time to have a chat with her. With any luck, I'd get her to open up about her life.

I cradled Max in my arms and set him on the floor. "We can do this. Right, Max?" I pulled on my jacket then clipped the leash to Max's collar and led him down the stairs. Put on the old Abbington charm and get Audrey to spill all the personal details that would tell me if she was the killer. I pulled my shoulders straight. That was the plan.

Opening the door, I stepped outside and stood on the porch, gazing at the lake. The calm waters framed the surface like sheets of blue glass. A flock of geese landed, disrupting that calm with tiny ripples, but only for a brief moment. "Come on, buddy." I tugged at the leash and walked across the lawn.

As we passed by Spill the Beans, I waved at Tom, who was sweeping the sidewalk entrance. Covering the next few blocks, we reached the park. It was a little past nine. My guess was Audrey had arrived early to work on the mural, hoping to make a good impression and assure the town council and Miles that they'd made the right decision. If Nick was with her, I'd have the opportunity to ask about his change of heart. After all, when we had met for lunch, he'd sounded eager to leave town and claimed Audrey was too upset to finish the job. Maybe the issue was money. I rolled my eyes. Unfortunately, for many people, their decisions were motivated by dollar signs. They often didn't give a thought about their health, well-being, or any other factors that should be considered, as long as their bank account benefited.

I stepped onto the path and passed through the hedges to find Audrey sketching one corner of the mural. The scene of musicians and instruments had taken shape and become quite impressive. From what I could tell, Audrey had added lots of details to Lana's sketching. No doubt, the young artist had true talent. As an artist, I could appreciate what she'd accomplished. Now, I felt guilty for suspecting she could have murdered Lana. She didn't need to use any scheme to advance her career. Her talent stood on its own. I shook my head. "Be objective, Chloe. Look at the evidence. Evidence counts. Not personal feelings," I mumbled. That's what Hunter would tell me. "Morning, Audrey. Gotta say, the mural looks great so far."

Audrey swiveled on her heel, but not before dropping the sketch pen and raising a hand to her chest. "You startled me. Hi, Chloe."

"Yeah, I guess everyone's somewhat jumpy after what happened." I swallowed but managed a smile. Any reminder of Lana's death made my heart sink. "While I was taking Max for his morning walk, I thought it would be a perfect opportunity to stop by and congratulate you on getting the job."

"Thanks. I…" She licked her lips. "I have to admit, I wasn't sure if I could. Do the work, that is. Not after…well, you know." She threw up her arms. "But here I am."

"Yep. Here you are." I drew a deep breath, anxious about what to say next. Asking too much, too fast could make her clam up and refuse to talk. I had to pace myself. "Are you okay with Izzie and I bringing a group here on Saturday? I'm sure Lana told you we made plans to hold a mixed event for our clients to paint an image of the mural."

"Sure. Tate is working on getting the grid paper to hand out. I should be done with the sketching and ready to paint by then." She tapped the pencil against her thigh. "I'd better get back to work. Gotta take advantage of the perfect weather."

"Oh, sure." I turned to the side, then swiveled back to face her. "You know, I was going through some old photos of me and Lana when we were in Paris. You're from there, right? Did you take art classes at the same university? I think that's what Lana told me." Even though it was for only a second or two, Audrey's jaw muscles tensed, then she blinked and lifted her chin to smile.

"Yes. Paris is my home, and I attended the university for a time. In fact, that's where I met Lana. During one of the art classes I was taking, she came in as a guest lecturer." Audrey took a seat in the chair positioned next to the mural. Her posture relaxed, and the stiff smile became warm and genuine. "She spent some time after the lecture to view students' paintings. I guess my work must've impressed her because she approached me and offered the internship, once I graduated." Her voice wavered. "One of my proudest moments and better days during that time. I was grateful for her help."

The guilt I'd been feeling churned in my gut. I believed every word she was saying. Audrey appreciated Lana, not resented her. I gripped the dog leash, reminding myself to keep on that path of objectivity. "I wasn't aware. Lana never told me. How long have you been out of school? Moving away from home has to be hard. Don't you miss it?"

"Sometimes. I left Paris last fall. The holidays are the worst. This was my first Christmas away from my family." Her eyes misted.

"I don't get it. The internship is over. Nick mentioned you were uncomfortable with how people were reacting to Lana's death, especially Rita, and all the stress that's giving you migraines. Why not return home?" As she glared at me, I braced myself for an angry reply.

"Nick shouldn't have told you. I'm fine. I'd get migraines wherever I lived. Besides, people like Rita don't annoy or intimidate me. She's a petty, jealous woman, someone I don't care for." Audrey stood. "You should know, this job is the sort of opportunity to boost my career. After I'm finished, I'll decide whether to return home, or maybe I'll stay in New York. Some artists manage to become really successful there." Her eyes narrowed.

I stiffened and rolled my tongue across the roof of my mouth. I recognized an insult when I heard one, indirect though it might have been. "Good for you. I admire your positive attitude and for sticking around to finish the job. Like I said, the mural looks great." I stepped toward the lake and tugged at Max's leash. "I'll let you get back to work. Talk later."

She probably would be a success in New York, Paris, or wherever she ended up. Maybe my time to become a recognized artist, if I chose to try again, would come later. I had no doubt about that. Positivity was my credo. That influenced my beliefs and actions. I shook off the moment to clear my head. The path leading to the lake took us through a thicket of greenery. I dodged thorny branches that were long overdue for pruning.

Max went off the path, his nose to the ground, until he buried his head in a nearby shrub. Backing up, he turned to face me. A piece of material with strings hung from his mouth. Paws moving forward, he dropped the object at my feet, then wagged his tail.

I frowned and bent to get a closer view. "What trash did you dig up, now, little man?" No doubt, from the shape and color, I recognized a face mask like the kind we used at the shop. I sniffed at the odor of pine. "Great find, Max." My brain worked to figure out what this could mean, if anything. A mental list of details spilled out. Close to the mural site. Hidden under a shrub. The pine scent was almost sweet and reminded me of turpentine, commonly used by artists. Maybe someone painting our mural? I reminded myself not to make that leap in deduction. I pulled out the doggie bag I'd brought along for just-in-case moments and covered my hand in plastic. Picking up the mask, I noticed the red smudge along the bottom. Lipstick? Paint? Or maybe blood. Holding the mask closer, I sniffed the faint scent of lavender. So, pine and lavender? A weird combination, I thought. Tucking the mask inside the bag, I knotted the opening then placed the item that could be evidence inside my jacket pocket. What if it was connected to Lana's death? Left behind by the killer because he or she had been in a hurry to escape the crime scene? I'd hand it over to Winsell. Of course, a tiny part of me reasoned that doing so was to my advantage. A murder suspect would never volunteer evidence if he or she was guilty of the crime. At least, that's what I hoped Winsell would think. Maybe then he'd stop putting me under his detective microscope and move on to someone else.

Traveling farther down the path and away from the overgrown shrubs, I could view the lake. A familiar figure was removing pieces of trash from the area with a grabber stick and dropping them into a barrel. Frank Benworthy focused on the task at hand, not glancing up as I approached. "Morning, Frank," I greeted.

He started and whipped his head around to stare at me. His lips parted, revealing a toothy grin. "Chloe! Good morning." Lines of sweat trickled down his forehead. He swiped the moist skin with the back of one arm.

"Busy doing your civic duty, I see." I waved an arm. "The park has never looked better."

Max sniffed at Frank's shoes. Frank reached down to pat his head. "I do what I can when I have the time."

"I'm sure the kids who come to play appreciate your effort." I chuckled. "Well, anyway, the parents do. Picnics where there's trash at your feet aren't very appetizing."

Frank tapped the grabber stick. "Kids do deserve a clean place to play. I wish the city could add some fun equipment like a slide and swings. Give the young people something to do instead of finding trouble, you know."

At once, Tom's and Megan's words came to mind. Maybe Frank's reason for filing the complaint about the amphitheater's return and for joining the protesters went beyond hurting his bed and breakfast business. I shuffled my feet and gave the leash a tug. "And joggers appreciate a clear path to run on. You jog through here often enough, don't you? I've seen you once or twice."

"Jog every day, morning and evening. I've covered practically every square inch of ground in Whisper Cove. Guess it's obvious I miss my days competing in races." He shrugged.

"Yeah." I sighed. "Sure is a shame the amphitheater will change things around here. I mean, you should know, jogging through here is so peaceful. Especially in the evenings. I imagine that's why you joined the protesters. Right?" I tossed a doggie treat to Max, but kept my eye on Frank's reaction.

He stiffened. "Lots of folks are upset about what that theater will cause. Not just me." Checking his watch, he added, "I should be getting back to work. I promised my guests a tour of Whisper Cove. You have a great day, Chloe."

I studied the back of Frank as he hurried across the park ground and toward the street leading to his bed and breakfast. Right or wrong, I'd become quite talented at pushing people's buttons. This time, Frank's reaction told me I was onto something. The question was what exactly? Sure, he made it clear to anyone who'd listen, but the amphitheater's return hurting his business was a flimsy motive to kill Lana and put a stop to the mural being finished.

I circled back to head home and dropped off Max. Hopping in my car, I drove to work. Frank's easygoing personality didn't fit the profile of a killer. On the other hand, given the right circumstance and armed with plenty of anger, most any person could lose control. "But if he did the deed, why kill Lana? Why not Miles?" I shoved my bag strap over one shoulder and walked to the shop. Wrong place, wrong time, wrong person. I shook my head. "There has to be a more serious reason to push Frank that far. Has to be." I pulled up short and gasped. "Hunter." He stood at the front door, ready to walk inside Paint with a View.

"Hey there." He smiled and pulled me to his chest for a hug.

I breathed in the musky scent of cologne and felt the warmth of his body.

I could stay here like this and be totally content to never leave. After a long, relaxing moment, I slipped out of his embrace. With my chin lifted, I stared at his face. "I've missed you."

"The feeling's mutual. I'm here, now, so let's get reacquainted." His lips brushed mine then pressed harder, demanding more.

My heart pounded, and I grew light-headed. Pushing against his chest, I stepped back to come up for air. "Let's not give the neighbors too much to gossip about."

"Who cares if they do?" He caressed my arms, pulling me closer again.

"Seriously." I chuckled. "Come and sit with me on the bench. I've got news I'm dying to share. And to give you this." I lifted the doggie bag from my jacket pocket.

His brow creased. "You want to give me dog poop?"

"Ha! No, of course not. Let me explain." I tugged his arm and led him to the bench overlooking the lake.

I explained what Max had found. "Maybe this mask is a clue."

"I'll turn it over to Winsell. Thank goodness I should be finished with my case by Saturday, but until Winsell asks me to join him on this one, I'm on the sideline." He pocketed the bag. "What other trouble have you been into?" The teasing humor in his voice failed to reach his eyes.

The worrying would always be there, but we had an understanding. He wouldn't ask me to stop snooping as long as I shared with him whatever I found. I'd managed to keep our deal at least ninety percent of the time. That amount seemed fair to me. Every couple kept some secrets, just not the murdering kind.

"I had a talk with Audrey." I related what I'd found during my internet search and the story of how Audrey had met Lana. "I asked her why she didn't return to Paris since she missed it. It's home, after all. After I mentioned how Nick thought she was too upset to finish the mural, she became so defensive."

His arms straddled the back of the bench. "Well, could be she's hiding more than she's letting on. Winsell will figure it out. He's a bloodhound when it comes to uncovering people's secrets." He stood and stretched. "I need some serious sleep. Last night's surveillance kicked my butt. How about dinner this evening? You, me, and maybe Izzie and Brody. We need some fun, relaxing time. Or at least I sure do."

I rose from the bench. Lifting on my tiptoes, I kissed his cheek. "I think that would be great. I'll talk to Izzie. Now, go get some shuteye."

After he left, I relaxed once more on the bench. Closing my eyes, I raised my head. The sunlight warmed my face, almost convincing me to stay rather than return to the shop. It was still early, but I needed to give Izzie the word about dinner plans.

"Chloe! Hey there. It's me, your aunt Constance."

I'd recognize that high-pitched voice without the introduction. "Aunt Constance, how are you?" I rose and folded my arms around her ample middle. She hadn't lost the weight from stress eating, even though she attended a senior aerobics class three days a week. Being accused of murder does that to a person, especially when that person was Constance Abbington. Food had always been her go-to when times were difficult. Yet, she still managed to look attractive and stylish wherever she went. "That melon jacket really makes your skin tone glow. Props to your fashion sense."

She touched her cheek with one hand and blushed. "Thank you so much, Chloe. I woman my age needs those kind of compliments, you know."

I chuckled. "Women my age do too. Even though we shouldn't need compliments to feel good about ourselves." I leveled my gaze at her. "You're beautiful. Don't ever doubt that. How's A Stitch in Time doing?" She'd taken over the business when her daughter left town for another job. There'd been financial and family issues in play, but everything worked out for the best. Constance was happier than she'd been in quite a while.

"Business is booming. And before you ask, here's a blank check to cover fixing that teensy ding I put in your car. Again, I'm so sorry. My mind wandered, and before I knew it your car popped out of nowhere, and, well, you know the rest." She shrugged with a sheepish grin.

Popped out of nowhere? I let that one slide and accepted the check. "Thank you."

"Now, what are you going to do about that man of yours? Have you decided to attend his wedding? Or are you planning to stop it?"

Her eyebrows wiggled. I could almost read the scenarios cruising along in her mind. Ones that had me conspiring to get revenge or maybe trying to get him back, but I'd resolved those feelings about him months ago. Ross and I had been a thing, then we weren't, and then almost became a thing again. That on again, off again scenario was stressful. However, now we were friends who occasionally got in touch, with phone calls or texts, but nothing like we used to do. I was satisfied with that, wasn't I?

"Aunt Constance. Stop. I would never...I mean, I'm happy for him." I fidgeted with the hem of my shirt.

"I get it. You deserve some time to grieve. Being dumped makes people sad. It can't be avoided."

"I wasn't dumped." I mumbled under my breath, not intending for her to hear me, then added, "As for the wedding, I haven't decided. There's still time." I tapped my pocket where I'd placed my phone. Over the past two days, he'd called, left me messages and several texts, and I hadn't answered any of them. I'd been busy. That was my excuse. I promised myself to call him back this evening.

Constance patted my shoulder. "You take all the time you need, honey. Now, I should get back to the shop. My new hire is still on a learning curve." She waved while walking the other way.

"Being dumped makes people sad. Really?" I shook my head. I couldn't stop others from seeing things through their own eyes. If she thought it was more plausible that Ross dumped me than me dumping him, why argue? Did it matter? No, absolutely not.

I retraced my steps to the shop entrance then suddenly stopped. "Dumped people are sad, and sometimes angry. How angry? Angry like murderous angry? Oh, boy." I reasoned aloud. What if that tense behavior between Lana and Nick I'd witnessed meant something more than the quarrels couples typically have? What if Lana and Nick had a blow out, and the argument came to a tragic end? I rubbed the back of my neck. "Couldn't be. Nick was truly devastated when he found out Lana was dead. I saw that with my own eyes. Didn't I?"

Chapter Nine

I spread the napkin across my lap, then took a sip of wine. While Hunter and Izzie laughed at the comical story Brody told, I relaxed to enjoy the pleasant scene. Disturbing thoughts and images of murder, and me being a suspect, faded for the moment. Not hearing from Detective Winsell for the past twenty-four hours provoked both relief and worry. At least my conversation with Hunter, yesterday, had calmed my nerves. I guessed even the strong, independent feminist in me needed some consoling on occasion. His assurance that Winsell would only consider concrete evidence and not rumors in charging someone with Lana's murder made sense. Another reason I loved this man. He approached every circumstance with rational and plausible thinking. In my defense, I was the one with Winsell's possible target on my back. A heap of panic and anxiety was an obvious reaction.

"Hey. Earth to Chloe. Are you listening?" Izzie nudged my arm.

I turned to face her, and heat flushed my face. "Sorry. What did you ask?"

"If you want to come with me to Buffalo next month on the eighteenth. Hunter says there's a Monet art exhibition."

"My mom told me about it. She's going, of course. I'd love to tag along with you, but work may interfere. We'll see," Hunter said.

"I'm in. Monet is one of my favorites." Hunter's mother taught art history at a university. He'd often spoken of being dragged along to those classes when his mom couldn't get a babysitter. To a young boy, her lectures were boring. Yet after a year or so, he'd learned to appreciate art and often attended exhibits with her. A detective with a passion for the arts. You didn't run into that very often. Or maybe not at all. I admired that about him.

"Well, if you three end up going, count me too. I have lots of vacation time left," Brody said.

"Speaking of plans, maybe we should talk about the May Fling at the Casino? I know it's difficult to celebrate after all that's happened, but we only have a week to prepare. Mom's counting on us to track down at least a dozen art pieces for the charity auction." Izzie sighed.

"I know. You're right. Let's save an afternoon early next week to go shopping. I hear Monique's Art Gala recently restocked their inventory with Latin American pottery and paintings. She promised to donate a couple pieces, if we'd give her business some serious advertising." I tapped my nails against the wineglass. One of my last conversations with Lana was to offer an invitation to the May Fling. She and her team would be the guests of honor. A joyous occasion marred by her death somehow didn't seem right to celebrate.

"Lots of business owners are donating coupons and other free stuff. We should—" My words broke off and eyes popped open. Detective Winsell was approaching our table. I winced and pulled my hands off the table to cradle in my lap, so quickly, I nearly knocked over my wineglass.

"Evening, everyone." He tipped his chin and gave Hunter a cursory glance. "Detective Barrett, I'd like a word with you, alone."

Hunter dabbed his lips with his napkin then stood. "If you'll excuse me for a moment."

Maybe this had nothing to do with me. As Hunter and Winsell stood a few feet from our table, I stretched my neck and leaned sideways, attempting to hear their conversation. Pointless, since the chatter of guests around us drowned out any of the detectives' exchange.

Hunter returned to the table and winked at me. Winsell followed.

I relaxed somewhat, but Winsell wasn't the one winking or even smiling. In fact, the creases in his forehead and squinty eyes hinted that he hadn't finished his business. I braced for the worst. Would this be a conversation about his theory? How I lured Lana to Whisper Cove for revenge?

"Miss Abbington." He shook his head and chuckled. "You mind if I call you Chloe? Seems reasonable since we've seen so much of each other, don't you think?"

I shrugged. "Nice to see you, Detective. Have you had dinner? You're welcome to join us."

"No, no. I grabbed a burger from Millie's, earlier." He rubbed his jaw. "I only wanted to compliment you on finding the face mask the other day. No results from the lab yet. They're backed up with evidence to analyze. Anyway, excellent sleuthing skills, Chloe."

I felt the heat rise in my cheeks. "Thanks, but the credit goes to Max. He sniffed it out."

"Max?" His brow wrinkled.

"Oh! Yeah, my dog. He's a bit of a bloodhound when it comes to finding things." I folded my napkin and rearranged my utensils.

"No matter. If the mask turns out to be evidence, I'll let you know." He patted Hunter on the shoulder. "Or Hunter will. I've invited him to be on the case with me. Another set of trained eyes always helps."

I eyed Hunter. No wonder he acted happy. I was too. And relieved. At least he believed in my innocence.

"Well, I should leave you all to finish your dinner." He tipped his hat and turned to walk away, but in seconds retraced his steps. "I almost forgot. Do you read the New York Times? I imagine having lived there for a while, you would still keep up on the news, especially the arts section."

I straightened. My breath held while my body tensed. He was going to say something after all. A glimpse of Hunter's face told me he was just as surprised. I guessed Winsell hadn't given him a heads-up. "Yes. The online edition catches my attention occasionally. Why are you asking?"

"Yesterday's paper had a story about the award Lana Easton received. Until the committee rescinded it, that is." Winsell scratched the top of his head. "And to think the award was for a mural that featured one of your paintings. Sad how she didn't get to enjoy the honor very long, isn't it?"

His eyes hinted at sadness, but underneath the look of sympathy, I suspected he was carefully calculating my reaction. I shivered. "I didn't read about that. In fact, I hadn't heard about the award. Lana never mentioned it."

"Really? You'd think since your painting inspired her work, she would've been excited to share the news. Oh well, who knows what goes through people's minds sometimes." He smiled. "Have a good evening."

"Well, that was awkward." Izzie spooned more of her sherbet. "He reminds me of that detective in the old television show Mom and Dad like to watch. Always asking questions or making comments in a weird way." She pointed her spoon at me. "Columbo. That's it. Sort of dresses like him too. Frumpy, wrinkled clothes. They could be twins."

"I'm sorry, Chloe. I had no idea he planned to bring up the award." Hunter squeezed my hand.

"I'm guessing someone brought the article to his attention. The question is who?" I said.

"My bet's on Audrey. Sounds like jealousy and revenge," Izzie added.

I puffed my cheeks and blew out air. "No matter who may have told him, the news gives Winsell yet another reason to believe I killed Lana."

A quick assessment of Hunter's face showed he was worried, too. Great. One of us needed to be the cheerleader, giving me hope and confidence, telling me this nightmare of a case would soon be over. However, no one spoke, and all eyes turned away. I pushed my chair out. "Enough of this. Let's go dancing at Duckies. Okay? I need some fun time right now."

"You bet." Hunter grinned ear to ear and draped my sweater over my shoulders. He brushed my hair to one side and kissed my cheek. "Everything will turn out fine. I'll make sure of it," he whispered.

I poked his chest. "*We'll* make sure of it."

He chuckled. "Understood. Now…" His feet shuffled side to side. "Let's go dancing."

"Dude. If those are your dance moves, I'm staying on the opposite side of the floor." Brody laughed.

"Hey! I'll have you know, I won a dance contest for having the best moves." Hunter twirled around.

"When you were like what, twelve?" Brody shook his head. "Sad. Really, really sad."

"Come on, guys. We'll finish this on the dance floor where it counts." Izzie tugged at Brody's arm while I linked mine with Hunter's, and we made our way to Duckies.

After a few hours of fun, we dragged ourselves home. Exhausted, I tucked myself into bed and closed my eyes with a sigh. The dancing was a success despite Hunter's awkward moves. Izzie and I even persuaded the band to play "Say Something" so we could sing along. Justin Timberlake, my senior year, and a great summer spent with Izzie before I headed off to college brought back memories with that song. I left Duckies feeling a mix of melancholy and joy, not to mention a spoonful of the gloomy doomies, as Izzie would phrase it. The sleuth sisters had to step it up, first thing tomorrow. I yawned. One thing was for sure: I had to put a ton of faith in Hunter and Winsell. As a team, they'd most likely figure out who killed Lana before we did. That was fine with me, too.

Chapter Ten

A warm breeze tickled the back of my neck. I closed my eyes and breathed the fresh air, giving into a well-deserved relaxing moment. I'd had a brief conversation with Ross this morning. Just a hello and how are you kind of thing. Of course, his nudge for me to RSVP to his wedding was thrown in there at some point. I skirted and evaded to stay clear of why I hadn't and when I would RSVP. Instead, I launched into an info dump about my life, Lana's murder—yes, I finally could say she was murdered without falling apart—and the amphitheater drama until our talk came to an end. His end, that is, because Miranda said it was time to meet friends for brunch. The friends he and I used to hang out with, but that was in the past, and I'd moved on. Even though it hurt when they didn't call or text me after the breakup. Funny how not having them in my life felt worse than not having Ross. Maybe because breaking up with him was my decision. Maybe because we still talked despite me ending things. I had to give the man credit. Some guys would've held a grudge, torn up all the photos as a couple, deleted phone numbers, social media accounts, and more. Sure, he'd kept trying to win me back, but when that didn't work, he still wanted to be friends. I loved and admired him and was grateful for that.

The murmur of conversation, along with the rhythmic thump of footsteps on the cement patio, interrupted my thoughts. I inched open one eye to view Izzie, Mom, and Dad, all carrying their refilled mugs of coffee to the table. Breakfast outside was a treat this time of year as the cool, often dreary, sometimes rainy mornings dictated the calendar months of spring. I sipped from my mug and stroked the back of Max, who snuggled on my lap.

"Just got off the phone with Brody. He and Rex are on their way. You hear that, Max? Your buddy is coming to play." Izzie sat in the chair next to me and fluffed the top of Max's head.

Max sat up straight and bellowed a howl.

I laughed. The word Rex had become an important part of his vocabulary. It was almost as special as saying dog food, treat, and walk. "Did you hear how Miles is planning a doggie pet day at the amphitheater in August? A double feature with *Lady and the Tramp* and *Beethoven*, plus dog treats and a blue ribbon contest for best outfit, are on the program. Then, in September, he'll schedule one for cats. Wise not to mix the two. Some dogs and cats can't get along. Right, Max?" I recalled how he'd run across five neighboring lawns to chase a cat up a tree. "Anyway, Miles wants us to bring some of the paint-your-pet portraits our guests did last month."

"Oh! Speaking of Miles, Megan told me he fired his music program director last night." Izzie blew on her beverage before taking a sip. "They had a full-blown shouting match in front of Claire's bakery shop. She heard the whole thing while picking up an order of donuts."

"Fired? Why? I thought he'd hired one of the best in the business. Like, famous all over New York." I leaned back in my chair.

"Money issues. Megan said the director spent way over the budget Miles allotted." Izzie pointed. "Wouldn't you agree, if you want the best—"

"You have to pay to get it. Yeah, I'd agree, but maybe that wasn't the only reason Miles fired her. Never know." I paused for a second. "In her place, I'd have gone to Miles and gotten his okay before spending that much. Seems like common sense."

Izzie stood. "I'm going upstairs to change. Be down in a few minutes."

I turned to Mom and Dad. "What do you think?" They hadn't said a word, which was unusual.

"I'd say it's odd." Mom's brow wrinkled. "I've never known Miles to penny-pinch on any project. Go big or go home is his motto."

Dad folded the Saturday newspaper and set it to the side. "I agree. He spends quite a bit, but he always manages to come out ahead."

"I'd think even people like Miles would have a limit on how much to spend." I tried reasoning why he did what he did, but considering all that had happened in the past week, "odd" certainly could fit his behavior.

The doorbell rang, and Max erupted into barks and howls as he scampered down the hall. I followed close behind and let Brody inside. He brushed back the windblown curls of hair caressing his face before kneeling down to unclip Rex's leash. Growing out his hair only added to his good looks. "Hi, Brody. Izzie will be down in a minute." I gave Rex a pat on the head, then led the way to the patio.

"I took the day off work so I could stop over for a visit. Ever since Lana's death, I can't stop worrying about how you and your sister are doing. Can't be easy," Brody said.

"You're right. It isn't easy. The sooner we find, I mean the sooner Detective Winsell finds the killer, we'll all be able to relax." If he only knew how much Izzie and I were involved in the search for answers, he'd worry even more. Besides, that was Izzie's right to tell him.

As we stepped outside, Rex and Max zoomed past us across the patio and leaped onto the lawn where they could chase each other from one end of our yard to the other. I laughed. No doubt, these pups would sleep well tonight.

"Have a seat, Brody," Dad said. "If I know Izzie, she'll be a while."

"Says who?" Izzie stepped out of the kitchen doorway and clip-clopped in heels across the patio, wearing a cream-colored sundress with pink flowers and earrings to match. She leaned down to give Brody a peck on the lips, then pulled a chair next to him and sat. "Hi." Her voice grew soft.

I sighed. Nothing like love in the air to make you feel warm inside. I thought of Hunter and smiled.

We chatted about the unseasonably warm weather, Winsell's unexpected visit during our dinner date last evening, and other safe topics until Brody ventured into the news about Lana's murder.

"I sure hope Winsell is as good at his job as Hunter claims. Like I told Chloe, I worry about you two." He squeezed Izzie's hand. Steeling his gaze away from her for a second, he glanced at Mom and Dad. "I worry about all of you, this town, and everyone in it. A killer could be living right here in Whisper Cove, free to roam the streets."

"Honestly, we're being careful." I didn't know if my words assured him any, or if they even assured me. "No late evening walks or traveling down dark alleys. Trust me."

"Our daughters will play it safe." Mom cast me and Izzie a steely-eyed glare that only she could manage to do well. "Right?"

I tipped my head to the side. "Or risk the painful sting of a Kate Abbington lecture? No thanks. We know better." I did my best to keep the teasing lilt out of my voice. Funny how we change. The child version of me would be shaking in my high top sneakers right about now.

"You know, it's a shame. Some folks won't stop talking. I hear them wherever I go in town to shop. They believe Lana brought all this trouble to Whisper Cove," Mom said.

"That's ridiculous." I crossed my arms and huffed in anger. "If trouble started anywhere, it was when Miles brought the amphitheater to town."

"Speaking of the theater," Brody interrupted. "It may not be a problem for your town very much longer."

My brow furrowed. "What do you mean?"

"I have a cousin who works in one of the offices at the county building in Mayville. He's hearing rumors that Miles Terrell has run into trouble with the zoning commission. My cousin wasn't sure of the details." Brody reached for a muffin.

"Hmm, well, maybe we should ask Aunt Constance?" I shrugged while facing Izzie.

"She's the best source for town gossip, and Mayville is her home, so yeah. Let's ask her what she knows." Izzie stood and clasped Brody's hand. "You want to take a quick walk down by the lake? I have about an hour before we need to open up shop."

"Take your time. Willow and I can get things started," I suggested.

Brody whistled for Rex, who bolted across the yard. Walking hand in hand, he and Izzie headed out of the house.

I finished lining the window floor with green crepe paper and scattered silk flower petals across the area. "All done," I shouted over my shoulder at

Willow. "Ready for the mural." Sunlight brightened the display. I shaded my eyes with one hand and appraised my efforts then added a few extra petals. More color never hurt.

"Here you go. This one's the better of the two, I think." Willow placed the canvas in my hands.

"I agree." The shading and the hues of blue and green accented the background of the focal point, that being the amphitheater's mural. Willow had imagined what the finished product would look like based on Lana's vision and description. Music instruments and notes scattered across the scene. In the center, the amphitheater sat floating on the lake. I had to admire her talent, although it came with a touch of envy because without formal training I could never have honed my talent the way Willow did naturally. Some artists were born with that gift.

Izzie walked out of the storage room, her tablet in hand. "Do you think we should use the mini canvases again? They worked so well at the winery. That way, we wouldn't need to haul the easels and—"

Izzie's words ended with a jaw drop while we all snapped our heads around to face the entrance.

Audrey stormed through the doorway, full of energy and emotion. Her face blushed while her eyes glowed an intense shade of green. A grimace thinned her lips, and a finger jabbed in my direction. "You! How could you?" She sniffed and swiped her mouth with the back of her hand.

I blinked, stunned by her accusation. I sat back on the window ledge. The perfectly placed petals scattered, and the canvas tipped over. "What?"

The finger wagged, and the head shook in unison. "Don't play innocent with me." Her other hand shot out, holding a newspaper. Opening to the front page, she read aloud. "Famous mural artist, Lana Easton is a fraud." Audrey's voice shook. Her chest heaved while she inhaled. "You killed Lana, didn't you? You knew she won that award for the mural she painted using your work. You must've been jealous, jealous enough to want revenge." She shoved the paper at me. "Read for yourself."

I read the first few lines of the article and my heart sank. Lana had been given an award, only last month for her mural painting of wildflowers along a lake. That was the work I'd given to her, the one we argued about when I'd learned she'd used it for a mural. We'd ended things peacefully. Yet, the moment left its mark on our relationship. I couldn't completely trust her after that. I read on and groaned.

The committee rescinded the award because they learned from an anonymous source that the image used in the mural had been stolen from a painting by new and upcoming artist, Chloe Abbington, who hadn't been reached for comment. The article continued to explain Lana met a tragic end earlier this week and suggested it could've been suicide after she learned her act of fraud would soon be made public.

I glanced up, speechless. Winsell hadn't told me everything. At least, not about the anonymous source. What I knew for certain was that Audrey accused me of murdering Lana. I also knew from experience that jealousy or envy was a popular motive and easily believed. "Audrey, I—look, I understand why you're upset, but I couldn't; I didn't know about the award until last night, and…" I hitched my breath, and upon release, it trembled through me. "Lana was my friend, a close friend. I could never hurt her."

"Excuse me if I don't believe you. In fact, I wouldn't be at all surprised to find out you were the anonymous source. Killing her wasn't enough. You wanted to ruin Lana's reputation." She leaned closer. Her gaze so intense, it could burn a hole through me. "Better be prepared. I plan to go to Detective Winsell with this news." She grabbed the newspaper from my hands. "This will put you at the top of his list. He'll be coming with handcuffs, ready to haul you off to jail." With that, she stormed back out as quickly as she'd arrived.

The unsettling moment spiked my nerves, and queasiness rippled through me. I peered out the window while holding tight to my stomach, willing the nerves to subside. Audrey marched down the alley, her arms swinging side to side. A woman on a mission, a mission that could turn my life upside down and out of my control to do anything about it. "She won't be in the greatest mood for our mixed event this afternoon, will she?" I chewed on a fingernail.

"No, probably not. But hey, we'll manage no matter what." Izzie pumped her arm skyward.

"She can't defeat me. I won't let it happen," I muttered.

Izzie squeezed my shoulder. "No, *we* won't let it happen. We'll figure out who killed Lana and stop this kind of crazy accusation. I mean, how dare she suggest such a thing?"

I sniffed and chuckled at the same time. With my chin lifted, I managed a half-baked smile. "Thanks, but what if we can't? Our snooping hasn't gotten us very far." My positive outlook had fizzled, and doubt muscled its way in to take over.

"Hey!" Izzie playfully jabbed my arm. "Toss that kind of talk in the garbage can. Right, Willow?" She twisted to look behind her.

Willow gave two thumbs up. "I'm in. Let's catch the bad guy and send him to jail. We'll give Winsell some competition in the detective business."

This time, a genuine smile lifted my spirits. "You two are the best. I feel better already." At least I tried. Maybe talking that way would convince me enough to scare away my doubts. I remembered Dad once telling me during my high school soccer tournament that if I visualized kicking that ball into the net and scoring the goal, then it would help make it happen. I closed my eyes and visualized Winsell leading someone in handcuffs to jail. I scrunched my forehead and concentrated, but no matter how hard I tried, I couldn't make out who that person was, not even if the person was male or female. I sighed. Positive vibes were going to take a lot of work.

Not that he could do anything to stop Audrey from spilling her theory to Winsell, and though I hated acting like the sort of female who needed to cry on a man's shoulder, I reached for my phone, and, with a shaky finger, I pressed the button for Hunter's number.

Chapter Eleven

"I've managed to fit all the mini canvases we need into one box. Do you have the paints, cups, and plates ready?" Izzie asked.

"We've got it covered. The cars are packed and..." I twisted my wrist. "We should be leaving to set up everything before people arrive."

"Almost showtime!" Izzie led the way.

Willow stayed in the rear and locked the door. She then hurried to catch up to my side. "How do you think Audrey will react when she sees you? I mean, you not being the jailbird she hoped for."

"Ha. Well, if she did follow through to sell Winsell her theory, she probably didn't get the answer she wanted." I shrugged. "Which means she won't be happy to see me or anyone else."

Willow sighed. "I got a hunch this event won't be the fun time we'd hoped for."

"Let's just hope Audrey concentrates on painting the mural." I pressed the start button, and the engine rumbled.

"We can always improvise. I know quite a bit about mural painting." Willow hopped into the passenger seat.

I raised my brow.

"What? I've been reading books and watching online videos. It's not that hard, really." She buckled in. "I can fake it. None of the guests would know."

I laughed. "Fake it until you make it, I guess."

While packing our vehicles, we discussed whether we had arrived any closer to who killed Lana. I certainly didn't think we had. Of course, Izzie insisted we should take a closer look at Frank Benworthy. Even so, I had a problem with pinning the murder on him. Everything fell into place, making him look guilty. It was almost too easy. Murder was messy and complicated. The cases of Fiona Gimble's murder and then Viola Finnwinkle's proved that much. I needed more from Frank to be convinced.

We worked our way through town and reached the entrance to the park. A crowd of folks were gathered on the sidewalk, most everyone carrying protest signs. One handled a megaphone. I moaned. Great. The sight of protesters would be accompanied by loud chants. I had to wonder if they would ever give up their fight. Unfortunately, the county zoning issues with all those complaints about Miles might fire up the protesters even more.

With armfuls of boxes, we skirted around the vocal group with their signs held high to get into the park where the mural stood. Surprisingly, Frank wasn't among them. Maybe he was busy with his B&B duties. I spotted Nick and Tate unloading chairs from the rental van. To my left, Audrey stood on the lift. With mask on and spray paint can in one hand, she worked on a top corner of the mural. Lined up next to her on the lift were several paint tools.

"That power handheld sprayer is for painting the big areas," Willow commented. "The rollers with extendable arms can reach pretty far, which is nice if you're standing on the ground or if the mural is like stories high."

I was impressed. She wasn't kidding about doing her research. My gaze traveled the length of the several feet that expanded the lift. Both spray cans and gallon containers of paint sat alongside the rollers, as well as rags and cleaning solutions for those accidents artists expected on occasion.

"Hey, Audrey! We made it on time. The mural looks fantastic," Izzie called out.

Audrey twisted to face us. The turned-down lips and narrowed gaze, told me she was still agitated. However, she greeted us with a stiff smile. "Thanks. It's been a smooth project so far."

"Well, the colors pop and give the mural that electric vibe. You know, the kind you'd want for a music theme," I added.

"Sure." The sour look accompanied her tightened jaw.

I swallowed hard, worried if others noticed. Turning to glance around me, I spotted Nick.

He walked over, wrapped an arm around me, and gave my shoulders a squeeze. "Absolutely right about the colors. And hey, we're all pumped to do this mixed event with you. Aren't we, Audrey?"

I glimpsed his face with its intense stare aimed at Audrey, like he was telling her to calm down. Or that's the way I read it. In any case, she ditched the vinegary attitude, relaxed the tight jaw, and thrust her free hand into the air. "Let's do this!" She forced enthusiasm into her voice, but I wasn't fooled. The anger and resentment were buried, not gone.

Dismissing the moment and her behavior, I walked over to where guests for our event gathered. Willow handed each one a mini canvas. The chairs were specially designed with retractable folding trays to hold supplies the guests would need to use. I passed around cups and plastic bags containing brushes and other items, greeting each person as I went.

Reaching the last of the chairs, I lingered. Tate and Nick stood nearby, and neither one looked happy, especially Nick. His scowl and clenched jaw were a dead giveaway. Straining to hear, I caught the exchange between them. Tate's question, which I didn't catch, seemed to upset him.

"I have more than one camcorder. You should know that," Nick snapped. His loud voice carried.

Tate shrugged. "I just asked. You've been using the other one all week. Thought maybe you broke it or something." He snapped open the legs of the stand to hold the projector we would use for the event.

Nick tapped the side of his camera. In a sporadic tempo, like someone with a nervous tic. "I take great care of my equipment. Nothing's ever broken. You should know that too. I just felt like trying out this one is all. You satisfied?"

"Geesh. Relax. I didn't mean anything by it." Tate finished setting the projector on the stand and securing the clasps before walking off toward the lake.

What happened to the cheery mood he'd shown a few minutes ago? And why react so defensively to a simple question? I shrugged off thoughts of the incident. My agenda right now was to find out all I could about Audrey, and Nick might be the one with answers.

Boosting my confidence with the lift of my chin, I walked over to Nick who sat on a bench, fiddling with his camcorder. "Hey, Nick. Thanks for stepping in earlier to soften the tension between Audrey and me."

"Huh?" A confused look in his eyes was followed by a smile of recognition. "Chloe. Yeah, sure. I mean, it was nothing. Audrey gets cranky sometimes when she's working."

So he believed. I sat next to him. Taking the direct approach might be risky, but why not try, I thought. "Are you sure her mood isn't about a certain talk with Detective Winsell?"

He leaned back. "What? No, that is, I'm not sure what you mean."

Blinking his eyes and dropping his jaw was a tad overdramatic, in my opinion. "Come on. Are you saying she hasn't told you? Audrey accused me of killing Lana. She claimed I was jealous of Lana's award. You didn't know about that, Nick?" I jutted my chin and pressed my lips, daring him to deny any of it.

His fingers splayed to rest on his knees. "Okay. I read the article, but I had no idea Audrey planned to accuse you of anything. Honest."

I almost believed him. Rather than pressing the point, I switched topics. "How well do you know Audrey? She's obviously got amazing talent. Is that why Lana chose her to intern? Paris is so far from the States. Until recently, I thought Lana hadn't returned to visit there in years." I almost expected Nick to tell me some details that would discredit Audrey's story. People tended to lie when they had something to cover up. Especially secrets that, if revealed, could get them in trouble.

"They met in Paris last year during some lecture." Nick shrugged. "Lana was impressed with Audrey's talent and offered to help her career when she finished her studies. That's all I know."

"You said she's been suffering from migraines and gets upset over stuff. Do you think she misses home? I know if she were me, I'd be on the first plane to Paris so I could be with family."

"Really, she doesn't talk to me about her personal life. Maybe she did with Lana." He raked his fingers through his hair. "Anyway, she's got the mural job, and to her, that's everything. She's all about her career. That much I do know. Say, why all the questions? You think she killed Lana? Because that's crazy. Audrey admired her like she was her idol. No way would she do anything to harm her."

I studied his face. I could almost swear his eyes teared. The emotions over losing Lana hadn't diminished, not a bit. I believed he believed what he was saying. Or wanted to believe it. He genuinely loved Lana and would never imagine anyone thinking badly of her. My shoulders sank. How was I supposed to believe he killed Lana? Keeping my mind focused, I returned to my questions about Audrey. "You're right about one thing. She must be extremely excited to have the mural job. Did you see how she's already taking credit by painting her signature at the bottom? In bright, bold letters, no less."

Nick choked on his laugh and then sniffed. "Yeah, sounds like something she'd do. Like I said, she's ambitious." He shrugged. "Guess you could say she's obsessed."

I chewed on my lip. "Well, it would be nice if she'd add Lana's name to the mural. Seems only fair."

Nick nodded. "You're right. I'll say something to her."

I thanked him and turned to leave. "One down and maybe three suspects left, Detective Winsell," I muttered under my breath. "That's not counting me."

As it was, I didn't have any more time to psychoanalyze Nick's or Audrey's or anyone else's behavior. Our team had work to do. Guests to impress. I pivoted on my heel to steer a path to the mural area. From the corner of my eye, I caught Izzie smiling and joking with a couple of the guests while Willow helped an older woman adjust her chair table. At least the three of us would put on a good show. However, the thought that Audrey could ruin it concerned me. Her presentation about mural painting was essential. I stared at her while she painted the top corner with blue music notes and tried to decide if she could pull it off. I seriously considered putting Willow up there, if Audrey flaked on us.

The chairs were all taken. A mental count told me the number of guests who'd signed up had showed, plus one more. I frowned, perusing each seat and face. My eyes widened when I reached the far corner of the second row. Setting my feet in motion, I hurried to where Willow stood. She was in charge of the guest list and confirmation emails on this event.

"Hey." The palm of my hand curved to cover my mouth. "What is Rita doing here? And why?"

"I don't know the why part. She signed up at the last minute. Since there was a spot left, I okayed it. Is that a problem?" Willow lifted her brow.

"No, of course not." I blinked. "It's just—never mind. This isn't the time. Your canvases with the instructions look perfect. Is there anything else you need?" Like I'd said, maybe this wasn't the time, but I couldn't keep my mind from spinning questions about Rita. If she resented losing the mural job, which made no sense since she sided with the protesters about the amphitheater's return, why attend this event? Was she playing both sides of the issue? And speaking of protesting, why wasn't she out there with the others, wielding a sign and chanting, "go home" or whatever they were saying?

"Chloe, are you listening? Izzie is signaling us." Willow poked my arm.

"Hmm? Oh! Sorry. My mind wandered for a moment." I gave Rita one last glance, then walked to stand by Izzie. No matter why Rita attended the event, as long as she didn't plan to cause a scene, I'd be satisfied.

"Hi, everyone. We're so glad you've joined us. This is a special event because painting a mural in our park is a once in a lifetime occurrence. Or, as far as we know, it is," Izzie chuckled. "If you'll look to your left, you'll see the mini canvases Willow has painted, showing the guitar, notes, and the amphitheater on the lake in the background. That's what you'll be painting today."

"As explained in the ad for this event, this project is for those with some experience in painting," I added.

"But if you have any questions or need assistance, the three of us will be taking turns to help you. Just holler or raise your hand," Willow said.

"To start things off, Audrey, who you see standing by the mural, will explain her process. We're quite lucky to have someone with her talent to finish painting what our dear friend, Lana Easton, started. So, let's welcome

Audrey Laurent." I took a deep breath to calm my emotions and clapped along with the others. The moment got to me, thinking of Lana and how proud I would've been to share the stage with her.

I stepped to the side while Audrey took the microphone. Gone was the surly behavior. Instead, she spoke with a calm and professional tone, sharing with our guests her impressive knowledge of art technique and the process involving mural painting. She even threw in some historical tidbits, including a reference to da Vinci's *Last Supper* painted on the refectory of the church in Milan. I was blown away.

Minutes into Audrey's presentation, I felt the sweat on the back of my neck. The sunlight showed through the trees and toasted the air with unseasonable warmth. I walked several steps to the table where bottles of water floated in a bucket of icy water. Grabbing a few ice chips, I sat on a bench to rest and rubbed my face and neck while staring out at the lake. Near the shore and seated at a table was Penny. I strained my gaze to get a clearer look. She had a camera in her hands and was loading film. A sudden impulse to have a chat about her part in the protest march came to me. I stood up from the bench.

"Chloe!" Izzie motioned to me.

I waved my arm. Audrey had finished her introduction. My chat with Penny would have to wait. Taking my place, I pointed to the gridded sketch I'd prepared and explained the significance to the guests. The lines squared off sections of the image that would be painted on the mini canvases. In the same way Tate had explained the process of how to place each detail in the proper location on a wall mural, ours would be a miniature of what Audrey painted. Grids weren't normally a part of our instruction, but I thought it would give people a better idea of how muralists worked, kind of like seeing through someone else's eyes.

The instructions went smoothly, and somehow the guests seemed to have little to no problems. With only a few hands in the air, we were able to linger and chat with people we knew. I loved that part. Getting to hear how Mrs. Tempio's dog Trixie was healing well after her surgery, and us arranging a play date next week with Max so they could play brightened my otherwise troubled mood.

"I'll call you next week to make sure Trixie feels up to the visit. Max will be super excited," I said and squeezed her shoulder. Mrs. Tempio was somewhere past eighty and widowed. I had a hunch she got excited, too, when company stopped by.

Izzie threaded her way between the rows of chairs to reach me. She tipped her head to one side. "Would you look over there? Penny is snapping photos of our event."

I shrugged. "So? What's strange about that?"

"From what I've noticed, the only direction that camera is pointed is at three people. Audrey, Nick, and Tate. Not us. Not our guests. Not even the mural. Don't you think that's odd?"

"Huh. Yeah, it is. So's her being involved in the protest. You'd think she'd see the uptick in business the amphitheater could bring as a positive."

As if she could hear us talking about her, Penny turned toward the lake and began snapping photos of the amphitheater and a couple of sailboats gliding by.

"If I could have everyone's attention, please." Nick held the microphone in one hand and a clipboard in the other. "I'm trying to get the word out about a scholarship started in Lana's name. I'm sure you know about her untimely death and maybe have seen some of her work. Check out her website and Facebook page. I think you'll agree how impressive and impactful her paintings are. The murals are found in almost every country in the world. She's touched the hearts of millions, and that's why I am serious about making this scholarship available every year for art students."

He held up the clipboard. "If you decide you're interested, sign up with your name and email address. I'll be in touch. And please, spread the word. There will be a website available soon where you can donate or write a check if you prefer." He paused for a second, then cleared his throat. "Lana was very special to me, and I'm honored to do something that keeps her memory alive. Thank you."

"You want to donate, don't you?" Izzie touched my arm.

"I think Lana would be really pleased with the idea of a scholarship. So yeah, I do," I said.

Izzie gestured with her thumbs up. "I agree. I'll go sign the clipboard."

I leaned against a tree behind the projector and stared out at the lake. Ripples of water washed into the shore and out again.

"I don't care. You shouldn't have called. I told you I'd be in touch when I'm finished here, Émile, and not before."

I peeked around the tree trunk. Audrey sat on the bench, hugging her knees. The phone lay at her side. All at once, she stood, swiped her eyes with the back of one hand, then stormed off toward the street.

"What do you think that was about? And who the heck is Émile?" I wondered aloud. No doubt a call from someone with words she didn't want to hear. One more puzzling detail to add to the list of people acting strangely. How many more would there be? The needle in the haystack analogy came to mind, along with the crime show *Unsolved Mysteries*. This looming, heavy sense of defeat could easily discourage me. What if we never figured out who killed Lana?

Chapter Twelve

With Max in the lead, I hurried across town. I had a quick stop to make before taking our walk to the park. Plenty of questions for Aunt Constance spun around in my head. Brody's news about the amphitheater made me curious to know more. At this early hour, and on a Sunday, she'd be at her shop, taking inventory.

I slipped sunglasses on and jogged the path across Artisan Alley. Several doors down from Paint with a View was the practically brand new building that housed Aunt Constance's shop, A Stitch in Time. After the fire last year, turning Sammy's Quaint Décor into ashes, Spencer Abbington, Constance's daughter, decided to build a new business, which ended up in our aunt's hands. She was eternally grateful to have something on her plate of things to do, after losing the position as the Sisterhood's chapter president.

I stood back to admire the tasteful exterior. Robin's egg blue paint covered the clapboard siding with white trim bordering the windows. On the sides and top of the doorway, wood carvings of spools, thimbles, needles, yarn, and material swatches added the right touch to announce what shoppers would find inside.

I tugged at Max's leash. "Come on, boy." I climbed the steps, and a cheery tune of chimes jingled as I opened the door to enter. "Hello?" I shifted my glance side to side to view the small interior and its narrow aisles with stacks of shelves that almost reached the ceiling. "Anyone here?" Somebody had to be. Constance would never leave the door unlocked if the shop was unattended.

A throaty cough echoed from the other side of the room while an arm waved above a tall shelf. "Sorry. The shop's not open for business yet. Come back at eleven."

I navigated the maze of aisles to reach the familiar voice. "It's me, Chloe."

She clutched a stapler to her chest and gasped. "Oh, goodness. I didn't recognize, that is, well, it's not important." She blew air upward to lift the wisp of hair away from her forehead. Laying the stapler on the shelf, she took my hand. "Come on, let's sit outside in back. I have two rockers sitting underneath the maple tree. Plenty of shade, which is what I need right now. That and a cool drink." She led the way and pulled two bottles of water out of the mini-fridge.

"Thanks." I took one of the beverages and followed her outside. Under the canape of leafy limbs, two wood rockers sat, painted the same shade of Robin's egg blue. I had to give my aunt credit for her decorative flair. "The place looks fantastic, Aunt Constance. I hope business is doing well for you." I'd heard otherwise, but those were rumors you couldn't put much stock into. Better to hear from the direct source to get to the truth.

Max plopped down under the maple tree and chewed on a fallen twig.

Constance shrugged and took a healthy swig of water. "I expected a slow start. Not to worry, though. I have my dear late husband's inheritance to fall back on."

I pictured Dad's tormented face and didn't comment. "I have a question or two for you. Do you have time for a break? I don't want to keep you from work."

She waved an arm and flipped her wrist. "I'm the owner. I take breaks whenever I like. Besides, I'm doing inventory. Boring as watching paint dry."

I smiled. "Right. Okay. I've been told there's word going around Mayville that Miles is having issues with the county zoning department concerning the amphitheater's relocation." I leaned forward. "Have you heard anything about that?"

She pursed her lips. "As a matter of fact, I have heard something to that effect."

"Are you sure these aren't just rumors floating around to stir up trouble? You know how those can be." I hated to think Miles' efforts to move the amphitheater would come to a disappointing end. After all that had been done so far to get the theater back in Whisper Cove. And the mural. What would happen to it if the zoning department changed its decision? No more amphitheater meant no mural.

"My source is reliable. She's a dear friend and neighbor who works for the Chautauqua County Planning and Zoning." Constance lowered her voice as if someone was close by and listening to our conversation. "I promised her I wouldn't say anything, but I trust you to be discrete."

I crossed an X over my chest. "What did she say?"

"Well, for one thing, someone raised a ruckus over Miles getting his proposal approved." Constance tipped her head to the side and narrowed her gaze. "The same person who earlier proposed building a playground and walking trail in that area of your park."

"Oh, wow." My jaw dropped.

"Trust me. It gets much worse. This person suggested there'd been unethical behavior, maybe bribery, to sway the planning commission. And the complaints haven't stopped there. He or she has also insisted shortcuts were taken to bypass the specific zoning codes for that area of the lake and park, which seems ridiculous since the theater had been docked in that general location before." She finished the last drop of her water and laid the bottle on the ground.

"Maybe zoning laws have changed since the amphitheater was here years ago." I made the suggestion but doubted the possibility as soon as the words came out. Zoning laws didn't change often. Besides, whoever lodged those complaints should know those laws. Why make such a fuss for the sole intent to cause trouble? Resentment over losing his or her playground proposal, perhaps. It took very little to provoke some people. The thought needling me was if this issue somehow tied into Lana's death. I couldn't let my mind venture too far into that theory, but knowing the recent history—comings and goings and acts that were suspicious—of every person who could've murdered Lana was worth my time to investigate. So, that's exactly what I planned to do.

"Does your neighbor know who complained?" I flashed back to the memory of Megan's news. Frank Benworthy had confronted the Whisper Cove town council about the amphitheater. Did he also lodge a complaint with the county zoning department?

"I never asked, not when I spoke with my neighbor. Besides, she didn't act comfortable telling me as much as she did." Constance stood. "Well, guess I should get some work done. The inventory won't check itself."

I finished my water. "You haven't mentioned how the new hire is working out."

"Oh, I let her go after two days. She accused me of being too picky. Can you imagine?" She bent to pull out a weed. "It's for the best. I prefer handling everything myself, and I've scheduled store hours in a way that gives me time for my private life. Like I said, money isn't really an issue. This place gives me something to do since I don't have the Chautauqua Sisterhood any longer." Her face wrinkled to a prune-like scowl.

I pressed my lips to avoid a response. She obviously hadn't gotten over losing the presidency. "Thanks for sharing the story about the zoning issues. Do you think your neighbor would be willing to give me more details?" I didn't want to cross Aunt Constance and cause a rift between her and the neighbor.

"Let me talk to my neighbor. If you call her without permission, she might take it as an ambush. Plus, I did promise not to tell anyone about the zoning issue. I don't want to ruin a valued friendship, so if she refuses to talk, we'll need to respect that." Constance tipped her head and squinted at the sun. "It's going to be another warm one today, I think." She turned her gaze back to me. "I'll call you tomorrow."

I gave her a hug and a peck on the cheek before leaving the shop. She hadn't given me a name, but "valued friendship" made the identity an easy guess. Trudy Fitzsimmons and Constance had been close for years. After Uncle David's death, Trudy visited Constance almost every day, bringing her casserole dishes, taking her to the movies, theater productions, shopping sprees, anything to get her out of the house and over her depression. The thing was, Constance put Trudy on a pedestal. In her eyes, she could do no wrong. As for my view of her, besides all the positive qualities, I recognized one that she didn't. Trudy tended to be gossipy, even embellishing stories at times. I doubted she would care that Constance told me her news. Oh, she might act hurt or offended, but that mood would pass as soon as Constance put on some sixties tunes and brought out the wine and charcuterie. Nothing pleased Trudy like food, wine, and music. I wouldn't worry about ruining their friendship, but I'd respect Constance's wishes and wait until hearing from her tomorrow.

I paced my steps to take some time to think about what to ask Trudy, first being the identity of the one who'd lodged the complaint with zoning. Drawing closer to our shop, I glanced over toward the lake. Near the shore and close to one of the docks stood a tall woman with her braid of white-blonde hair trailing down her back. A denim blue dress and turquoise jewelry covered her from head to toe. Penny Swenson. Alongside her was a man, bald head, tall frame, and wearing black-rimmed glasses. Wink Lawrence, the owner of the *Whisper Cove Gazette*, appeared to be carrying on an intense conversation with Penny. His arms pointed in all directions, including at Penny's ample chest. Penny's arms, on the other hand, locked close to her sides, with fists on her hips, looking mean as hell.

I didn't know what to make of it except to be totally puzzled. As far as I had observed, the two of them did not get along. Wink had printed an article in the Gazette about Penny causing a brawl at Duckies and threatening to sue the owner. She claimed the owner was ruining her business by selling the same aromatherapy products Penny sold at her shop, The Healing Touch. As a result, Duckies would no longer sell those items. In my opinion, the article was rather gossipy and not appropriate news for the Gazette. In any case, Wink wrote a retraction to explain that Penny did not cause a brawl, but rather had words, a totally civil conversation with the owner. Old news, but from what I'd heard, Penny continued to give Wink the cold shoulder. So why they were talking really did puzzle me. I clicked my tongue as my thoughts wandered. The image of Penny snapping those photos of the mural team at the park yesterday puzzled me too.

"Let's get on with our walk, Max." I steered a path away from Artisan Alley and into town.

I unzipped my jacket and pulled up the sleeves. Picking up the pace, Max and I jogged across the boulevard. The traffic in town was sparse. On Sunday mornings, most folks I knew living in Whisper Cove liked to kick back and take it easy unless you were the owners of For Sweet's Sake and Spill the Beans. The weekends brought in the most customers and sales so good they couldn't ignore the opportunity.

Max stopped to lift his leg on a corner tree. I scanned the shop fronts and smiled at Picasso, the adopted town mascot, sitting on the corner bench, licking its fur. I'd aptly named the feline Picasso, one of my favorite artists and a totally free spirit in his painting. Plenty of folks attempted to coax the stray home and make it a house pet. Picasso would have nothing to do with the idea. The most anyone could do for him was to set out a dish of milk or tuna on the porch.

Resuming our walk, we neared the park. I was anxious to see how the saxophone and guitar Audrey had sketched turned out after adding color. Each detail of an artist's work excited me, how they transformed the images into something beautiful. Like writers who put words on a page with all the twists and turns of a plot, at times with a surprise ending, the finished painting would be unique and somehow personal for each person who viewed it.

Only several yards away, the sounds of raised voices could be heard. I tightened my grip on Max's leash and picked up the pace. Rounding the corner, I spotted Audrey and Rita, standing toe to toe. Rita shook her head as Audrey wagged a finger. The mural formed a backdrop and was partially hidden by the two of them.

Max and I entered the park. I pulled to a stop and gasped. The beautiful mural, now in full view, had transformed, all right. Transformed with swirly streaks of crimson red paint marring the surface with the message *GO HOME!* My gaze volleyed from the mural to the quarreling duo and back again. I defeated the anxiety doing battle with my nerves, and stepped forward.

"Hey, good morning, ladies. What's going on?" I maintained a calm tone, hoping to defuse whatever was happening between them.

Audrey stabbed a finger in Rita's direction. "I arrived at the park to get an early start on the mural, and I found her." The muralist's voice quivered. "And that." This time, her finger pointed at the mural. "I mean, how could she?"

Rita held up her hands, one holding a power paint sprayer. "I came here to help. I'd never destroy someone's artwork. It's sacrilegious, a violation of everything an artist stands for."

"Bull. You were holding that paint sprayer when I got here. And it's dripping with red paint. Don't tell me about violations and claiming you're innocent. You came here to ruin the mural because you're jealous or angry or whatever. And that warning? Who knows? Maybe you killed Lana." Audrey was screeching by now.

"Me? Are you insane? I'd never. That's, that's ridiculous," Rita sputtered.

I stepped between them, worried someone would throw a punch or be turned into a human tomato, sprayed from head to toe with red paint. "Rita, would you like to explain what you are doing here and why you're holding that paint sprayer?" I attempted to give her a chance, even if she did look guilty.

Rita swiped hair from her face. "I was taking my Sunday morning ride, on my way to visit a friend, when I drove by and saw the mural. I happened to have cleaning supplies in my car that I'd recently bought. I couldn't leave it this way. I know how to fix it. And that's what I'd planned to do." She dropped her head and sniffed. "Such a disgrace."

"Can you believe this?" Audrey threw up her arms. "Like I said, bull."

Rita dropped the paint sprayer and clenched her fists. "I'm not lying." Her voice quivered.

I'd heard enough. Worry coursed through me because Rita wasn't looking too well. As for Audrey, her temper had reached the point where I imagined she'd resolve the issue with bodily harm. Glancing around, I found no one else in the park to help me. Taking the risk they wouldn't kill each other for at least a minute, I stepped several feet away and punched buttons on my phone to call for help. Maybe the authorities could handle the situation better.

As if my wish for a helping hand sent a telepathic message, Nick and Tate walked into the park. I waved my arms like a frantic, crazy person. At once, Nick dropped the coffee he carried and ran toward Audrey and Rita while Tate jogged over to me.

"Thank goodness. I didn't know how long I could keep those two from boxing each other with punches instead of words." I released a rattled breath. My nerves fizzled and popped like kindling in a firepit. I'd had enough drama this past week to last a couple of lifetimes.

Glimpsing behind me every few seconds, I explained to Tate what I learned of the situation. I could hear Nick's calm voice. His words attempted to pacify Audrey as he pulled her to the side. Meanwhile Rita grew louder and her tone more agitated. She insisted she could clean the mural without ruining Audrey's work. "Maybe I should go see if I can help." I pointed at Rita.

The scream of a siren grew louder as a cruiser barreled down the street. I winced. "Is that really necessary?" I whispered and hurried toward Rita, whose expression showed both fear and irritation. Not a good sign. A groan escaped my mouth. A rhythmic clickety clack, along with the mantra "go home, go home," came from the other side of the tree line. I peered through an opening. In unison, the half-dozen or so protesters hit the posts of their signs on the concrete sidewalk, the sound accompanying their words. I braced my shoulders and stepped next to Rita.

"Don't worry, Rita. We'll get this sorted out." I patted her arm.

"Worry? I'm not worried. Nope. I did nothing wrong." She shouted the last words over her shoulder in Audrey's direction and pointed a finger.

"How about you call Lou?" I swore Rita's husband had some kind of magic in the way he alone could calm Rita when she got in this mood. "I'm sure he'd like to be here to support you."

She gestured with a flippant wave of her arm. "Already did. He'll tell Miss I-Know-Better-Than-Anybody a thing or two. She has no right accusing me. I'm a skillful artist. Just as good as her." Another finger pointed.

"Okay. Maybe we should take a breather. Especially—oh, boy." I tensed as Deputy Daniels marched authoritatively across the lawn. His eyebrows knitted together, and those lips penciled in a thin line, which hinted he meant business. Not exactly in a bad way, but something to be weary of, nonetheless. "Morning, Deputy. This really isn't as bad as it looks."

"Oh really? I get two phone calls from dispatch. First, yours telling us there's a scuffle brewing between two individuals. And the second?" His arm lifted and palm faced upward toward the mural. "Someone ruined this fine piece of work. To me, that looks bad, Miss Abbington." He plucked a notepad from his pocket and gave his chin a curt nod.

I couldn't argue. He was right on both counts. Before I opened my mouth to try another approach, Rita broke in with her defense. I stifled a second, or maybe it was a third groan, and when Max tugged on his leash, I let him lead us toward the walking path. The protester group had grown to include others. Gawkers, curiosity seekers, nosy bodies, or whoever they were, stopping by. My guess was they hoped to peek at what disrupted their otherwise quiet Sunday morning.

A second cruiser pulled up to the curb. A deputy I didn't recognize got out and motioned the crowd to disperse before arrests for disturbing the peace were made. I blinked. Disturbing the peace? Audrey and Rita already had that issue covered. In any case, one by one the gawkers moved on, leaving one or two protesters who spoke up to defend their first amendment rights. I had to smile at that argument, even if I didn't agree with their opinion about the amphitheater.

In seconds, a blue minivan pulled behind the cruiser. The barrel-chested man exiting the vehicle spoke to the deputy for a few seconds, then left him to enter the park. Lou Morgan smiled and waved as he passed by me. I pivoted on one heel to catch sight of Rita running to her husband. He wrapped arms around her small frame, and with only a tip of his Mets cap directed at Daniels, he then led Rita to the minivan. From what I could tell, Daniels almost looked relieved.

I sighed. "Well, Max. I think we can finish our walk now. What do you say?"

He emitted a tiny bark and tugged again at the leash. I steered away from the mural. Audrey, Nick, and Tate left the scene after Deputy Daniels.

Fortunately, no one was hurt in the morning chaos, except for the mural. That would need some work. As for Rita, I was certain she'd have her day in court to argue her innocence. I myself wanted to believe her. She'd said destroying a work of art was sacrilegious and swore she'd never do such a thing. Her words sounded totally sincere. One thing for certain, someone vandalized the mural.

Max snorted, his nose buried in the dirt as if something important caught his attention. I finally pulled the leash and Max to the side. Leaning over, I examined the ground. A large shoe print with the same grooved pattern and size I'd found the night of Lana's murder. I chewed the inside of my cheek. The print could be nothing. I followed what led to more prints, all leading to the lake. Lots of joggers and walkers came through here. No significance to draw from that.

"Right, Max?" I glanced down at my feet. Max panted while cocking his head. "We should check it out anyway. Is that what you're trying to tell me? Fine. Let's go." I yanked on the leash and pursued the trail of prints. Almost the same exact path someone had taken that night. "Coincidence. That's what Winsell would tell me. Without real proof, we have nothing." My sleuthing energy deflated. Nothing to call home about, as Dad would say.

I moved to turn around and head out of the park, but a sudden thought stopped me. Smart detectives collected all the evidence, even when they weren't sure it meant anything in the case. I fished my phone out of my back pocket and snapped photos of the shoe prints, including one with my foot next to it. Logical or not, the print reminded me of our hunch that Frank could be my mystery runner, and I wondered how much we really knew about him. He never spoke about his past or anything personal. Most people shared some stories about family, holidays, memories. Not Frank. Could he have something to hide about his past or personal life? I mused over the possibilities and steered a path home, looking forward to a relaxing breakfast with my family.

After making a few stops for Max to sniff the trees and mailbox posts along Sail Shore Drive, we finally walked up to our front porch. The ring and vibration of my phone made me pause to answer. "Hi, Aunt Constance. That was quick. Did you speak to Trudy? Will she talk?"

"No go, Chloe. She won't, and not even to tell me who filed the complaint. I'm sorry, but she suggested you file a request for that information with the zoning department."

I plopped down on the bottom step. "That will take too long." I knew how government offices like the zoning department worked. The wait to get results might take weeks.

"It's the only way, sweetie. Besides, Trudy is taking family leave to help care for her mother, who fell and broke a leg. She lives in Florida."

"Okay. Thanks for trying, though. Have a good day, Aunt Constance." I glanced at Max. "So much for that lead."

He whimpered and wagged his tail.

"I appreciate the sympathy, buddy. Let's get you and me some breakfast, okay?" I opened the front door and listened to the sounds of chatter and laughing. At least I had them to cheer me up.

"Nothing new, but the mood seems to be worse." Mom chewed on a bite of grapefruit.

We took breakfast on the screened-in porch. By now, the sun shown bright and the temperature had inched up but remained comfortable. I settled in my seat with coffee, grapefruit, and a toasted bagel. Dad had made his standard trip to buy an assortment of bagels and donuts. For the past few months, Sundays became our lazy days. We'd take it easy, and with no mess in the kitchen to clean up, we could enjoy spending more time talking about our week. In this case, the conversation went beyond the usual town gossip or plans we had, trips to take, movies or plays we'd like to see. When a murder happened in our small town, that's all anyone wanted to talk about. Anyone included the Abbingtons.

"I'm worried if the authorities can't manage the protesters, someone will eventually get hurt," I said.

"I'm more interested in those shoe prints." Izzie scooted to the edge of her chair. Her eyes gleamed with excitement. "They have to be Frank's. He has big feet, doesn't he? Always wearing sneakers."

I lifted my shoulders. "Lots of joggers run through the park, and I've never known anyone doing that in dress shoes."

"He told you he runs that way. Plus, he's the one who complained to the town council about the amphitheater. And he talked about sprucing up the park with a playground, additional trails, and other stuff. Wasn't he picking up trash when you ran into him? Seems to me he spends more time in the park than about anyone else." Izzie took a huge swig of her juice.

"Still doesn't mean those prints are his, or that he's my runaway jogger." I twisted my mouth. "Even if he was, we can't claim he's Lana's killer." We didn't know, and us proving anything about those prints was impossible. I fiddled with my phone, thinking of the photos I'd taken.

"We can't claim he isn't, either. If only there was a way to get a look at Frank's shoes, see whether they match your pics, I don't know. Wouldn't that be proof?" Izzie glanced around at all of us.

Mom dabbed her lips. "You know my friend Mattie, the one who went through a divorce last year? She goes to the local gym every Sunday to work out. I had to chuckle when she told me how she keeps an eye out for available men. She's lonely and wants to date again. Anyway, she sees Frank there, usually taking a swim or working out. Now, wouldn't that be the perfect opportunity to sneak into the locker room, maybe get a look at his shoes?" She glanced at her watch. "Mattie's invited me to meet her there this morning. She gave me two free passes to use. Why don't you go in my place?"

"Kate Abbington, aren't you the bold and sly one. I never knew." I winked.

"Oh, stop." She blushed.

Dad's brows arched as he held up his fork. "Don't let your snooping get you in trouble or put you in danger. If Frank is guilty and catches you tracking his comings and goings, well, you know what I mean."

"I'm sure the girls will be careful, Joe." She tapped her chair arms with both hands. "Now, you should hurry. I believe Mattie spends an hour or so at the gym, which means she's there right now."

"We'll give it a try. Thanks, Mom!" Izzie stood and tugged at my arm.

"Come on. You heard her."

"Yeah, all right. Even though the odds of catching Frank there are slim to none," I said.

"Or getting an opportunity to take a peek at his shoes that might not even be the shoes you found this morning or the ones he wears to the park? Probably no chance, but we have to try." Izzie practically sang out her words with an optimism I wasn't feeling as she dragged me along toward the stairs.

"I have nothing better to do, so let's waste some time on our only day off," I grumbled.

"Negativity won't get things accomplished."

"I'm looking at the situation realistically and practically. No negative vibes involved." I brainstormed to come up with a more efficient way to find out whether his shoes were the right shoes, but got nothing.

Within ten minutes, we were out the door and on our way to the local gym. Sully's Fitness was sort of like a YMCA, only smaller and privately owned by Tuck Sully. Locals loved the place, especially when Sully ran his specials for discounted memberships or free trial days.

We hadn't spotted Mattie, but the free passes got us in. "Let's check out the work room first to see if he's there. We can use the equipment while waiting for him to hopefully head for the locker room and showers," I tugged at my athletic wear bottoms. Whoever said these were comfortable didn't know me. "If not, we'll go on to plan B."

"What's plan B?"

"I have no idea. I'm making this up as we go." I entered the workroom behind Izzie. A quick glimpse showed Frank in the far corner, lifting weights. I stepped onto a treadmill that faced him while Izzie chose the elliptical trainer next to me. With any luck, I wouldn't be draining bucketsful of sweat before he finished and headed to the locker room to shower. I lowered the speed on the treadmill. Just in case.

"Look! He's wiping himself with a towel. I think he's done," Izzie whispered.

The five minutes we spent here seemed like five hours. I really needed to get into shape. Hadn't I been saying that since last summer? I rolled my eyes.

With the flip of a switch, I gladly turned off the treadmill.

We hid behind the corner wall, waiting for Frank. As luck would have it, he passed us without a glance and entered the main hall. Keeping a safe distance behind him, we ended up at the men's locker room just as he disappeared inside.

I stared at the closed door. "Now what?"

"We give him a few minutes, and then we sneak in." Izzie chewed on her fingernail.

I dropped my jaw. "What if there are other men in there? Like naked or something. I can't, Izzie. It's too risky. Not to mention creepy."

She threw up her arms. "How else are we supposed to get a look at his shoes? Isn't that why we came here?"

"It sounded like a good plan before we left the house." I scratched my head. "Let's leave. We don't have to keep snooping, do we?" Boy, talk about a change in my attitude. I'd let that tiny voice in my head get to me. That and Dad's warning.

"Nope. We're here, and we're going in." Izzie grabbed my arm.

Before I had a chance to resist or react, she pulled me into the locker room. I hitched my breath and shut my eyes. In seconds, I eased them open, one at a time. The room was empty. The only sound I could hear was running water in the shower. A guardian angel had to be looking out for us. Nobody should be so lucky.

"Let's find his locker and fast." I began opening doors in the row of lockers closest to me while Izzie worked on the other side.

"Found it," Izzie whispered.

I circled around to see her standing with a pair of sneakers in her hands. Pulling out my phone, I opened my photo gallery and clicked on the pictures I'd taken this morning. My eyes widened. "Oh, wow." The grooved pattern in my photo matched the soles of Frank's sneakers. I placed my foot next to the shoe. And the same size. I couldn't see any evidence of paint stains, but the smoothed, worn areas on the outsides of the soles were the same.

"I know what you're thinking, Chloe," Izzie started. "Look at it this way. Would you wear sneakers with blue paint stains, the same blue paint found at the crime scene, that would implicate you in a murder case? No, you wouldn't. You'd either clean them up or throw them away and wear another pair. Don't you see? We can't rule out the possibility Frank was there that night. I feel it in my gut, Chloe. Frank is your runaway jogger."

"We can talk about that after we get out of here." I snapped photos of the sneakers, tops, and bottoms and one with my foot next to them. I tensed and strained to hear. The patter of water from the shower suddenly stopped. "We need to leave. Now." I shoved the shoes in the locker, then yanked Izzie's arm, practically dragging her to the exit. I still wasn't convinced. Frank might only be someone who'd been in the wrong place at the wrong time. In any case, I wasn't comfortable sticking around to talk to him about it.

Chapter Thirteen

I twisted the sponge dipped in paint onto the canvas to create a pattern of flowers, blurred forms that imitated Impressionists like Monet and Renoir. I promised one of our frequent paint party guests that I'd create the painting for her mom, who was also a fan of the Impressionist style. Adjusting my rear to get more comfortable, I sat in the shop window seat, looking out at the shoreline for inspiration. Fortunately, the on-again, off-again showers that lasted from late yesterday afternoon until early this morning ended. The window was cracked open just enough to let the cool breeze carry the fresh smell of spring inside. I took a deep breath and relaxed.

"I still don't know how you two managed not to get caught." Willow busied herself with adding up invoice amounts of all the items we'd ordered for the month.

"A total miracle, if you ask me. I'm still wondering if anything we gathered will amount to evidence. I mean, sure the shoe prints match, the size and the grooved pattern, but that only suggests they could belong to Frank who was jogging in the park." I sat back and examined my progress on the painting. "I refuse to jump to any conclusions. None of it means Frank is the killer or even the jogger I saw that night."

"Geesh." Izzie tossed a wadded rag at me. "Would you stop? Repeating the same argument again and again doesn't make it any more or less credible. We should at least consider showing Winsell the photos. Let him decide."

"I could say the same to you about your argument. And no way are we showing him." I tossed the rag back at her. "Because we'd also have to tell him where we found the second set of prints. I don't think he'd approve of us sneaking into the men's locker room or how we're interfering in his investigation."

"Hmm. Got a point. Then what should we do? Sit on this news and wait for the right time to tell him, which I admit I don't like. What's your idea, Chloe?" Izzie sent me a pointed stare.

"We wait. That's the only safe choice. After all, Winsell has tons of evidence on Frank. His protest poster with those paint stains, for one. In fact, I'd bet our detective in charge has photos of the shoe prints from the crime scene and has already approached Frank about them. Seems like he's doing a thorough job investigating." I lifted from the window seat. "Let me talk to Hunter. I might persuade him to tell me how seriously Winsell is targeting Frank as a suspect."

"He won't tell you. When it comes to his cases, his lips are sealed shut," Izzie said.

"I think you underestimate me." I crossed my arms over my chest. "Just wait."

"How about we change the subject?" Willow tapped the projector with a pointer stick.

I turned to face her. While Izzie and I were debating the news about Frank, Willow had created an impressive list, illustrated with diagrams. "What's this?"

"It's a timeline. I may have missed some details, so you'll have to fill them in." Willow grinned proudly with her chin lifted. "Takes us from the moment you found Lana's body to the present. I also made a list of our most likely suspects and their alibis, if they had any. What do you think?"

"Wow. That's amazing, Willow." Izzie smacked palms with her in a high-five moment.

"Chloe?" Willow handed me a dry erase marker. "You should be the first to add anything I missed."

I hesitated while scanning the board. "I found Lana that night closer to eight forty-five. And it took me time to..." I swallowed, emotions threatening to take over my voice. "To settle the initial panic and get control of myself. Anyway, I called for help, and I'd guess the medics arrived within fifteen minutes, so let's say a little after nine?" I scribbled on the board.

"I think you left out some facts about one suspect. Rita Morgan."

I spun around. Penny stood at the entrance. Her hair was swept back into a tight bun with two pencils protruding from either side like those stick barrettes you see women wear. She held a notebook in one hand, which she waved at us.

"Rita Morgan, aka Rita Labinski, was born in Poland. Her grandparents were imprisoned in a Jewish concentration camp during the war. They had been celebrated artists before that. In fact, they were famous for their work. Rita's parents fled with her to the States and New York City, where Rita spent her childhood, attended the fine arts school known as LaGuardia, and later graduated from NYU. The first college graduate in her family, by the way. She moved to Whisper Cove after marrying Lou Morgan." Penny closed her notebook and smiled. "Pretty good, huh?"

I dropped the marker on the table next to me. "Nice to see you, Penny, but what does all you said have to do with this?" I waved at the whiteboard.

Penny nibbled on her lower lip, and lines creased her forehead. After a few seconds, she snapped her fingers. "Wink says every bit of research about someone's background helps. When the time comes, you weed out what's relevant for your article. So, I can't really say whether those details are important. Not yet."

I blinked. "Say what?"

"Oh!" Penny chuckled. "Guess I should explain. I'm writing an article for the *Whisper Cove Gazette*." She straightened and puffed out her ample chest, as if the announcement was the most important news ever.

"Um, okay. Why? Are you selling your shop to switch careers and become a journalist or something?" Izzie asked.

"Oh, goodness, no. I could never quit aromatherapy. I love it too much. I, er, I'm hitting a dry spell in sales, so I thought I'd give this gig a try to supplement my income. You understand rough times, don't you?" Her smile wavered for an instant. "Wink says if I can get the scoop on Lana's murder and write a spiffy article, he'll pay me and print it in the Gazette." A dreamy-eyed expression glazed over her. "And maybe take me on as a regular contributor. Who knows? I might get my own column. Something like 'Penny for Your Thoughts' would be a catchy title. Don't you think?"

I actually did think the title was clever, but my mind was stuck on the other news. "That's why you were talking to Wink yesterday morning?"

"And taking photos at our mixed event in the park," Izzie added.

"Exactly." Penny rolled back on her heels. "I plan to crack this case wide open, as they say, and win a Pulitzer for this article."

"High expectations." I wagged a finger at her. "But you don't think she's the guilty one, do you?"

"We know Rita has a habit of blowing her top when she's upset and reacts to situations with too much drama. What little I witnessed of your friend Lana, she seemed a bit on edge, almost angry, I think. Put the two of them together, and something tragic could've happened." Penny tapped one of her pencils. "However, my bet is on Nick, the boyfriend. He and Lana snapped at each other, or at least she did at him. His reaction was sulky and the quiet kind of anger, which is a lot more dangerous, if you ask me. Trouble in paradise is what went on with those two. I'd bet on it."

A sense of dread soured my stomach. What if she was right? Nick was alone during the time Lana was murdered, supposedly in his hotel room. Was he telling the truth? "Sounds like you've given this a lot of thought. But I'm not ruling out any of those others just yet." I pointed to the board. "Each of them had plausible motives, or ones just as strong as Nick's."

"Or none of their motives work. You gotta look at it that way too." Willow tapped the pointer stick on the board. "The killer's name might not be on the board. Could be someone none of us knows, like an enemy Lana had from the past who took the opportunity to kill her, thinking the authorities would blame one of these people." The pointer tip touched each of the names.

I groaned. "Oh, please don't go there again. I can't stand the idea of starting over or maybe never finding out who did it."

"Or worse, sending the wrong person to jail." Izzie let out the words in a soft, barely heard whisper as she covered her mouth.

"Well, I should be going. Just wanted to drop in and say hello. Have a great day!" Penny beamed a wide smile and waved as she went outside.

"Drop a gloom and doom conversation on us, then tell us to have a great day? Geesh." Izzie plopped down in a seat. With elbows on the counter, she cupped her chin in both palms and glanced wearily at Willow. "You sure didn't help."

Willow shrugged. "Sorry, but it had to be said. I watch that show about cold cases. Lots of murders never get solved. More than you'd imagine."

"Not this one." I smacked my side. "I'm thinking if we eliminate a few of these names, narrow done the list, we have a better chance of figuring out who did the crime." I scanned the board. "Of course, Rita, Nick, and Audrey have the more likely motives."

"Don't forget. Frank falls into that right time, right place category. Plus, there's the physical evidence. The shoe prints, the paint-stained poster, the tall, athletic build that match so well. Hard to dismiss all of that," Izzie said.

"And he went to the town council to file a complaint about the amphitheater." I sighed.

"Why kill Lana? Why not Miles? He's the one who brought the amphitheater to Whisper Cove. It's his fault, not Lana's," Willow said.

I'd already covered that in my mind and wrote another scenario. "Let's say Frank came to the park looking for Miles to confront him because he was angry, really angry, but found Lana instead. Lana tried to calm him, or maybe she argued with him. One thing led to another, and he caused her to fall. Intentionally or accidentally, that might have happened."

"Fine, then how do we eliminate any of them if they all look guilty?" Willow asked.

"We need to dig deeper and find out their secrets. They must have some we're missing," Izzie added.

I snapped my fingers. "I'm calling a friend in Paris. Muriel is a faculty member at the University of Paris and knows many in the academic world. She might be able to find something on Audrey." I walked to the storage room and dialed Muriel but had to leave a voicemail.

With nothing else to do but wait for her to return my phone call, I offered to make a lunch run at Bob's Barbecue Pit. Orders in hand, I sprinted out to my car and traveled down the road into town. The place was always packed at lunch time and dinner time.

The line was long, but from my experience, it would move quickly. I pulled to the curb in front and killed the engine. Slipping out of my seat, I stood facing the Pit. Nothing fancy about the building, which from the front gave the impression of a food truck. A wide roof extended several feet as a protective overhang in case of rain. No room inside the tiny shack except for a kitchen. Still, a few tables surrounded the area for those customers who preferred to stay and eat instead of grabbing takeout orders. Bob kept his business open from April through October. He spent his winters in Florida, where he co-owned and ran a restaurant. Life was satisfying in Bob's world.

I reached inside the car for my bag and the order list. Locking the door, I peered at the line once more. A tiny gasp slipped from my mouth. Detective Winsell stood next to the order window, talking to Bob. He kept the line waiting for a minute or two before moving away and with no bagged order in his hands. An obvious hint that his visit had nothing to do with barbecue or a thirst for Fizzy Orange. I ducked back into my car. Was I being overly suspicious? Winsell was talking to people all over town. That's what I'd heard. I also had told Winsell I stopped at Bob's before heading to the park the night of Lana's murder.

As soon as Winsell disappeared, I sprinted across the lot and got in line which had dwindled to a half dozen people. Twisting my head to view behind me every second or so, I must've looked like someone with a nervous tic. No sign of the detective reappearing.

"Chloe? Do you have an order for me?"

Bob interrupted the paranoid ramblings, somersaulting in my head. "Oh! Ha. Sorry, Bob." I shoved the list of food items across the counter. "I, um, I noticed Detective Winsell speaking with you."

"He was." Bob held the order, then leaned close to me. His voice dipped lower. "He asked about you."

"Oh?" I gulped.

"Don't worry. I told him the truth. You stopped here that evening to order a Fizzy Orange. I remembered the time because I was closing up early. You were in a big hurry and me too. So I was glad you didn't order a barbecue

126

sandwich because I'd already put the food away."

Relief warmed my insides. "That's good. Anything else? I mean, did he say anything more?"

Bob rubbed his jaw. "Chloe, he's been talking to lots of folks in town. I heard people at Millie's. In fact, that artist who's painting the mural. Audrey, is it? She's been spouting off at Duckies and Millie's that you probably murdered Lana over some painting award. Sorry to tell you."

"Yeah, I'm not too surprised." I bristled as heat rose to my face, thinking how that news influenced Winsell's investigating. Had I become the focus of his case? Just because Audrey decided I was the killer and had to broadcast her opinion to everyone in town? "I know he's asking a lot of questions about Frank Benworthy too, so I guess he's doing a thorough job. Can't blame him for that. I want Lana's killer caught more than anybody."

"You bet. Now, let's see what you got on this list." He slipped his reading glasses back on and squinted. "Gotta get my prescription updated. Darn glasses aren't much help anymore. Give me a minute. I'll be back with your order."

I willed my heartbeat to slow down. Winsell asking questions about anyone he considered a suspect in the case wasn't unusual. He investigated every detail, which I had to respect. Still, the idea of being put under a microscope, analyzing every move I made, every comment, made me uneasy.

"Thanks, Bob." I smiled as I took the bagged order and the cardboard bottle holder containing three bottles of soda. Filtering my thoughts and sorting which to keep in mind and which to shelve for later review, I hopped in my car and sped down the road to Artisan Alley.

Once parked, I grabbed my cargo and hurried to Paint with a View. I'd spent more time than planned away from the shop. After lunch, I'd help Izzie and Willow with finalizing the agenda for tomorrow evening's event. Shimmers had been my idea, inspired by my love for Monet's art. When I found the time, I'd give Hunter a call. With any luck, he'd share what he could about the case. Any news was better than no news. I hated being kept in the dark. Not knowing what Winsell thought, what he planned to do next, and how close he was to finding the killer flustered me. I tightened my grip on the food order. "I need answers." The words came through gritted teeth as I shoved open the door.

"Hey! Slow down. You almost kicked over your beautiful canvas," Izzie said. A frown quickly set her lips in a tight line. "What's wrong? And don't say nothing is because I can read you better than anybody. I'm your sister." She wrapped an arm around my shoulder.

I shook my head. "Just more trouble. I caught Winsell talking to Bob. Seems he's asking questions about me. Or at least that's what Bob told me. Oh, and it gets better." I set the bag of food and drink carrier on the counter and plopped down in a chair. "Audrey has been spouting off to everyone in town that I killed Lana. Great day, right?"

"Aww, sweetie. No one will believe her. She's practically a stranger in this town. People know you. They trust you, not some crazy-talking stranger."

I patted her hand. "Thanks for the vote of confidence, but let's face it. Winsell has got it out for me. Until someone proves otherwise, I'm on his whodunnit list."

"What about your friend from Paris? Maybe she'll give us something to show Audrey had more than enough reason to get rid of Lana," Willow said.

"We'll see. Meantime, let's eat before the food gets cold." I munched on my barbecue sandwich while finishing up the outline I'd started for tomorrow evening. At least keeping busy with work stopped me from thinking too much about Winsell and finding Lana's killer.

The afternoon flew by. One minute, my watch said noon, and the next time I looked, it was five. We'd promised Mom to be home for dinner. She enjoyed celebrating holidays and other significant dates. Today was the thirtieth anniversary of Mom and Dad's first meeting. The evening would include the story about a college party, wine, poetry, and how two awkward, shy students had a conversation and fell in love by the time the party ended. Romantic with a few cheesy moments, but still a good story.

"You go on ahead. I'll finish locking up, after I give Hunter a quick call," I said. "Tell Mom I won't be late."

"You sure?" Izzie questioned with her raised brows.

"Yeah. I won't be long."

Once she and Willow disappeared through the doorway, I pulled out my phone, pressed a button, and sat down. His number rang twice and then went to voicemail. "Good grief. Seems no one is available when I need them." I left a quick message. Leaning back against the wall, I closed my eyes. Life shouldn't be like this. Lana turned twenty-seven in March. Twenty-seven years didn't give you time to do all the things you had planned, all the goals, all the relationships you hoped to have. I couldn't get my feet to move. Not for several minutes, as my mind reeled with all those lost plans.

I blinked, then swiped my eyes dry before starting for the door. Cleaning up could wait until morning. I picked up my bag and slung the strap over my shoulder. In a fair world, Lana would get some kind of justice. I'd do everything I could to help. And afterward, I'd make sure that award taken away from her would be reinstated.

I flipped off the light switch and opened the door. Stepping outside, I gasped. Cerulean blue paint graffitied the front walkway with huge letters. *Killers get what they deserve.* I spun around. My hand trembled as I attempted to put the key in the lock. Safely back inside, I clicked the bolt, then dialed nine-one-one.

Chapter Fourteen

"Whoever did this sure worked fast. I was only twenty minutes behind you." I chewed on my fingernail while tapping my foot. My nerves were shot. I flinched each time Winsell's team member snapped a photo of the painted message.

Izzie touched her upper lip with the tip of her tongue. "You know, the message might not be meant to accuse one of us. Maybe this person wanted to let us know he or she is on our side. After all, killers do get what they deserve. You see what I mean?"

"I thought of that. Still…" I tensed once more at the snap of the camera. Winsell approached as he'd finished questioning someone who supposedly had exited her condo and noticed the graffiti bandit at work. Her excuse for not doing anything to stop the person was lame, in my opinion. She thought maybe one of us was painting some kind of decorative sidewalk art. Wearing a black hoodie and running away from the scene afterward? Yeah, that sounded like something an innocent person would do. Geesh.

"Okay, Miss Abbington." He smiled and held up his finger. "Chloe, can you remember anything else that might help us catch the person who did this?"

I shook my head. "When I stepped out of the shop, I didn't see anyone, only that message." A tremor of fear shuddered through me.

"Well, the witness believes the person is male because of their build. Tall, rather thin, and a pretty fast runner because he sprinted across the park. But you know my opinion about conjecture."

"Only tell what you're sure of. Got it." I paused. "What I am sure of is that paint is the same color found by the mural the night Lana was murdered and smudged on the poster belonging to Frank Benworthy. I'm also sure whoever painted the sidewalk is pretty damn bold because he or she took a chance of being caught in the act. The lights inside were on, which should've implied to our graffiti artist that someone was still in the shop." I folded my arms and hugged them tightly against my chest. "Maybe he or she watched Izzie and Willow leave and knew I was alone. Maybe that person was even willing to hurt me if I came outside at the wrong moment."

Izzie squeezed my shoulder. "I think we've had enough drama for one night. How about we get you home? I didn't tell Mom and Dad why you called me. They're probably anxious by now."

Mom and Dad. I groaned. I didn't know what to say, or if I should say anything about this to them. I hated the idea of making them worry. But was keeping them in the dark any better? I looked at Winsell. "Are we through here?"

"If I think of more to ask, I'll call. Meantime, take that message as a threat. Both of you. Be vigilant and let me or Hunter know immediately if you think you're in some kind of danger." He sighed. "I shouldn't have to tell you to keep your distance from this investigation. Right?"

Neither one of us answered. Distance was not what we'd been keeping.

Winsell tipped his hat. "You have a good evening, and stay safe."

I awoke Tuesday with a splitting headache. Last evening's scary incident left its mark, both physically and emotionally. I popped a couple of pain reliever capsules in my mouth and washed them down with a swig of coffee. Nothing like a caffeine jolt to amend the problem. After this case was solved, I would need a long vacation, somewhere on a beach or in the mountains. I took a couple of deep breaths to calm myself, then headed downstairs. Izzie and I planned to stop by the mural site and see how much progress Audrey had made. Rain had slowed the effort to erase all the mural damage and wait for it to dry. I worried she'd gotten very little done, and even worse, we'd find Miles causing a scene, complaining about deadlines and losing money.

I stepped into the kitchen. Izzie finished up her coffee and set the cup in the dishwasher. "You ready? It's almost eight." I tapped my watch.

"I doubt anyone will be at the park this early. We have time to make a quick stop at For Sweet's Sake to grab a dozen bagels. Food always cheers people up," she said.

"You're referring to Miles? In that case, he'll need the whole dozen to turn him into a cheery person. I feel sorry for Audrey. I'm not sure she has Lana's nerve to stand up to him."

"You mean like the nerve she has to spread those lies about you?" Izzie sniffed. "Hard for me to feel sorry for her, after that."

"Izzie." I scolded her with the point of my finger.

"Okay, a little sorry. I'll manage that much. Can we leave now?" She grabbed her jacket, hanging on the chair, and led the way.

Minutes later, we pulled in front of the bakery. The white and coral exterior was warm and inviting. Claire definitely had applied artistic flare to give the place a nostalgic feel. The windows were dressed with scalloped canopies like you see in those movies from the fifties. She'd given attention to the tiniest detail. The interior carried the white and coral colors on the walls, tablecloths, and even the cloth napkins.

Claire's assistant waited on us, so there wasn't the usual chatter and gossip we always had to start our visits. Leaving a generous tip, we bid goodbye and walked out with a dozen assorted bagels and tubs of cream cheese.

The Land Rover fit snugly into a tight parking space between two utility vans. I inched myself sideways to exit the vehicle. My footsteps squished in the soggy grass as I made my way into the park. I waved the bag with containers of cream cheese. "I don't hear any screaming or shouting. That's good news."

Izzie trailed behind me, clutching the bagel bag in one hand.

I turned and laughed. She tiptoed in a zigzag path to obviously keep from stepping in puddles of water. "The white on those sneakers won't last the day."

"The price of dressing fashionable, I guess." She shrugged. "No biggie. I'll just toss them in the wash. I see Audrey. She's on the lift, painting."

"And I spot Miles below her. He's doing a lot of arm waving." I groaned.

132

"Is that a good or bad thing that she's ignoring him? I can't decide."

"Maybe he's just excited to see how far along the mural is."

"Huh. Maybe so." I worried that Miles being here would prevent me from opening up a discussion about the graffiti bandit with Audrey. I might get some kind of guilty reaction to hint at her involvement. Audrey matched the description the witness had given. She was rather tall and thin. So was Frank. Plus, he was a fast runner. Even Nick worked. Though his build was not thin, he certainly wasn't heavy. I had to face facts. Tall, thin, and able to run could match a lot of people I knew. Still, I'd confront Audrey and Nick while I was here.

By the time we reached the mural where Miles stood, I heard laughing. His cheeks puckered with a smile. I jerked my head back. This was not a look I'd seen very often.

"Stop. You're flattering me too much. I'm just doing a job the best I can." Audrey's tone took on a coy and flirtatious lilt.

I'd underestimated her skills. In fact, her pleasing approach to handling Miles and his mood was better than Lana's somewhat surly comebacks. "Hey, guys. What's going on?" I laid the bag I carried on a folding table set up near the mural.

"Oh, I was telling Audrey how pleased I am with the mural. She's doing a fantastic job. Don't you agree?" He rolled back on his heels. The grin and puckered cheeks remained.

I scratched behind one ear. "Yeah, she really is. Glad to hear you have no complaints, Miles."

"How about that? Complimentary and nice." Izzie sprinkled her voice with a bit of sarcasm.

"What my sister means is you seem really happy with things, which looks good on you." I glared at Izzie, who rolled her eyes.

He waved an arm. "It's fine. She's right. I've been too cranky. Lots on my plate and a load of problems, too. Now, if you'll excuse me, I need to have a word with an electrician about this lousy sound system." The smile deflated along with his puckered cheeks, replaced by a creased scowl.

I guessed becoming nice took some time and effort. I shielded my eyes from the glare of sunbeams with one hand to look up. "Hi, Audrey. Can we help in any way?"

"Does it look like I need help?" She stared down at me. Pulling a handcloth out of her pocket, she wiped away the sweat on her face and dabbed her lips.

I shivered. Her hard, cold stare implied all that coy, friendly attitude was for Miles alone. "Ha. No, it doesn't. But since you're so far along, maybe I can have a word?"

"Fine." She lowered the lift without protest. Facing me, eye to eye, she threw up her arms. "What can I do for you?"

I shifted my gaze to Izzie, who mouthed words of encouragement. Taking a deep breath, I gave Audrey a quick summary of what happened last evening. "It rattled me, and I'm worried someone is out there wanting to do some vigilante justice kind of thing. I thought you should be aware, just in case."

"Just in case of what?" She crossed her arms and tightened her jaw. "I'm certainly not worried because I didn't do anything to hurt Lana. You, on the other hand, should be concerned."

I blinked. Her eyes burned with anger. So much for taking time to reconsider her accusation about me. "I see. Well, if you hear or notice anything concerning, please let Detective Winsell know. Okay?" Agitated, I grabbed the cloth she'd dropped on the ground and waved it. "Wouldn't want to litter the park grounds," I said and hurried away before I could add anything I'd regret later. If Audrey had told the truth, she deserved to be upset about Lana's death. I was, too. I wished I could make her understand that. I shoved the sweaty handcloth in a trash bin before marching across the lawn.

Izzie dropped the bagel bag on the table and hurried to catch up. "You don't believe all that nonsense, do you?" She scoffed as she stepped alongside me. "She's using her anger and accusations to cover up. Maybe not for killing Lana, but I'd bet she's feeling guilty about something."

"I don't know what to believe anymore." I clenched my fists. None of what we tried got us anywhere. I searched for Nick and spotted him near the walking path. He was staring at Miles, and a man who I figured must be the engineer. "Why don't you take a break, and I'll go question Nick."

"You sure?"

"If I'm alone, he might open up more. Besides, you're kind of intimidating." I poked her in the side and grinned.

"Me? Never." She drew out the last word and giggled. "I'll wait in the jeep. Don't be too long." Her phone beeped with a message. She quickly read it. "Oh, wow. That was Willow. She's locked herself out of the shop. Do you mind if I leave you here for a while? I can easily be back in ten minutes."

I shook my head. "Stay at the shop. I can walk there after I'm done talking with Nick."

She waved and skirted around the hedges to reach the parking lot.

"Now, let's try this again. Maybe with a lot less snark involved." I muttered under my breath. Getting closer to where Nick stood, I could hear the raised voices of Miles and the engineer. I cleared my throat. "So what do you think that's all about?"

Nick swung around. "Oh. Hi, Chloe." His face relaxed. "I'm not sure. Something about sound systems and not enough bass."

"Well, as one would say, it's certainly all about that bass." I grinned.

"Ha. Good one. So, what are you up to?" He sat on the ground and crossed his legs.

I did the same and attempted to look at ease. "Oh, Izzie and I delivered you guys some bagels. In case you needed a midmorning pick-me-up. Lots of carb energy in bagels." I bounced a curled knuckle against my mouth, thinking how to bring up what I'd planned to say.

"I heard. About carb energy, I mean." He stared intently without blinking. "Is there something you want to say, Chloe? I'm guessing that's why you're here."

"Oh. Yeah, I um…did you hear about what happened last night at our shop?" I stifled a moan. Way to be cool, Chloe.

"Actually, I did. Detective Winsell came to visit me late last night. He had a few questions about the incident. He thought I might know something. Not sure what gave him that idea." His brows inched up while he tipped his head.

I tucked my knees close to my chest. "What did you tell him?"

"That I was surprised to hear about the painted message and had no clue who put it there." He finally looked away and motioned with one arm toward Miles. "Seems the two of them resolved their difference of opinion."

"Always a good sign."

"Projects like this can get people worked up, cause arguments, even destroy relationships." He turned once more to face me. "Not all of them have a happy ending, even if the project gets done."

"I suppose not. Say, meant to ask how you enjoyed your lunch with Miles at Tasty Spirits. They have an excellent menu and some of the best local wines in the Five Finger Lakes area." I held my breath. Would he admit to being there, I wondered. By the frown on his face, I guessed he wouldn't.

"I don't know what you're talking about. Must've been someone else you saw." He stood and brushed off his pants.

I followed suit. It was time to embellish a little. "That's funny. I overheard Miles talking about it at Millie's the other evening. He even mentioned you by name." A total lie, but I was desperate to know what that lunch was about.

His face reddened. "You heard wrong. I've never been there. Never plan to go. In fact, I hate wine. Besides, I have too much work to do to drive two hours to lunch at a winery. Work that I should be doing now. Have a great day, Chloe." He hurried off toward Audrey and the mural.

I'd certainly got a reaction. For one, I was sure he'd lied about the winery. How else would he know that it took two hours to get there, if he didn't go? Too bad that bit of information didn't help me get to the truth about their meeting. I was dying to know because the secrets people kept were driving me crazy. And one of those secrets must have something to do with Lana's death. I was sure of it. "More than one way to tackle this." I straightened and marched over to where Miles sat on a picnic table facing the lake.

I followed his gaze and smiled at the picturesque view. Fishing, swimming, sailing, canoeing, the lake was filled with activity. After the rain yesterday and the return to milder temperatures, people were anxious to enjoy some early summertime fun. I envied them. Instead, I remained stuck in my discouraged mood, worried over this case.

I scooted onto the table and pointed. "Looks like everyone's having a great time."

Miles braced both arms behind him and anchored his hands on the table. "Lucky souls, aren't they? Meanwhile, you and I have to slave away at our jobs. Speaking of, how is your paint party business doing?"

I was surprised he remembered we had a business. "Doing okay. The first couple of years are the hardest, I hear."

"True. It will get easier, though. You'll see."

"I had a conversation with Nick a moment ago. We talked about the Finger Lakes and all the wineries. What a coincidence it was seeing you two together at Tasty Spirits." I scooted closer to him. "Izzie and I were hosting a paint event, you see. I came outside, and there you two were." I twisted my mouth into a frown. "You seemed to get angry at one point, though. Did you and Nick have a falling out? Not a good sign for a working relationship."

Miles laughed. "Not at all. Only a momentary lapse of mood. Call it artistic temperament. We creative types all have it, don't we?"

Only some of us were artistic types. That didn't include Miles, but why argue? "Sure. I get it."

"We had a delicious lunch, and their wine selection is excellent, tasty like the name. Even Nick agreed."

"That's a relief to hear. Fighting amongst yourselves won't get the mural finished, will it?"

"We're good, Chloe. Don't you worry. The mural will be done and the amphitheater will be showcasing all those wonderful concerts as planned, right on schedule. Now, if you'll excuse me, I have a meeting with an investor. One with deep pockets, which is the kind I love." He released a deep belly laugh and hopped off the table to walk away.

"Somebody or both somebodies are lying. The question is why." I pulled out my phone to give Hunter another try. He hadn't returned my call from yesterday, and I was anxious to talk. Listening to the ringtone, I headed out of the park.

"Hey, Chloe. I'm so sorry for not getting back to you. We've been swamped with tips about the case, which we've been following up on. Too bad they lead nowhere."

"Not a problem." I had felt a tinge of hurt, though, because I expected to hear from him after what happened last evening. Wasn't that what couples were supposed to do? Comfort each other in moments of stress and traumatic experiences, like a threatening message painted on your doorstep?

"No, I owe you an apology. A big one for not calling after the scare you got. No excuses, just me being an inconsiderate heel. Forgive me?"

I relaxed my shoulders. "Of course. It's fine. Look, I'm just now leaving the park. Izzie's expecting me at the shop." I stepped into the crosswalk. "We can talk—" I gasped at the abrupt sound of tires squealing. From the corner of my eye, I spotted the blurred image of a car barreling down the road and directly in my path. At once, I fell back on my heels and landed on the curb, inches away from the vehicle as it blew by me. My heartbeat raced, and blood rushed to my head, making me dizzy. I clutched my chest, taking deep breaths, and willed myself to keep from fainting.

"Chloe, Chloe! For God's sake, Chloe, answer me." Hunter shouted into my phone.

I gulped another breath of air and strained to speak. "I'm okay, but I think I'm going to need someone to come get me. I don't trust my legs to walk anywhere."

I dropped the phone to my side. What happened suddenly hit me. A whimpering cry shuddered throughout my body. I couldn't help but think this wasn't an accident. Whoever drove that car intended to hurt me.

Chapter Fifteen

While I sat huddled in my living room chair with Max in my lap, Hunter paced the room for the tenth or maybe hundredth time. His agitation made my anxiety rise. And asking me to repeat what happened several times didn't help. No, I didn't see the license plate number. No, I didn't catch any details to describe the driver. Yes, the vehicle was a dark blue sedan, make unknown to me. Maybe foreign. I knew his mood was to cover up how scared he was for me. I appreciated the concern but wished he'd dial it down a bit.

"Maybe we could take a break and talk about something else?" I tried on a friendly face to assure him I was fine and ready to move on. "Honestly, going over what happened, again and again, is upsetting." Throwing in a true confession might work, too.

"I'm sorry." He dragged his fingers through his hair, then knelt in front of me. Folding my hands in his, he breathed a sigh. "You gave me quite a scare. I don't want anything to happen to you."

I slipped one hand out of his grasp and touched his cheek. "I love you too. Now, how about I make us lunch? Chicken salad sandwiches sound okay?"

"Nope. You sit tight, and I'll take care of it. Besides, you look a wreck." He winked.

"Gee, thanks." I leaned back in my chair, shut my eyes, and stroked Max's fur with one hand. "In that case, I should catch a nap while *you* fix lunch and wait on me." I pressed my lips tightly to keep from laughing.

"Yes, ma'am. One sandwich with loads of chicken salad and a dill pickle on the side coming up." His phone rang in his pocket. Fishing it out, he opened the call. "Hey, Rico. What do you have?"

I sat up and strained to hear his side of the conversation as Hunter now took over the hallway to pace back and forth. Within only a minute, though, he was finished and came back into the room.

"That was Rico. He located the traffic cam footage from the road in front of the park." He shook his head. "Even though he could see the moment when the car sped by you, it's too grainy to make out the license number or any details of the driver."

"Great." I fell back against the chair again. Max jumped to the floor and trotted off down the hall. I wrinkled my nose. Obviously, he'd heard the word lunch and went to check out his bowl.

"Hold up. Rico's sending the footage over to Buffalo. The department there has a specialist, and his equipment is way better than ours. Maybe he can get results. Don't you worry. We'll catch the man or woman who did this."

He didn't have to say what we both were thinking. Identifying the driver could also mean identifying Lana's killer. We wouldn't know if the incident was intentional or the act of some reckless joyrider, not until we had more information. My worry was this happened less than twenty-four hours after the graffiti warning. Why wouldn't I think there was a connection? I stood. "Sorry, but I can't just sit here and do nothing. Keeping busy is what I need."

"Fine, but there's no way I'm letting you hold the knife to slice bread. Your hands are still shaking." He tapped my nose and grinned.

"Ha. Funny you." I linked my arm with his and walked down the hall to the kitchen. Mom and Dad had left early to meet friends, and when I called Izzie to let her know what had happened, I made her promise not to say anything to them. Last night, after giving careful thought to the matter, I'd told them about the vandalism at the shop. They'd freaked out enough then. Adding more to their worries wasn't something I was willing to do. Besides, they'd find out soon because of small-town gossip. Plenty of drivers and those walking by had witnessed the near collision I'd had with the speeding car. By lunchtime at Millie's, everyone in town would have heard the story. Fortunately, Mom and Dad wouldn't be home until this evening.

"I've been meaning to ask you something." I handed him the loaf of bread and cutting board, then took out the container of leftover chicken salad from the fridge. I picked out a small bite of chicken and dropped it next to Max who stood on his hind legs. "I spoke with Bob yesterday while ordering lunch. He says Winsell was asking questions about me. In fact, Bob claims your detective partner has been questioning lots of people and mostly asking about me." I pried open the container and stirred the contents, more than needed. I let the spoon drop, and it clattered on the counter. "Should I be worried?"

Hunter gave the slightest headshake. "No. You have to understand Winsell is thorough. I'd say probably the most detailed investigator in the field. As I've told you before, he covers all the bases, digs into any lead, and dishing out questions about suspects is a part of that process." He grabbed the container of chicken salad out of my hands when I picked the spoon up again. "He's asking about Audrey, Nick, Rita, and anyone else connected to Lana, just as much as about you. So, stop letting him get to you."

"You're right. I should focus on other stuff, like work. We have the Shimmers event this evening." I licked the spoon, then dropped it in the sink. Pulling a clean one out of the drawer, I handed it to him. "No need for me to—" My phone vibrated, and the muffled jingle sounded in my pocket. I turned away as soon as I read the name on the screen. "Hey, Ross. How are you?" Taking a deep breath, I faced Hunter once more and shrugged.

"Chloe. Boy, it's good to hear your voice." A soft chuckle came across the receiver.

"Ah, yeah. You too." I flushed with heat. This was awkward. The memory of Ross and Hunter making nice with each other last summer came rushing back. I'd felt awkward then, too. When your ex and current boyfriend are friendly, like over-the-top friendly to one another, and maybe sharing stories about you, what girl wouldn't be uncomfortable with that? I walked to the other side of the kitchen and avoided eye contact with Hunter. "So, what's up?"

"Oh, sure. I thought I'd call to remind you that our RSVP deadline is approaching. I mean, you haven't replied, and I just thought I'd check." He paused.

His words were rushed. I bit down on my lip. That meant he was nervous. We were usually relaxed when we talked. After one more tentative glance at Hunter, I steered my steps into the hall. "Okay, what's going on? You sound off," I whispered.

"I don't know." His voice rose. "I'm a wreck, an absolute wreck. I'm messing up at work, which you know isn't like me. I'm a total professional, the best lawyer this firm's got."

I rolled my eyes at that comment. Modesty wasn't one of his personality traits.

"Chloe, I'm having second thoughts about going through with this." He barely got out the words.

I sat down on the bottom step. "What you're having is pre-wedding jitters. That's all. You love Miranda, right?"

"Of course I do." His voice sounded more assured.

"And she loves you, so what's the problem? Afraid of losing your bachelor status?"

"You, of all people, know that's not the case. In fact, I've been thinking about you lately. What if we made a mistake? I mean, what if—"

"I'm gonna stop you right there, Ross. We, you and I, were not going to work out." I stood and paced the hall. "Our priorities are too different. Did you forget that? Look." I tucked a stray lock of hair behind one ear and sat once more. "Ross, come on. We are the past. You and Miranda are your future. Don't throw that away. Please, trust me. You belong together." I tore off a loose thread on my jeans. There was total silence on the other end of my phone. "Ross? Are we good?"

"Sure, Chloe. Everything you said is…right. Don't forget to RSVP, okay? I should get back to work. Got an important client to take care of."

"You always do. Bye, Ross." I ended the call. Pivoting on my heel, I walked to the rear of the house and paused in the doorway. This didn't have to be awkward. I squeezed my eyes shut and took a huge breath of air. My tension soon eased. I stepped into the kitchen to find Hunter leaning his back against the counter ledge, ankles and arms crossed. I swallowed. "That was Ross."

"Oh? How's he doing?" His voice was calm.

"Good." I sat at the table, facing him. "He's having some of those pre-wedding jitters, but that's normal." How easy it was for me to leave out the part where Ross questioned if we could've kept trying to salvage our relationship. A slight, yet intentional omission done not because I felt the same way, but because I worried Hunter would believe I did. I deflated with guilt. What happened to total honesty and transparency between us? Was keeping secrets really the way I intended to go? I stood and walked to him.

"Actually, there's more to his doubts than pre-wedding jitters." I spilled that part of the phone call, and even included my feelings, which I didn't really confess to Ross, then pressed my lips to keep from blathering.

"But you didn't tell him you no longer felt the same. Why?" His head tipped sideways.

"He knows how I feel, or don't feel." I jutted my chin forward as if defending my actions.

Hunter let go of my hands, his brow furrowed with creases. "Should I be worried?"

"No! Why would you even ask that?" My voice raised. In a quieter tone, I added, "I'm sorry. I shouldn't yell. It's just…" I threw up my arms. "I love you, not Ross. I want to be with you, not him. Can we leave it at that?"

His tongue trailed along his teeth. He took my hands once more and pulled me close. "Of course. I don't want to argue or turn this into one of those mountains out of molehills, but can you promise me one thing?"

I leaned my head against his chest. "Name it."

"Answer that RSVP and tell them we'll be there for the wedding. If you and I are truly over this thing about Ross, then we should be comfortable attending. Right?"

"Absolutely." I kissed his cheek. "I love you, Detective Hunter Barrett."

"I love you too, Miss Chloe Abbington, artist extraordinaire. That's French, isn't it? Extraordinaire."

I laughed at the poor attempt to mimic a French accent. "We should get out of here. I need to earn my keep, and so do you."

He pulled on his jacket and helped me slip into mine. "Talk to you this evening after your event?"

"Yep." I pointed. "Or sooner if you hear from that specialist in Buffalo." I gave him a peck on the cheek and turned to lead the way out of the house. Once in my car, I waved goodbye and sped down the road.

The air was brisk with the taste of lake water carried across the shore and inland. Gulls cried as they soared up and then dove to the ground. I traveled along the gravel surface of Artisan Lane and found an empty space to park. I jerked when my phone suddenly rang. This sure was the day for phone calls. Hopefully, this one would bring positive news. I killed the engine. Picking up my phone, I smiled at the name lighting up the screen. "Hello, Muriel. *Ça va?*"

"*Ça va.* I hope you are doing fine as well. I read about Lana's passing. I'm so sorry, Chloe. I know you two were close."

"Thanks. It's been an emotional couple of weeks, I admit. Did you also know Lana's death has been classified as a homicide? I'm still processing that detail."

"Is that why you asked me to search for info about Audrey Laurent? Quite an interesting bio she has."

I reclined my seat to settle in. This could be what I'd been waiting for. "I'm listening."

"First, my search led me to L'Ecole des Beaux-Arts. It's a very prestigious school of the arts."

"Yes, I remember hearing a lot of stories about it during my time in Paris. Audrey attended and graduated from there. Right?"

"Not exactly. She attended for three years. It's not easy to be accepted. The exam is rigorous, and students must have exceptional talent. Very few receive a scholarship," she said.

"That explains a little why Lana would've chosen her to intern." I remembered how Lana was such a perfectionist. Only the best talent would do.

"*Oui, bien sur.* I agree. The tuition cost is extremely high, too. I've found no record that Audrey received a scholarship. I'm guessing she either has money or comes from money. I will check into it more, but I haven't told you the most interesting part of the story."

My heart raced. I had so many questions. Audrey never tried to hide where she'd meant Lana. She'd only mentioned the word university. Beaux-Arts was a school for older students, those beyond what we in the States call high school. "Go on." I managed the words.

"She suddenly dropped out of Beaux-Arts last fall semester. Only a year before she would have graduated, which was puzzling to me."

"Last fall. That's when she told me she met Lana."

"Makes sense since she came to the States soon after. Anyway, I managed to do more digging into why this happened. I must say, it was not easy. The scandal had been covered up well. Someone had great influence to manage this."

"Scandal?" Pulling the lever on my seat, I sat up straight. In my rearview mirror, I spotted Izzie sitting on the front stoop of Paint with a View.

"*Oui.* A scandal. Your mural artist had an affair with a professor at Beaux-Arts. When this was discovered by the administration, the professor was fired, and Audrey left school. This all happened during the fall semester. Surprising, no?"

"Very." I absently rubbed my chin with the pad of my thumb. "Muriel, would you check to see if Lana had been a guest lecturer at Beaux-Arts during that semester?"

"I don't need to check."

"Oh? Why?"

"Because I was there. I attended that lecture. Very impressive presentation. All about mural art and its history."

"Well, I have to say, when you deliver information, you do it in a big way." I smacked my hand against the dash. This news could be important. I just hadn't figured out how yet. Did Lana know about the scandal? If she did, hiring Audrey was surprising. Lana didn't like messy situations, ones that could taint her reputation. Then again, she had used my painting for her prize-winning mural. That marred anyone's reputation.

"If there is anything else you need, call me, *mon amie.*"

"You are a good friend, Muriel. I'll be in touch, and we can have a more pleasant conversation." I ended the call and remained in my seat, sorting through everything she'd told me. I didn't blame Audrey for keeping her affair with the professor a secret. It wasn't something to shout out to the world. In fact, all that Audrey had told me was the truth. However, those tiny details left out of the story were what concerned me. I could come up with all kinds of scenarios. What if Lana knew about the scandal? That could explain the rather harsh way she treated Audrey. If the scandal had been buried like Muriel implied, maybe Lana threatened to expose Audrey. Comply with every order she gave or else. I shuddered, thinking of Lana being that cruel. The Lana I knew was kind and considerate, the person who took care of people, protected them. That person would be the kind to offer the internship to someone who'd just dropped out of school and needed a friend.

I got out of the car and walked to the shop. Maybe I was going down the wrong path with making something out of Audrey's story in order to pin the murder on her. I pulled open the shop door. I felt like I'd only scratched the surface, and only a bulldozer could dig deep enough to find the answers I needed. Meanwhile, the Shimmers event was waiting. The anticipation of laughter and a fun time painting made me smile. I recalled the line from a Dr. Seuss book Granddad Abbington used to read to Izzie and me. *Today was good. Today was fun. Tomorrow is another one.* I hoped tomorrow would bring news that Winsell had solved Lana's murder. In the meantime, I'd enjoy this moment.

Chapter Sixteen

"It's almost time." I set the final canvas from last evening's event in the display case and stepped back. "I'd say Shimmers was a huge success. The talent here could rival Monet's. You see what I mean?" I pivoted on one heel.

Izzie slung her bag strap over one shoulder. "You delivered the instructions like a Monet. That's also why it was successful."

"Thanks, but I think I'll give our guests most of the credit."

Izzie's head cocked to the side as she stared intently. "Do you want to talk about Ross? I know he's on your mind. Or what he said is."

"Nope. I'm good." I almost regretted telling her about the phone call or the part where Hunter and I had discussed the issue of Ross. If she pushed too hard, I'd either blow up at her or cry. I didn't want to do either one. I loved Hunter, not Ross. How many times did she need to hear that?

I turned the knob and shoved the door wide with the force of one hand. "Besides, we need to hurry. The meeting is starting at noon." All of Whisper Cove's residents had received word that a special council meeting had been scheduled because of urgent circumstances involving the amphitheater. Not at all surprising. The floating entertainment venue seemed to take up most of the council's time in the past few months. Today, items on the agenda included brainstorming ideas to promote the grand opening of the theater, particularly those sales events merchants could schedule to attract visitors. For that reason, shop owners were urged to attend, if they could arrange for staff to run their businesses for an hour or so. In our case, Willow would be here, not that we ever got that much traffic during the early afternoon.

Megan stood on the sidewalk, facing the lake. As we stepped outside, she turned and smiled. "Morning, ladies. Are we ready to take on the town council?"

I frowned. "Why would we be taking them on? Do you know something we don't?"

"Yeah, what gives, bestie?" Izzie linked her arm with Megan's.

"Oh, just some town gossip I heard from one of my sources," she said.

"You have sources? I'm impressed." I chuckled.

"Okay, you caught me. It's only Penny dishing out the scoop." Megan skirted around a parade of ducks that waddled across our path, pulling Izzie along with her into the grass.

I followed them as we ended near Whisper Lane. Recalling our conversation with Penny, I was curious to know about the scoop, as Megan called it. In fact, I'd put a lot of faith in what the newbie reporter had to say.

"Well, come on. Let's hear it." Izzie popped open the car door.

"She heard that Miles is knee-deep in troubles. He hasn't hired someone to fill the music program director's position yet. And there's the issue with zoning. You know about that from your aunt."

Knee deep? More like up to his neck, but feeling sorry for him was difficult to do. For one, he'd brought those problems on himself by firing the original director and possibly cutting corners or making a special deal with zoning. People wouldn't forget, especially the protesters who looked for any excuse to criticize the amphitheater and the person who initiated the move.

Personally, I wanted to see if any of those issues connected to Lana's murder. That's why I was anxious to attend the meeting. Who knew? Something might come up.

I hopped in the back seat of the Land Rover while Izzie and Megan sat up front. We road across town and arrived in time to hear the opening remarks, but not soon enough to grab seats. The place was packed. I strained my neck to view the front row of chairs. Sure enough, most of the protesters, like Rita and Frank, sat together. All across the room, the buzz of whispered conversation didn't stop, even when the council president, Stanley Thornacre, asked for quiet. Emotions peeked. I imagined tempers could boil over at any minute. Some of those in the crowd were those who supported the amphitheater and viewed its return as a business opportunity or to simply add more entertainment. Either group could fuel an argument. Within this crowded room, I doubted even the council president would manage to keep control of the meeting.

"Over there." Izzie poked my shoulder. "I wonder why Detective Winsell is here?"

I followed her gaze and spotted him standing in the far back corner of the room. He seemed attentive, shifting his head from one side to the other, not speaking to anyone. "Probably still on the clock to investigate Lana's murder." Our eyes met for a second. I quickly faced the front. By now, Stanley was hitting the microphone. The loud feedback caused most everyone to cover their ears and abruptly stop talking.

"Thank you. Now that I have your attention, we will first address the issues about the amphitheater. Mr. Terrell, would you please come up?" He motioned Miles to the podium and stepped to the side.

Miles walked up the middle aisle, carrying papers in his hands while nodding left and right at the crowd. The response he received was mixed. Some gestured with a thumbs up while others scowled. "Thank you all for attending this meeting and taking time out of your busy morning." He shuffled the papers and laid them on the podium. Tugging at his shirt collar, he then smiled.

"Do you see that? He's nervous. Miles Terrell is never nervous. Angry, yeah, but he doesn't act this way, ever," Izzie said, cupping her hand over her mouth.

I gave a slight nod and put a finger to my lips. I wanted to hear every word.

The room grew loud once more. Miles held up his hand. "Please. What I'm going to say should answer all your questions and concerns, if you give me time to speak." The noise quieted to a whispered drone. "Thank you. First, I've hired a new music program director. She's smart, experienced, and a pro with budgeting, which pleases me since I'm trying to keep costs within reason. Second, a new investor from Rochester has generously contributed an amount that will help make the rest of this project run smoothly and with no more delays."

"Who is this director? Do we get a name? How about a bio with her credentials? It'd be nice to assure folks with that kind of information. You know, in case someone wants to check her out."

I smiled, hearing the familiar voice. Penny stood off to the side and near the front of the room. She had her pen and pad ready.

"Yes, well, her name is Amelia Heart, and she's worked for various music venues all across the country. I'll post a link to her bio on my website." Miles gave Penny no more than a second before turning. "Anyone else have questions?"

"What about the investor? Does he or she have a name? Will you be providing a link to their bio on your website as well?"

Penny was relentless and all business in her demeanor. If I was a newspaper editor, I'd hire her on the spot. "She's good, isn't she?" I whispered to Izzie.

"Conrad Meeks. And yes, I'll link his bio, too. Is that all, Miss Swenson?" His voice edged along with the hint of a scowl he failed to hide.

"Thank you, Mr. Terrell, but that's not all. There are rumors that you're having trouble with the county zoning department. Is there a problem keeping the amphitheater here in Whisper Cove? Or will we be seeing it towed back up the lake to Mayville?" Penny lifted her chin.

An audible echo of voices spread from every corner of the room. Several hands flew up. I leaned against the wall and sighed. At this pace, the meeting might go on through dinnertime. Though I had to admit, anything Miles had to say about the zoning could be worth hearing.

Miles waved an arm. "Now, now. There's nothing to that story. I've spoken to zoning about a complaint that's completely unfounded. It's been settled. So, no one needs to worry."

All the hands dropped, and the noise faded to mere whispering once more.

That was disappointing, but who knew if he told the truth? Maybe he was hiding a few details. I'd filed the request for information about Miles's permit to move the amphitheater and for the identity of whoever registered the complaint with zoning. I was right in estimating how long it would be to hear back. Two to four weeks at least. The person who handled my request

150

commented the department was backed up, which wasn't encouraging news either.

"If there are no more questions, I can announce that the amphitheater grand opening will be on Saturday, June seventeenth, three weeks after the May Fling charity event. In the evening, from seven to nine, the tribute band, Poker Face, will perform a set list of Bruce Springsteen songs." Miles gestured to those seated behind him. "Also, I hear from the council that plenty of activities are planned for the day, including rides for the kiddos, games, canoe, sailboat, and speedboat races, an obstacle course competition, and of course plenty of food vendors. Let's make this the best opening Whisper Cove has ever had. Thank you for your time." Miles quickly left the podium and exited through the front door, giving no one a chance to comment.

From the back row, one arm raised. I turned to peer over several chairs and recognized Ira Gibbs who ran the Whisper Cove Casino. It didn't take much speculation to figure out what he wanted to talk about.

"Yes, Mr. Gibbs?" Stanley gestured, pointing his finger.

"Thanks, Stanley. I was wondering if you and the other council members will have enough in the pot to support both the May Fling at the casino and the amphitheater festival. Ours is only three days away. You've already committed to help out our event, you know." Ira crossed his arms over his chest and leaned back in the chair.

"Absolutely. Through some very generous donors the kitty has grown. We have enough funds to help with both events as well as our fall festival." Stanley grinned. "Now, let's talk about sales events. I'm sure all of you store owners have fantastic ideas to share."

"I'm gonna visit the ladies' room." I circled around the back row. As I neared the hallway, a man sat in the corner, wearing a tweed jacket, hat, and shades. The shades were puzzling. Why keep them on inside? He leaned forward in his seat, staring straight ahead. I followed his gaze. Audrey was talking to Penny. Suddenly, she turned and glanced my way. The scowl on her face wasn't surprising. She held on to her belief that I killed Lana. Before turning to find the ladies' room, I caught Audrey's expression change. Her eyes widened, and the scowl twisted into something even angrier.

A chair squeaked as the stranger took off the shades and stood up. He moved quickly, weaving around people in his way, closer to the front of the room, while Audrey whispered to Penny, who stepped into the stranger's path. Audrey took the opportunity to leave the room.

It didn't take me more than a second before I picked up my pace, choosing my route through the doorway closest to me and into the hallway. I hurried around the corner to reach the front exit, where I nearly collided with a stack of chairs. Gripping the top to keep from knocking the towered obstacle over and me along with it, I inhaled to catch my breath. Within seconds, Audrey emerged and the stranger along with her. Obviously, Penny's efforts to stop him failed. I squatted to hide behind the chairs and peered through a space between them.

The stranger stood close, removed his hat, and placed a hand over his chest. I had the chance to get a better look at him. Average height, I guessed, since he was slightly shorter than Audrey. His mousy brown hair stood out in tufts. I strained to hear any of their conversation, but being nearly twenty feet away, I couldn't. Audrey kept shaking her head as he spoke. Maybe he was interested in mural art or wanted to hire her for a project. However, those guesses were just that, guesses. Within a few minutes, Audrey waved her arm and stormed off toward the building's rear exit.

With nothing more to see, I entered the main room once again, forgetting about my restroom visit. People were gathering their things and filing out. The meeting had ended while I was busy snooping, but totally worth my time. I mulled over the scene between Audrey and the stranger. My gut told me something more personal caused what now seemed to me as an argument. That something only added to the mystery of Audrey's background. Why had the strange man upset her? Could he know about the affair she had and planned to blackmail her? That didn't make sense, though. If Muriel was able to uncover the story with a little extra effort, so could others. I had a hunch, but I would need to call Muriel again to learn more. Meanwhile, I'd ask Penny if Audrey had said anything about the man, like who he was and how Audrey knew him.

"What took you? You missed all the great ideas people suggested for the grand opening. I'll fill you in on our way back to the shop." She clutched her bag to one side.

"Where's Megan?" I asked.

"She's catching a ride with her parents." Izzie threaded her way through and around the groups of people who lingered to chat. "The family is helping her rearrange merchandise in the shop. Her mom has ideas on what to showcase up front, I guess. Megan was frustrated when telling me about it. She loves her parents, but since they've invested lots of money and time into the business, they probably deserve a say in what to do with it." Izzie shrugged as we reached the Land Rover. "It's a touchy situation."

"I bet." I slid into the passenger seat and buckled up.

Once we were on the road, Izzie explained the part of the meeting I'd missed. After hearing all the suggestions made for store sales and promotions, I was excited to begin planning ours. The event was only a little over three weeks away. Of course, we'd already submitted items for the charity portion of the May Fling at the casino this Saturday. I'd yet to pick up a dress for the affair and check to see if my black pumps were clean—those were the only dress shoes I owned. To top it off, I couldn't dismiss the murder hanging over my head, with me being one of Winsell's suspects. I pressed a hand against my chest and felt my heart pounding. Too much to handle was overwhelming me.

"Are you okay?" Izzie glimpsed sideways for an instant. "Why are you breathing so hard? Don't worry about the grand opening, if that's what it is. I already have some great ideas for promotion. You won't have to lift a finger."

I blew out the last breath and forced myself to relax. "It's not that. Well, not only that. Guess I'm reeling from everything that's happened in the past couple of days. I'll be fine."

"Good. Now, you didn't tell me why you were gone so long from the meeting."

"Oh! Right. Listen to this." I dove into what happened between Audrey and the stranger who upset her. "I need to speak with Penny. She and Audrey were talking at the time. Maybe Audrey told her something to explain who the man is and why he's in Whisper Cove."

"Hmm. Wouldn't hurt to keep an eye on Audrey and watch out for the stranger, don't you think?" Izzie pulled into a parking spot.

"Yeah, good idea." I grew queasy with the sense of feeling overwhelmed again.

"I'm sure Willow would want to team up with us. Sleuth sisters plus one on the case." Izzie giggled and exited the vehicle.

"You are such a cheeseball." I laughed and followed her to the shop. My steps slowed as we neared, and eventually froze in place. Detective Winsell sat on the bench situated across from our entrance.

As if hearing us approach, he turned and stood. Brushing crumbs off his shirt, he then held up one arm. His forehead creased, and lips narrowed in a thin line. "Chloe, Izzie. Your assistant said you'd be back soon. May I have a word?"

I licked my lips. Not greeting us with the usual friendly demeanor put me on alert. "Will it take long? We have lots of work to do."

"Won't take but a few minutes." He waved an arm, gesturing us ahead.

Izzie squeezed my hand. "We've got this."

Entering the shop, the chimes tinkled. I cringed as if the melodical sound suddenly annoyed me. "So, what is it you have to say, Detective?" I didn't mess with niceties like offering a beverage or for him to take a seat. At this point, my nerves couldn't handle it.

Willow excused herself. She had a couple of errands to run. Once she left, the room grew silent. I tried on a smile as I shifted my attention. "Detective?"

He pulled a photograph from his jacket pocket and handed it to me.

I studied the image of a camcorder for a second then gazed at Winsell. "Is this supposed to mean something to me?"

"Not without an explanation. I received a visit from Nick Poling. He filed a report with the authorities, claiming his camcorder had been stolen and missing since the morning after Miss Easton's murder." He scooted forward in his chair. "What he's concerned most about are the videotapes stored inside the camcorder bag. They are very valuable, according to him."

"Okay, but I still don't understand. What does the theft of his equipment and tapes have to do with me?" I had relaxed, though not completely. In my frazzled state of mind, I actually had imagined Winsell had come to arrest me. That serious stare with his creased brow and narrowed lips had left me frightened and unnerved. Still, I had no idea where he was going with this conversation.

"Mr. Poling suggested maybe you saw the camcorder in the park that night Miss Easton died?" Winsell steepled his fingertips to rest under his chin.

My heart somersaulted a few beats. Was he serious? Was he implying I stole the camera, on top of possibly murdering Lana? I waited until I got control of my voice. "I never saw the camcorder, have no idea what happened to it or who could've possibly stolen it." I messaged him with a calm stare that I wasn't about to let him rattle me. I'd keep that reaction buried deep inside.

"What I do know puts a few holes in Nick's story." I recounted the conversation between Tate and Nick I'd heard the other day. "You see, he never mentioned the camcorder being stolen, only that he liked to use different equipment on occasion. Strange to not say something about it being stolen then, don't you think?"

"I'll talk to both men and see what they have to say." Winsell scribbled in his notepad.

"My sister has no reason to lie, Detective." With an edge to her voice, Izzie jumped into the conversation. "Maybe the runaway jogger Chloe saw that night stole it."

I gave her a slight shake of my head. She wasn't helping. She was poking the bear.

"One can always find a reason to lie, Miss Abbington." Winsell narrowed his gaze before standing.

A chill caused me to tremble. Rubbing my arms, I stood and walked across the room to open the door. "I'm sure you have a busy schedule, Detective."

"Yes, of course. Thank you for your time and cooperation. Have a good day." He tipped his head and walked outside.

"Wow. Thank goodness he's gone. Can you believe that?" Izzie shut the

155

door and slammed the palm of her hand against the frame.

"Izzie, he was just checking on Nick's story, that's all. I didn't hear him accuse me of anything." I sat down once again. The wind had been knocked out of me after his visit. Maybe he hadn't accused me, but the message was implied. I closed my eyes and pictured that quiet beach and blue ocean water again. The smell of ginger tea tickled my nose.

"Thought you could use this." Izzie handed me one of two steaming mugs and sipped from hers.

"Thanks." I cradled the mug while letting the warm steam soothe my face.

"I was thinking maybe Nick didn't tell Tate about the theft because he was embarrassed."

"Hmm. Could be. I mean, admitting that would show he's been careless with his equipment." I tapped the mug. "Or maybe he didn't tell him because it wasn't stolen."

"Right." Izzie sat next to me. "All we need to do is find the camcorder and prove which of his stories is the truth. Easy stuff."

I laughed though it sounded shaky. "Easy, huh? I hope you have a plan in mind to make that happen."

The door chimes jingled once again, and Willow stormed inside. She dropped the shopping bag to the floor. "You'll never believe what happened." She panted and raised her arm. "Sorry. I ran all the way from that boutique on Main Street."

"Come sit down." I led her to the closest chair and motioned to Izzie. "Another cup of tea, maybe?"

Izzie hurried to the microwave.

"Now, what happened?" I stared attentively.

Willow's breath eased out. "It's Rita. When I came out of the boutique, I saw a police cruiser across the street and Rita's car in front of it. Chloe, it was awful. The deputy handcuffed Rita. The poor woman was screaming, then crying. That's the last of her I could see because she was taken away. They arrested Rita."

Chapter Seventeen

"Oh boy." I raced to digest everything Willow had said. The thought of Rita behind bars painted a disturbing picture. I'd suspected something could turn up to connect her to Lana's murder, but when the reality of those speculations hit you, it was shocking all the same.

"Her husband is out of town on a fishing trip." Izzie's eyes popped. "Lou is out of town. That means she has no one to come to the station or even bail her out, if that's the case. Poor Rita. Keeping her in a jail cell is sad."

"That's it. I'm going to the station." I grabbed my bag and jacket. "No matter what we think she may have done, she's a friend, or maybe not as much friend as acquaintance and fellow Whisper Cove neighbor. We help out each other."

"I'm coming with you," Izzie said. She set her mug of tea on the counter. "Willow, please cover the shop. We'll be back soon."

"Sure, but there's one more thing I should tell you." Willow bit one of her fingernails. "Before Rita threw a fit, she tried to bribe the deputy. She offered to make a generous donation to the department, if he'd let her off with a warning."

"Great. Bribery on top of whatever else she was arrested for." I led the way outside.

The trip north to the sheriff's office took a little over thirty minutes. Izzie attempted to get ahold of Lou by phone while I drove.

"This is so frustrating. I've tried five times and still his phone goes to voicemail." Izzie tossed the phone in her lap. "What if there was an emergency? If Rita or someone else close to him was hurt, maybe dying?"

157

I snorted. "Melodrama is your thing."

"Sorry." She sighed. Her head slammed back against the seat. "Yeah, well, he should answer his phone once in a while."

I turned the corner and pulled into the parking lot next to the sheriff's department building. I'd only been here a half dozen times or so. Mostly to say a quick hello to Hunter but never on a business matter until now. "Let me do the talking. I'll ask for Hunter. That's our best bet to get answers."

"What if he's not in? Then what? Detective Winsell wouldn't be so willing to spill the news about whatever Rita's been arrested for." Izzie walked alongside me.

"Besides bribing an officer, you mean. Yeah, let's deal with that when or if it becomes an issue." I pushed open the entrance door. The pungent odors of burnt coffee and sweat permeated the air. I wrinkled my nose. At the front counter, a female officer stood behind a plastic shield, sipping her coffee. I stepped up to a box-shaped opening and cleared my throat.

"Good afternoon. I was wondering if Detective Barrett is in? I'd like to speak with him." I smiled and studied the woman who smiled back at me. Rather tall, a wide face, and expressive brown eyes. I'd never met her the few times I'd visited.

"Sure! He's in his office. Let me ring him, Miss..." Her brows lifted, waiting for what came with the title.

"Oh! Of course. Let him know Chloe is here to see him," I said.

"Okay then." She punched a button on her phone. "Hi. This is Rachel. There's a Chloe here to see you." She hung up the receiver and smiled again. "Be right out. Take a seat."

A woman of few words. I had to admit that in my circle of family and friends, especially the female gender, wordiness was key to a conversation. "Thanks." I turned and bumped into Izzie.

"Hey!" Izzie hopped aside. "Give a girl time to move, would you?"

"Sorry." I chuckled. "I almost forgot you were with me."

We took empty seats situated along the front wall to wait. Within a minute or two, Hunter came out of the hallway and into the waiting area.

"This is a surprise." He gave my shoulders a squeeze. "And you brought

Izzie. Doing some shopping and decided to stop by?"

"Shopping is one way to put it." I kept my voice low. "Is there someplace we can talk without being heard?"

He frowned. "Yeah. My office. Hardly anyone is in right now. What's this about?" He led the way across the hall to the very last office door.

Once we were inside, Hunter closed the door. "Okay, what's going on?"

"Rita Morgan. She was arrested earlier today, and we're here to help bail her out if she needs it." I nibbled on my bottom lip. "Of course, it would be better to know why she was arrested in the first place. Right, Izzie?" I turned.

"Right. If it's something really serious, you know." Izzie covered her mouth to muffle a hiccup.

Hunter leaned back in his chair. "Is that all? You both gave me a scare."

"Huh? Why?" I tilted my head.

"Thought you might've gotten in trouble again, snooping into Lana's murder."

"Seriously? Is that all you think we spend our time doing? Snooping in your murder cases?" Heat rose up to my cheeks. He was right, though. We did spend a lot of time snooping, just not all of it. "We want to help Rita. Her husband is out of town, and they don't have kids or relatives living close by."

"So, what happened?" Izzie said.

"It's no secret, ladies. Rita was stopped by Deputy Brennan for speeding. When she started shouting at him and threatening to report him for badgering little old ladies, Brennan recognized Rita from the mural vandalism incident. He asked for permission to check her car. She claimed she had nothing to hide. That's when Brennan found the rag and arrested her."

"The rag? What rag?" I puzzled over why she'd be arrested because of a rag.

Hunter sighed. "He found a rag in the backseat on the floor. It was stained red. The same red color of paint used to vandalize the mural. You see where I'm going with this?"

I did, and the direction wasn't promising. Plus, the sudden thought when I connected dots between the mask with the red stain and Rita's rag wasn't helping. "What did Rita have to say about it?" There were always two sides to a story.

"She claims she cut her finger and used the rag to stop the bleeding, then tossed it in the backseat and forgot about it."

"Sounds reasonable to me," Izzie said.

"Reasonable or not, the lab will test it, and we'll know then. Meanwhile, she received a speeding ticket, and I know the judge won't look too kindly on the bribe."

I slouched. "She offered to make a donation to the department. That's a nice gesture, isn't it?"

"In exchange for letting her off with a warning? That's called a bribe, Chloe. You know this." He rubbed his eyes with the tips of his fingers. "In any case, she has to go before the judge on the bribery charge, resisting arrest, and withholding crucial evidence in the vandalism incident."

"But she forgot about the rag! That's hardly withholding evidence," I argued.

Hunter stroked his jaw. "Look, I have no say in the matter. She's lucky the judge will see her later this afternoon, instead of making her wait until tomorrow morning."

Izzie's phone vibrated in her bag. She pulled it out and gestured with a thumbs-up. "Hi Lou. I'm so relieved you called."

I stood. "Thank you, for what it's worth. Will you let me know what the lab finds out?"

Hunter came around his desk and embraced me in a tight hug. "You bet. Being a simple test to see whether it's blood or paint, we should get results quickly."

"Sure. Thanks." I reminded myself that even if the results turned out to be proof that Rita could be the mural vandal, that didn't mean she killed Lana. Those were two different crimes. Connecting them was conjecture, an assumption with no real evidence. That's what Winsell would say.

"Great. We'll get someone to let her know so she won't be too worried. Thanks, Lou." Izzie hung up. "Lou is on his way home. He should be here at the station around four. You think that will work so Rita won't have to face the judge alone?" She glanced at Hunter.

"I'll see if I can send along word to the judge that Rita's husband is on his way and would like to be present in court. No promises, though." Hunter walked to his door and opened it.

"You'll let Rita know that Lou's coming? And call me when you learn about the test results?" My questions stumbled over each other as he led us into the hall. "And if you hear anything more from Winsell about Lana's murder? Don't forget. Oh! And if Winsell tells you he talked to Nick or Tate about the camcorder, you'll share that too?"

Hunter laid a hand on my shoulder. "Yes, Chloe, to all the above. Now, go home or to the shop or wherever you can relax. You're wound up tighter than my team on inspection day. Please?"

He kneaded the stiff muscles in my neck that proved what he said was true. "Okay. I'll drink a cup of Mom's soothing tea and tag along with Izzie to one of her yoga classes. Promise."

Izzie tugged at my arm to hurry me out of the building before I could spill out another string of questions. We hopped in the car, and I sped down the road toward Whisper Cove. "At least Lou will be with her. I would've refused to leave if he wasn't coming."

"Yeah, I know." Izzie tapped her knee. "Hey! We did a good deed today, and Karma rewards kindness, you know. Maybe Buddha will help things along to find Lana's killer and put you in the clear." Her eyes widened as she gripped the seat. "Maybe even cast some kind of good luck on our shop too. Wouldn't that be awesome?"

I sucked on my tongue. "I have no words, other than to agree we did do a good thing for Rita. However, part of our good deed was self-serving, wouldn't you say?"

"You mean we needed to know the details of her arrest and if she is the art vandal." Izzie nodded.

"Yep." I turned into the parking lot.

"And if that would make her more likely to be the killer." Izzie exited the car.

"Sister sleuths do think alike." I sighed. Being suspicious of so many people

161

we knew made me feel lousy and guilty. I had to wonder if this would be the last murder we'd face for a very long while and if our lives would return to normal. The truth was, I couldn't remember any time or place in my life where this much tragedy happened so close to me or put me in danger, or fingered me as a killer. Whisper Cove definitely hadn't been living up to its reputation of the popular relaxing and tranquil place to visit. Not by a mile.

After dinner and a warm bath, I curled up in my favorite chair in the living room with a mug of Mom's special tea in one hand and Max snoozing in my lap. Hunter had been right. Taking time to relax soothed my nerves and slowed all those thoughts racing in my head. Heavy eyelids threatened to take over and end my day sooner than I wanted. Before bed, I planned to walk Max through town. Some cool night air would also help.

When my phone rang, I winced. Why hadn't I silenced it? I didn't want interruptions, but if Hunter called with news, I didn't want to miss that either. I fished the device out of the chair cushion where it had wedged. Hunter's name lighted the screen. "Hi, Detective. I hope you're calling with some good news."

"Nice to hear your voice after my hectic afternoon."

"Why? Is everything okay?" I sat up straight and put Max on the floor.

"Too many leads that didn't pan out. It's a case I'm working on, not Lana's." He hurried to add the last part.

I eased back into the chair and breathed easier. "That's too bad. About the leads, I mean. So, did Rita get released? I've been worried all afternoon."

"The judge was lenient. She got off with a speeding ticket and a warning to hold her temper better. What helped the most was the lab report. It came back right before Rita was scheduled to appear in front of the judge."

This time, I sprung out of the chair. "She told the truth, didn't she? Blood stained the rag, not paint." I struggled with whether to be pleased or disappointed.

"Yep. That's what it was."

"Well, this sends us back." I walked to the front window and stared at the lake. The water had grown choppy as tiny ripples washed to shore. The full moon shone brightly on an otherwise starless black night.

"For both the vandalism and the murder case is what you mean." Hunter made a tisk-tisk sound. "Winsell would be disappointed in your sleuthing. Never make assumptions. The two crimes might not be related or committed by the same person."

"I know. That's exactly what I told myself." My voice carried a heavy tone. "I'm trying to keep a proper view of things. Just desperate, I guess."

"We all are. Summer is almost here, and the idea that a murder will be hanging over our heads beyond springtime is discouraging."

"Okay, any other news?"

"Nope. Sorry. Winsell couldn't track down Nick or Tate this afternoon. Audrey told him they'd taken a trip to Buffalo to check out another mural job."

"Oh? I guess that means the three of them plan to stick together and keep painting murals. Interesting." I sat on the window ledge.

"Why interesting?"

"Well, for one, the three of them don't act like they want to be working together. I mean Audrey and Tate get along fine, but Nick and Tate seem on edge a lot. As for Audrey and Nick, I keep getting this vibe that something between them isn't right. Like they are hiding things that keep them on guard with one another. Does that make sense?"

"It's possible, but without getting them to admit they're having problems, you can't know."

"Yeah, yeah. I hear you. Look, I've got to go while there's still time this evening to walk Max."

"Be careful out there at night. There's a killer on the loose, and your pooch isn't exactly equipped to defend you."

"His bark is pretty mighty. That scares off plenty of people." I reached down to scratch Max's head and smiled. "Besides, he's the right height to sink his teeth into someone's ankle."

Hunter laughed. "Absolutely. Talk to you later. Love you."

"Love you too. Night." I stared at Max. "Are you ready for that walk?"

He bounced and pawed the air, giving added emphasis with a high-pitched bark.

"All right then." I grabbed the leash off the hall rack when my phone rang once more. "Seriously?" I glanced at the screen and the unfamiliar number. However, the area code was one I knew well. I tapped to answer. "Hello?"

"Hi, is this Chloe Abbington?"

A man's voice carried over the receiver. "Yes, this is she."

"I'm sorry to call so late. This is Carl Easton, Lana's father."

"Oh, I see. My sympathies about Lana's death. You must be so devastated." I sat in my chair and gave Max an apologetic shrug. "It was a shock for all of us."

"Yes, I still can't grasp the reality of it. I won't keep you, but there's a reason why I called. Do you have a minute?"

"Sure. Anything I can do, I will." I reached for my mug and sipped the last dregs of tea which had since grown cold.

"You see, I was cleaning out Lana's apartment and found an envelope tucked away in her desk drawer. It has your name on it with no address or stamp. I'm assuming Lana may have written to you and forgot to send it. I didn't pry, so I'm not even sure what's inside. Anyway, I found your phone number in Lana's address book. Odd, isn't it? Hardly anyone keeps an address book nowadays. Lana was old-fashioned in that regard. One of her endearing qualities." His voice caught, and a moment of silence went on.

"I'm sure it was. She always had nice stories to share about you and her mom. I loved the ones about your summer trips to the family beach cottage. You had wonderful times there."

"Yes, they were special." He sniffed. "Okay, I should let you go, but if you give me your address, I'll mail it to you. It might be comforting. Lana always said you were one of her dearest friends."

My breath hitched along with my heartbeat. "Yes, of course. Thank you." I gave him the address and then said goodnight. A dozen or so questions invaded my thoughts. What could the contents say? Why hadn't she mailed the envelope? Would I find some information inside that helped me to figure out who her killer was? That last one was a stretch, but I found the possibility intriguing.

I clipped the leash to Max's collar, snatched my jacket off the rack, then led the way outside. The breeze was rather cool. I slipped on the jacket and zipped it to my chin. I jogged across the lawn and slowed when we reached the sidewalk. Finding out whatever was inside Lana's envelope would have to wait. The problem was, everything at this point was timely. The May Fling was this Saturday, only a few days away. Nick, Audrey, and Tate would leave after that if Winsell couldn't find reasonable cause to keep them in town. He might let them go with giving him their contact information as a condition. I wasn't comfortable with that idea. After all, someone who was guilty of murder would be anxious to escape and go where they couldn't be found. I knew I would. I had to trust that Winsell knew how to handle the situation.

Walking through town on Whisper Cove Boulevard at night lifted my spirits. Shops were closed at this hour, but most owners left a few lights on for security purposes. When I was a child, I'd get a thrill peering inside those shop windows, pretending I was on an adventure, exploring other worlds and making up stories about them. My first sketches were windows and the insides of those shops. I'd stored them away in a box and kept them underneath my bed.

Nearing the next block and closer to Main Street, a few businesses remained opened. Claire's For Sweet's Sake never closed before ten. She loved serving those customers with a nighttime craving for donuts or a caffeine pick-me-up for people working a night shift. As I neared her shop, the silhouettes of two men stood out in front of the picture window light.

I stopped at the corner. On a hunch that something was amiss, probably because of all the disturbing events that had been happening lately, I hid behind a wooden trellis covered with hanging flower pots. Peering through a small opening, I was able to see them, but when I strained to hear, only the muffled sound of voices was audible. Their gestures, however, told me plenty. As they moved more into the light of a streetlamp, I gasped. Miles leaned toward Frank and pointed at his chest. With a shake of his head, he threw up his arms and laughed before walking away. I held my breath as Frank sank onto the bench in front of Claire's. He lowered his head into both palms.

"Come on, Max. We need to check this out and maybe do another good deed today." I tugged at his leash, and we jogged across Main Street to reach Frank, who hadn't heard us approach.

"Why do I even bother to reason with that man?" He muttered into his palms.

I caught the gist of his comment, though. "Hello, Frank. Is everything okay?" I sat next to him on the bench and pulled Max onto my lap.

"Hmm?" He glanced over at me, groaned, and lifted his chin to stare at the sky. "Chloe. Would you look how beautiful that moon is? So far away. Sometimes I think how peaceful and quiet it must be up there. Don't you?" He glimpsed me but then quickly turned away.

"I don't know anything about the atmosphere around the moon, but it sure is a spectacular view."

His fingers splayed across his knees. "So, how much did you see or hear?"

"I'm sorry. I didn't mean to eavesdrop or snoop on you and Miles." I ruffled Max's fur. "We were taking a walk, and, well, it was a total coincidence finding you." If I handled the situation carefully, he might share what was going on between him and Miles. "Anyway, I didn't hear anything you two said. Just saw Miles throwing up his arms and laughing as he walked away." I pointed behind me. "That's all I noticed when we got to the corner. Did you have an argument of some kind?"

"Something like that." He grew silent.

I had a hunch he wanted to talk but was afraid to. The little voice in my head told me I couldn't force a good deed to happen, not if I wanted the deed to be truly good. "Frank, if you don't want to tell me what all that was about, I won't pry." I put Max on the ground and stood. "You have a good evening."

"No, wait." His hand touched my arm. "Having someone to talk to would be nice. And you're a lot better looking than the priest in my church confessional." He managed a smile.

"Hey. You're not supposed to peak." I teased.

"No, he's not supposed to see who's on the other side. Confession means remaining anonymous."

"Okay. I don't go to confession, so I trust you're telling me the truth." I tipped my chin.

"Thank you." He hitched his breath, then released it slowly. "Miles and I have history, and not in a good way, unfortunately. I'll be honest. I don't have much respect for the man. He's done things that I'd call unethical, and he's done some pretty shameful things in his personal life."

I steadied my gaze. "How so?"

"Well, I have evidence he cuts corners when it comes to his business deals. The kind of behavior that could easily get him in trouble with the law." He let out a bitter laugh. "Miles Terrell either has enormous luck or the type of friends who help keep his record clean."

I thought for a moment. "You mentioned his personal life. What is that about?

"I've heard he disowned his son, Shawn."

"Oh, wow. That's horrible. Why?"

"Miles had declared his bid to run for mayor of Whisper Cove. Then, he dropped out soon after, claiming health issues. However, the real reason was because he thought Shawn had betrayed him." Frank rubbed his jaw.

I straightened. "Miles ran for mayor? I never knew."

"I think you weren't living here at the time. It was a couple of years ago."

"Wait. I'm confused. How would you know his son betrayed him?"

"Shawn threatened him. Unless Miles dropped out of the race, he'd go to the newspaper with the story that Miles had cheated someone in a business deal. So, Miles dropped out." Frank raked fingers through his hair.

"How did you know about this if the story was never published? I don't—"

"Wait, and I'll explain." Frank's eyes pleaded. "It was my story. I was the one in that deal with Miles. I was the one who was cheated."

I frowned. "I still don't understand. Shawn made the threat, not you? How did he even know about the deal between you and Miles?"

"I'd been trying to figure out a way to stop Miles from running for mayor. Think about it, Chloe." Frank scooted closer. "If you knew a person was that unscrupulous, cheating to get what he wanted, even breaking the law, wouldn't you be afraid to see him in such a position of power? Who knows what Miles could've done while in office."

My heart hammered against my chest. Maybe Frank was being harsh and overcritical of Miles. Then I recalled that meeting between Miles and Nick at the winery. Also, the questionable actions he had with zoning for the amphitheater move. What if that was also proof of how Miles cut corners?

"What happened with Shawn?"

"I went to him. I figured if he had any influence over Miles, maybe he could reason with him, convince him to drop out. Otherwise, I planned to go to the newspaper with my story. Shawn begged me not to go. He agreed Miles as mayor would only cause trouble. Not only for the town, but also for Shawn and the rest of his family. He promised to talk with Miles and get him to quit the race. Then, later, I heard about what Miles had done. He disowned his only son." Frank shook his head.

"And about tonight? What you've told me so far is in the past. Old news. I'd guess that it has nothing to do with this evening's conversation with Miles."

"No. You're right, but old news becomes new news. Miles hasn't changed any. I begged him to reconsider moving the amphitheater here, arguing how the attraction would overcrowd our town with visitors. Heck, local authorities can't handle that kind of chaos, and the county won't spare deputies every time a music event is scheduled. I argued that, too. What about the noise and the traffic, I said. We're a peaceful place, and people around here don't want that to change. Adding to that are the protests, the financial problems, staff problems, and, on top of it all, a murder. I asked him if he couldn't see that as a sign to drop the project." Frank smacked the bench with one hand. "The man laughed and told me I was a pathetic whiner. I tell you, he's a horrible individual."

Frank certainly had reason to despise Miles, and I could see how agitated he'd become just talking about him. Time to wrap up the good deed gesture. "Say, I could use a cup of hot cocoa and a donut. How about you?"

Frank's smile covered the frown. "Sounds comforting. And thank you for listening."

"Anytime. Be right back. Come on, Max. I bet Claire would love to see you, too."

Chapter Eighteen

"I tell you, he's looking more and more like a victim rather than a killer." I sat on a patio chair, one of three we'd set up in the area behind our shop. Walls made of weathered hardwood, reaching seven feet high, gave us plenty of privacy. Izzie and Willow pulled their chairs out from under the overhang that shaded the area. The warm rays of morning sunlight felt comforting.

We'd arrived early at my request. Well before the shop would open. I'd shared last evening's conversation I had with Frank and waited for their feedback. The itch to keep sleuthing urged me on, even though Winsell and Hunter were handling the case. I'd told myself to step back and leave them to it, but new discoveries continued to pop up, like Frank's story about Miles. How could I not want to dig and find out more about Miles? He was in the middle of everything going on with the amphitheater drama and the mural painting.

"Yeah, but couldn't someone be both a victim and a killer? Bitter about being wronged might push a person to murder. The revenge motive at work," Izzie said.

"Why kill Lana and not Miles? I can't get that question out of my head. I'm almost convinced Lana's death was a mistake. What if the killer—and yes, I know I put Frank in this scenario too—if he came looking for Miles, found Lana, then, in a rage, murdered her instead? That's misplaced revenge, but those kinds of murders happen all the time. Think of mass shootings or random killings. The killer doesn't have a grudge against his victim, just a lot of pent-up emotions." I sighed.

"I'm gonna play devil's advocate." Willow leaned forward, her mug of chai tea cradled in her hands. "Let's say Lana was the intended victim, and this had nothing to do with the amphitheater. Maybe the murder was something personal, like payback or revenge? Anyway, that would mean the killer used this whole situation about the amphitheater controversy as a diversion. You know, a way to hide his identity and his motive for killing her."

"Hmm, that theory actually makes sense." Izzie's eyes widened. "Oh, wow. I just thought of something. The killer might murder another one of those involved, Miles, for instance, then the motive would look even more like something to do with the amphitheater. We should warn him. He could be the next victim."

"Let's not get carried away. I'm sure Miles is already aware of the danger. Winsell probably warned him to keep alert. He's the kind of detective who covers every angle." I drummed fingers along the side of my coffee mug. "If your theory is right, Willow, that brings us back to Nick and Audrey. They could have more personal reasons for killing Lana."

"In that case, we should include a third suspect. Unknown to us but someone who had a connection to Lana," Willow suggested.

"An unknown suspect would be a discouraging possibility because then Lana's murder might end up filed away as a cold case." I sighed and set my mug on the cement floor. "Let's stick to focusing on Nick and Audrey."

"And Frank. We shouldn't dismiss the theory of him being both a victim and a killer." Izzie spoke with a firm lift of her chin.

I struggled to comment on that one. "You know, I can't stop thinking Miles fits into this case somehow. Who knows? He may have had an ugly confrontation with Lana, and it ended badly. Not exactly murder, but causing her death all the same. The idea has teeth. We witnessed how much they quarreled. How about his alibi? I don't remember hearing if he has one for that night," I said. Nothing like adding yet another suspect to the list.

"Can't forget Rita either. This isn't getting any easier, is it?" Izzie's tone flattened.

"You're right, it isn't any easier. How about we make a list? We'll start with choosing one task for each of us to tackle. Audrey had an affair with a college professor. What if Lana knew about it and held that over Audrey's head? It would be a way to force Audrey into doing what Lana wanted, maybe she even threatened to make that affair public news if she didn't cooperate." I hated believing Lana would stoop so low, but I had to consider all possibilities. "I'll check to see if that stranger at the meeting yesterday, the one talking to Audrey, is still in town. Maybe I can get him to tell me how he knows Audrey. There might be a story in that."

"Let me talk to Audrey and ask about him. I bet she's still pretty miffed at you." Izzie wrinkled her nose.

"You're right. Besides, I want to have another talk with Frank before doing anything else. If he's the mystery jogger I saw that night, which we're almost certain he is after we discovered those matching shoe prints, he might have seen something or someone that could help with the investigation," I said.

"Or he could be the killer and not just some random jogger." Lines furrowed Izzie's brow. "I don't like the idea of you confronting him alone. What if the questions provoke him, and he attacks you?"

"I'll be fine. I'll make sure to speak with him at the B&B and where his guests are close by." I shifted in my seat. She might have a point, but I was determined to confront Frank.

"Slim chance he'll talk if anyone else is listening. Seriously, Chloe, what if he follows you home and then cracks you over the head with a weapon when no one's around?" Izzie paced in front of me and Willow. "You should wait until I can go with you."

"No way. He's less likely to talk if there are two of us confronting him." I reached out to grab her wrist when she passed by. "I'll be careful. Besides, Audrey is scarier than Frank. You better make sure you aren't alone with her." I winked.

"Okay. I'll drop it, but you better call me right after, so I know you're safe," she said.

"Tell you what. I'll call as soon as I leave the B&B. Does that idea satisfy you?"

"If you two are done, I have an idea," Willow said.

I relaxed my shoulders, relieved to switch topics. "Let's have it."

"I keep thinking about Nick. The camcorder incident seems suspicious." She pushed a few strands of pink and green hair off her forehead. "I don't buy his story about it being stolen, at least not totally. Why wait several days before reporting it? And why lie to Tate? I say he got worried after Tate questioned the camera's whereabouts. That's why he followed up and reported it stolen. He's hiding something. I'd bet on it. Remember the tapes Winsell mentioned? Nick said they were valuable."

Willow stood and hurried back inside the shop. When she returned, she held her laptop. "If the camcorder was stolen, there's a good chance the thief wants to sell it for cash. Facebook Marketplace, Craig's List, and eBay would be perfect places to list it. I can check, see if I find a match. What do you think?"

"I think that's a genius idea, Willow." I grinned. "You make a good point about the tapes. If Nick is guilty of Lana's murder, the tapes might be what would incriminate him. Maybe that's what he's hiding."

"What if the one who stole the camcorder is your runaway jogger, who we know most likely is Frank? He may be hiding it," Izzie added.

I huffed. "You won't let go of the idea that Frank is guilty of more than taking an innocent, evening jog, will you? I'm pretty sure the person I saw running away wasn't carrying anything in his hand."

"Pretty sure or absolutely sure? It was getting dark. The camcorder isn't that big, and it's black." Izzie's brows curled in question. "Don't dismiss my hunch so quickly."

I stood. "I won't. Thinking of Frank as a killer or even a thief is hard for me to believe, but I should keep an open mind."

"Then we have our agenda for the day. I'll stay at the shop and brainstorm promo ideas for the amphitheater's grand opening. Maybe we should include a couple of the canvas paintings from the mixed event. I have to admit, Rita's is exceptional." Willow clutched the laptop. "Meantime, I'll check out those websites to see if I can find any camcorders for sale locally."

After our discussion, I grew more confident that we could make headway in Lana's case. With any luck, we'd come up with some hard evidence or clues that led us closer to identifying the killer. Even Detective Winsell would be pleased. I tensed as a queasy feeling rippled through my stomach. Someone was obviously watching me, maybe even trying to scare me off from sleuthing and seeking answers. The near collision with a reckless driver and the painted message outside the shop had me somewhat worried. However, I couldn't let that stop me. Like I'd told Izzie, I'd be careful and extra cautious and take no risky action that could put me in danger. Or at least I'd try to do all those things.

The drive across town to Frank's B&B was quiet and uneventful. I had to admit Izzie's concerns rubbed off on me. I kept flitting my gaze left to right, and every second or so, checking my rearview mirror. Pulling in front of Frank's place, I gripped the steering wheel and breathed steadily. "See? No problem. No creepy stalkers following or waiting to attack me. Yep. I'm all good." I exited the car. My pep talk renewed my confidence.

The B&B was a decades-old building with early twentieth-century charm. I loved that Frank hadn't modernized the look. When he bought the house, he hired people to refurbish it, both the exterior and interior. Last fall, I'd brought a friend from New York whose passion was historic architecture to visit various residences that represented the origins of Whisper Cove. She'd practically salivated over Frank's. He'd blushed with pride. Too bad this visit wasn't light-hearted like that one.

I opened the door and stepped inside. Homey décor covered the foyer walls, including a sampler with the words "A place to relax and enjoy." No wonder Frank worried about the amphitheater bringing noise and chaos. He advertised his place as a restful and quiet stay. Hearing voices from the kitchen, I took a path down the hallway.

Frank tucked his phone in his pocket as he stood close to the fridge, pulling out items and laying them on the counter. He turned and smiled, one fist anchored to his hip. "Chloe. It's been, what? Less than twenty-four hours since we spoke and enjoyed our hot cocoa and donuts."

My smile wavered a bit. I hated ruining his obviously happy mood with my questions. "Claire's treats are the best, and I enjoyed our conversation. I hope it helped calm your worries." I took a seat at the table and patted the chair next to me. "Do you have a few minutes to talk again?"

He blinked. Without hesitating, he approached, slid the chair away from the table to sit. A shaky titter escaped. "Am I in trouble?"

"Oh! No, I…This might sound rude or intrusive or whatever." I licked my lips, working on how to ask him. "Frank, has Detective Winsell spoken to you about the night Lana died?" I purposely avoided the word murder.

He furrowed his brow. "He did. A couple of times. Why?"

Like pulling teeth, as Granddad would say. I leaned forward. "I'm not accusing you of anything, but if you were the one I saw running toward the lake, I'm hoping you saw something or someone. Some detail that could help discover who killed Lana." I sucked in air and held it for a second. Every muscle in my body tensed. "Even if Winsell already knows, I need to hear what you told him. I'm struggling so hard, and it pains me to think Lana's killer hasn't been caught, or worse, never will be." I reached to take his hand in mine as his shoulders trembled. "Frank, please tell me." My voice barely made a sound.

His composure broke down completely. Sobbing, he stared up at the ceiling.

I squeezed my hold on his hand. I hadn't expected this reaction. Anger? Yes. Even a cold, silent stare. Not this. "I'm sorry. I didn't mean to upset you."

He dropped his head and swiped the moisture from his eyes. "You didn't. I've just been a mess with everything going on. The protest marches, the fight with Miles, my plans for the B&B, and your friend's death. I'm sorry. I never expressed my sympathies. It must've been a shock losing her like that."

I looked away for an instant, refusing to fall apart. One of us had to stay strong. "She was one of my best friends. We'd pretty much been out of touch since I left New York, but she was like a sister to me. Did I mention Lana and I roomed together for a year in Paris?" I sniffed. "I miss her, and I'm hurting for her. That's why I'm here. I need answers because not knowing who did this and why is sheer torture."

He pulled his hand out of my grasp and patted my arm. "I am your mystery man. You see, I returned to the park, hoping to confront Miles if he was there. I'd just read how he'd won another battle with the zoning department. I knew he was up to his usual schemes, cutting corners, cheating people, and all that. I'll admit I was fuming." He stroked his jaw. "I didn't see Miles, but I found my protest poster. I thought somebody had taken it by mistake. Then I heard a scream. Honestly, I wasn't sure what to make of it. Kids playing hide-in-seek? Teens horsing around? Then I noticed someone running away from where the mural is located. A tall person who moved pretty fast toward the tree cover. I was too far away to make out any other details, which is regretful."

"That's okay. I couldn't make out you clearly, either. I mean, tall and athletic were all I managed to tell Winsell." I settled back in my chair and pictured the scene from that night. "Did you find Lana? Were you the one who knocked over the paint can? That would explain the paint on the poster and in the shoe prints found on the ground."

"Yes." He rubbed his neck. "I don't consider myself a coward, but when I saw her lying there on the ground, looking so lifeless, I stumbled back and knocked into the can as I fell. I couldn't make a sound. Chloe, I've never experienced such fear. So many thoughts raced through my head. What if someone killed her? What if I was in danger being there? When I heard someone call out Lana's name, I ran. Like a coward, I ran and didn't look back. I worried the killer was coming for me."

"It's okay. You were scared. People panic and sometimes do things they're not proud of. We've all been there at least once."

"No. I only thought of myself. I worried they'd blame me for her murder. After all, I'm one of the protesters who oppose the amphitheater. I'd be looked at as angry enough to lash out and kill anyone associated with it. That's what the authorities would say." He wagged his head.

"I stopped when I reached the lake. At least I had a moment of conscience and started to call for help. But then I heard the sirens and knew help was on its way, even though it was too late." The last few words trailed off. He gazed at me. The pain mirrored in his eyes shown. "I haven't been able to sleep.

The guilt has consumed me. That's why I called Detective Winsell early this morning to tell him the truth. Until today, I kept denying everything. I wasn't in the park. I didn't see Lana. I insisted someone else must've found my poster. That's what I'd told the detective. It doesn't matter, though. I've become paranoid, believing everyone thinks I'm guilty. I even threw away my shoes, not because they were evidence. I convinced myself that if I threw them away, that would help me forget I had been there. I'm not proud. It will take a long time for me to forgive myself."

My heartbeat skipped. I squeezed his hand once more. "I forgive you. That's a start. Thank you for sharing your story. It helps me deal with all this." I looked around the kitchen and all the colorful touches he'd made. "You have a beautiful place, Frank. Making your guests feel welcome shows how much you care about people. Don't forget that."

"Thank you, Chloe. Your words mean more than you know."

We shared a hug, and then I left. My spirits lifted a bit, even if I was no closer to identifying the killer. Maybe talking to Frank, helping him to work through his feelings, and giving him some encouraging words explained my mood.

Standing on the front porch, I clutched my jacket as a gust of cool air breezed by me. Hurrying to my car door, I suddenly froze. A thought came to me. Late, but they're all the same. One detail Frank put into his account of that night didn't make sense. Why would hearing someone shout Lana's name make him think the killer was close by and coming after him? The killer wouldn't do that. After all, dead people can't answer back. That one tiny detail gave me pause. Maybe it didn't matter, and like he said, he'd panicked and wasn't thinking rationally. I got behind the wheel and turned the vehicle around to head back to Artisan Alley. I'd save mulling over that detail for later.

After giving Izzie a quick call to let her know I was alive, I made a left turn onto the boulevard. A glance in my rearview mirror showed me a green Toyota SUV followed rather closely. I gripped the wheel and made a sudden turn left onto the next side street. The SUV followed. I tensed and tightened my grip on the steering wheel. "Stop. You're letting Izzie make you crazy and paranoid."

Main Street came into view. I took another left. I hadn't found a dress for the May Fling dance yet. I could stop at the boutique and see if anything appealed to me. It was an excuse to get off the road and away from that car, which continued to follow me. Intentional or not, I didn't have time for this kind of thing. Plus, I refused to let paranoia join my already mounting list of emotions.

I parked in front of Gloria's Frocks and Frills. Grabbing my bag, I slipped out of the car and dashed to the entrance. Not looking back to check for the SUV took considerable effort. Once inside the boutique, I peered out the window pane. The vehicle moved at a crawl, passing in front of Gloria's until it was out of sight. I breathed easier and made a mental note. "Toyota, license plate GR3 something. Drat. Why couldn't I catch the rest?" I muttered, then shoved open the door. Dress shopping was really the last thing on my mind. I clicked my remote to unlock the car and hopped back inside.

Killer or innocent victim, I couldn't be one hundred percent certain which Frank was. However, I considered a third option. What if he was lying to cover for the real killer? Someone he was close to and cared about? The first step I planned to take was finding out what he'd told Winsell, which meant talking to Hunter about Frank and my stalker on wheels. Maybe the Toyota meant nothing, but after my near-miss collision with the reckless driver a few days ago, I couldn't dismiss my suspicions. I loosened my tight grip on the steering wheel. What was it with me and car incidents?

I pulled onto Whisper Cove Boulevard and sped up to reach the shop. Within seconds, the high-pitched ring of my phone blared through the car speaker. My pulse skipped until I glimpsed the display. Hunter. "I was just about to call you."

"Hey, are you okay? Your voice sounds off," he said.

"Well, I guess off is better than freaked-out." I explained the incident with the Toyota and gave him a description. "Probably nothing, but with everything going on, I'm on edge and maybe a bit paranoid." I turned right on Whisper Lane and slid into the first open parking spot.

"A bit paranoid is probably wise at a time like this. Keeps you alert.

Meantime, I'll see what I can come up with. Good chance the owner is from Whisper Cove. I'll start there."

He sounded confident, which made me relax. "That incident isn't why I wanted to talk to you, though." I sorted and shifted through my words and decided on the full disclosure approach. "I paid a visit to Frank's B&B this morning." I tapped my index finger against the wheel and paused. Still rattled, I gazed outside my car window, as if expecting someone was watching, but no one lurked or peered in my car. I shook my head. I was totally bonkers and needed to get a firm hold on myself. "He told me some things, stuff he hadn't previously mentioned to authorities, I guess. Anyway, he said he spoke with Winsell early this morning. Has Winsell said anything to you about it?"

"I haven't seen him or talked to him since last night. Why?"

"Frank confessed to me that he was the one I saw running away the night Lana died and that he'd been looking for Miles, ready to pick a fight." I elaborated, giving him a detailed playback of Frank's account.

"I'm sure he wouldn't lie to you. He knows you could check on his story." A sigh came through the receiver. "Chloe, stay away from Frank. I don't like how he's been acting lately. Until we can prove he had nothing to do with Lana's murder, it's not safe."

I puffed my cheeks and let the air out. "Lots of people have been telling me that. I'm careful, Hunter. No need to worry. Now, before you lecture more, is there any news about Lana's case from your end?" I understood his concern. I'd feel the same way if our roles were reversed. Admittedly, I had worried about him in the past. Only my way of worrying didn't include telling him what he should and shouldn't do.

"Seems to be the day for news about car drivers. My tech contact in Buffalo got back to me. He was able to take out the grainy look on the video. The license plate number was clear enough to read, but not enough to make out a decent description of the driver. Anyway, I ran the plate and got the owner's name and address. You'll never believe this, but the car belongs to a ninety-year-old widow who lives in Jamestown. She hasn't had a driver's license in over five years. Her husband passed away several months ago.

She's having a difficult time and keeping the car for sentimental reasons."

I scratched the nape of my neck in thought. "Then who was driving the car?" My eyes widened. "Did someone steal it? Oh, that poor woman. First, she loses her husband, now their car."

"Hold on. No, it wasn't stolen. The woman checked and found it safely stored in her garage. However, after giving the vehicle a thorough look, she found a sizable dent on one side."

"Then does she know who drove it?" At this point, the idea the near hit was intended for me seemed slim to none. Someone involved with Lana's murder who drove to Jamestown, stole a car, then came here to run me down sounded too farfetched, even to the paranoid me.

"The only person she could come up with is her granddaughter, who's always begging to drive the car. She knows where the keys are kept, and she already took it for a ride without permission once. Only one problem. She was in Ohio visiting relatives on the date in question."

I pushed open the car door and got out to stretch my legs. "Are you planning to speak with her? Maybe she snuck away somehow when her relatives weren't watching."

"And drove all the way back to New York to take her grandmother's car for a joyride? Come on, Chloe."

"Or maybe she returned home Monday, and her grandma wasn't aware?" I rubbed my face with the palms of hands. "Yeah, yeah. Probably not. Okay, well, the fact the car is from Jamestown pretty much kills any connection it has to Lana anyway. Thanks for checking."

"I still want to have a talk with the granddaughter. I'll let you know if I learn anything new." He paused. "How are you holding up?"

"I'm fine. I'll be glad when the case is solved, and life goes back to normal. Or as close to normal as life seems to get, that is." A half-hearted chuckle escaped from my throat.

"You've got me whenever you need to talk or give you a hug or just be there for you." His tone grew softer.

"I'm glad to hear you say that. You, Izzie, Mom, and Dad are always there for me." I hurried to the shop and stepped to the door. "I've got to go. Lots of shop work to do."

"Me too. You be careful and stay out of trouble."

I laughed. "As if that can happen. Talk soon. Love you." We ended the conversation as I entered the shop. Music echoed from the storage room, and the off-key melody of someone singing along to Stevie Wonder's "You Are the Sunshine of My Life" caused me to wince. Willow might be artistically talented but not in carrying a tune. Before I could announce my return, Izzie slammed through the door, and we nearly collided.

"Woah! Where's the fire, as Granddad used to say?" I studied the frown on her face. Creases furrowed and deepened enough to swallow her whole.

"That woman is infuriating." She smacked the counter with her handbag.

"What woman?" I said.

"Audrey. I tried talking to her but all I got was her sour, snarky attitude for an answer."

"No info on the mystery guy at the meeting, huh?"

"She refused to talk about him. Told me to mind my own business." Izzie grabbed a bag of chips from underneath the counter and ripped it open. She chewed on one and mumbled her words. "Anyway, I followed up by calling Penny. I figured she might tell us something, but that lead is a dead end too. I hope you had better luck."

"I did." I pointed. "Didn't you remove salty snacks from your diet?"

"Give me a break. I'm stressing right now and don't have time for lectures." She licked crumbs off of her fingers.

"It's not a lect—never mind. Let me tell you about my morning." I relayed the conversation with Frank but left out the Toyota incident. No point in adding another brick to the stack of worries unless it amounted to something significant.

"That supports my theory, doesn't it? Frank is the killer. He was angry. He came looking for a fight with Miles, but found Lana instead and killed her in a heated moment." Izzie ticked off the key points with her fingers.

"I know you want to solve this case. I do, too, but it's not worth rushing. We're talking about a man who could be innocent," I reasoned.

"You're right. I am anxious to end this whole mess." She plopped in a chair and rested her cheek on one hand.

"Well, I have some news that should cheer you up." Willow walked out of the storage room.

"We could use some cheer," I said.

"Then hear this." Willow slid onto the counter and sat cross-legged. "I found a local listing on Marketplace posted this past Sunday for a slightly used camcorder. If it's Nick's, the thief didn't waste any time. He or she is probably afraid of getting caught with it."

"We should contact the seller to ask questions. If it sounds like the camcorder could be Nick's, we can make arrangements to meet. Oh!" Izzie bounced off the chair. "We should pretend to be the authorities when we get there. Flash a fake badge, act official, get the thief to tell us where he found the camcorder, and then make him turn it over."

"It's been four days since the ad posted. Even if the camcorder is Nick's, someone may have already bought it." After all the disappointing leads, I struggled to see this one turning out any different. I straightened. Would Hunter or Winsell give up or keep trying? "Make the call. We've got a date with our would-be thief."

We spent the next few hours, until dinner time, fixing up the window for our next event. Canvas paintings from the mixed event surrounded a mini replica of the amphitheater Willow created. Quite the show display.

The call from Lana's dad had consumed my thoughts. Even though he promised to mail the letter by express for next day delivery, I was impatient. I must have checked the mail a dozen times this morning. Enough was enough, I decided. My impatience wouldn't make the letter get here any sooner. Right now, my plan was to take a quick shower before our meal.

Following Izzie into the house, I sniffed the aroma of roasted chicken. My stomach growled. "Oh my. I am starving."

"Don't even think of nabbing a bite or two before dinner," Izzie said.

When Kate Abbington took her turn cooking meals, it was "hands off" until we sat at the table. Dad always managed to sneak a sample when she wasn't looking. If he caught him, we'd laugh. She'd playfully smack his hand with a wooden ladle, then plant a kiss on his cheek.

"What's this?" I spied an envelope on the foyer table addressed to me. My eyes widened as I read the words priority mail in red letters at the top. It had to be what Lana's dad promised to send. I tore the strip to open the envelope. Inside was a smaller envelope with my name scribbled across the front. Goosebumps on my arms made me shiver. This was like Lana sending me a message from beyond the grave. Exciting but somewhat scary.

"What is it?" Izzie bumped shoulders with me and leaned closer.

I slit the envelope with my fingernail and unfolded the contents. It was in Lana's handwriting. I scanned the words, then read them once more, but slowly to digest what she had written. My stomach lurched with that sick, queasy feeling you only get when something unpleasant crosses your path.

"Chloe?" Izzie whispered.

I clutched the letter in my tightened fist. "I think Nick must be the killer."

Izzie dropped her bag to the floor. "What do you mean? What does she say? It's from Lana, right? The letter her dad called you about. Oh, wow."

I motioned for her to step back outside, where we sat on the porch. "Hold on. First, she writes how she'd like to make amends and apologizes for being so distant. Then she goes on to say she hasn't been herself...because of Nick." I glanced over. "She couldn't think of anyone who wouldn't judge her for being foolish and trusting the wrong person other than me. I was her person." My breath hitched, but I kept my emotions in check. "Listen to this. 'I knew he'd been distant, and quite honestly, I was relieved. I guessed something was seriously wrong when I heard from my broker, who asked why I hadn't been investing money in my mutual funds account for the past several months. Right away, a red flag went up. I'd had a lot going on in the past year and so little time. Nick was supposed to help me out. He made sure my business expenses were paid, and every month, he'd put money in my retirement portfolio. I trusted him, but after that phone call, I had a gut feeling. I suspected Nick was stealing from me.'"

"That's horrible," Izzie said. "I can't imagine what she was going through. No wonder she acted snappy around him. I'm surprised she didn't dump him right away." Izzie scrunched her forehead. "Why didn't she?"

"I'm getting to that part." I held up the letter and read more. "'I knew what I had to do, even if I felt guilty. I hired a detective to follow him and someone to hack his computer. I was determined to confront him, if I got the proof. What hurt the most was my love for Nick. If he did steal from me, I needed to hear an explanation. No matter how pathetic his reasons would sound.'"

"Well, did he explain? I can't believe it. What a worm." Izzie shook her head.

"Wait. There's more to this worm's story. Even more hurtful than stealing, in my opinion. Get this. 'I heard from the detective a few days later. He had photos of Nick and some woman I didn't recognize. They'd met twice at a local coffee shop. Nothing too suspicious. People meet for coffee all the time. I hoped she was a business associate or maybe a real estate agent. We had talked about selling his condo and moving in together. The detective had an address and phone number of where the woman worked. So I called but from Nick's phone. Her name is Melissa. She answered by demanding the money Nick promised to come up with, otherwise the deal they'd made was off. At that point, I'd heard enough. I decided to finish the next mural job we had already scheduled, and then I would break up with him, tell him to keep the damn money he'd stolen, and get the hell out of my life.'"

I folded the letter. "She wrote a few more words about hoping we could get together next time I came to New York." I stood. "She must've written the letter and planned to mail it, all before she found out about the mural job in Whisper Cove. My guess is she shoved the letter in a drawer and forgot about it."

"Poor Lana." Izzie trailed behind me as I led the way inside. "She seemed so out of sorts during her short time here, and now we know why."

"Like someone carrying a lot of anger that she had to vent." I knew that kind of anger, that feeling of betrayal. It was difficult to keep it under control. Right now, what made me angry was not knowing who killed Lana. I was frustrated, discouraged, angry, all rolled into one hot emotional state. I headed upstairs for that shower, a cool one at that.

Chapter Nineteen

The shop was buzzing with conversation while guests greeted each other before settling down to paint the Whisper Cove ferry crossing the lake to the town of Stow. Izzie distributed the last of the items at each table seat while I stood close to Willow and filled her in on my letter from Lana. Including the mixed event at the park, this one was our third event this week, and we still had one Friday. Great for business, but I was exhausted both physically and mentally. The murder case, our sleuthing, and preparing for paint parties used up all my energy and then some.

"What a tool. Do you think that's what happened? Lana confronted Nick before coming to Whisper Cove? 'Sorry, babe, but I can't be with you any longer.' It sure would explain why they were snapping at each other." Willow flipped the switch on the projector.

"Possibly. I guess the only one who can tell us now is Nick." I'd take that scenario a step further. Lana might have told Nick the bad news that fateful night, which led to him killing her. A crime of passion would explain the murder. I didn't miss the curious gaze from a guest sitting close to us. Tugging on Willow's arm, I moved us closer to the storage room doorway.

"Say, what about Melissa? What if she came to town and killed Lana?" Willow air quoted. "Jealous rage turns deadly when scorned woman decides to end her rival's life."

I laughed. "Okay, reign it in a little. I doubt that happened. However, Melissa does make me wonder. What if Nick was in serious financial trouble? He owed money to some very scary people, maybe because he bet on horses or gambled at a casino, and Melissa was the messenger."

Willow snorted. "Now who's adding too much drama to explain things? You must be watching those same late night crime shows I do."

I rolled my eyes. "Point taken. If Detective Winsell could hear us now, he'd have a good laugh."

"Or remind you never to speculate or accuse someone without solid proof."

I jumped hearing the familiar voice behind me. My cheeks warmed with embarrassment as I turned. "Hi, Detective. What brings you here this evening?"

He pressed his lips tightly, but a smile surfaced despite the effort. "Definitely not to hear crime show drama. I came to tell you the mask you found had no prints or blood stains on it. The red smudge is from lipstick. According to the lab, crimson red. Nothing that tells me it has to do with the case."

I stifled a gasp. Images flashed in my head. Audrey's signature on the mural. The handcloth she'd used to wipe her lips. Bright red. Crimson red. Why hadn't I thought of it before?

"Might we go into that room for a little privacy? Just for a minute or two. I know you're busy with the event." He pointed at the storage area.

"Your lab tech didn't happen to mention anything about pine scent or maybe lavender, did he?" I led the way. Willow and Winsell followed. My heart pulsed in staccato-like beats, loud and formidable. I willed myself to calm down and think rationally. Even if the mask belonged to Audrey, I shouldn't jump to any conclusions. It could've fallen out of the trash, blown across the lawn. Any number of explanations were possible other than purposely hiding it there. Besides, guilty people weren't usually careless with evidence.

His brow curled. "Keen observation. The lab tech did mention both the fragrance of lavender and residue of turpentine in his report. Is there something more you need to say, Chloe?"

"No. Not really." I remembered the detective's motto. Never assume or speculate. Go by the evidence and tell only what you know for certain.

"Keep in mind. This report doesn't mean the mask has nothing to do with the case. For instance, a careful person would make sure not to leave prints. Just as I'm a careful detective who studies every detail. Leave no stone unturned, as they say."

I scratched my lip, giving some thought to what should come next. "Speaking of the case, I hear Frank Benworthy came to see you this morning to talk about it." I couldn't help but comment. My curiosity trumped taking the risk to ask, even if it made him annoyed. However, he didn't shift his mood and grow irritated. Or maybe he did. His was one of those hard-to-read faces.

"He did speak to me. And I won't ask where or who you heard that from, and as you well know, I can't divulge anything about an ongoing investigation. Have a good evening, ladies." He nodded at both of us before turning to leave the room and circle his way to the front door.

"That man is a strange one," Willow commented while walking alongside me to rejoin our guests.

"Might be part of what makes him, you know."

"A careful detective. So what was all that about crimson lipstick and turpentine and lavender? You looked ready to pass out when Winsell mentioned it," Willow said.

"Probably nothing. I guess I'm overwhelmed with all that's happened." I dismissed the topic, hoping she wouldn't push. I needed a moment to process what the lab report revealed. At least Frank had told the truth about contacting Winsell, but I had learned nothing to verify what he claimed to have said. Thanks to Winsell's tight lips.

In between instructing and helping out guests, I filled Izzie in on the conversation with Winsell. She wasn't surprised how close-lipped he'd been. Before I knew it, the event wrapped up. After the last guest left, I relaxed in a chair and closed my eyes. "I'm totally spent."

"Sleuthing by day, painting by night. We do it all." Izzie sang out her words, waving a paintbrush in the air.

"You're a goofball." I laughed.

"A goofball you love." She skipped to me and tapped my nose with the brush. In the next second, she sank into the chair next to me. "Seriously, I'm just as tired. You think we're taking on too much? I mean, there's Lana's case and managing our shop, which is a full-time operation. Maybe we should call it quits."

I gasped. "Quit the shop?"

"Ha. Of course not." This time, she poked my arm with the tip of the brush. "I'd never do that."

"The case." I groaned. "I have a gut feeling we're close to figuring things out. We can't back out now."

"Close, huh? With four possible suspects—the same ones we came up with almost two weeks ago mind you—and we haven't been able to eliminate even one of them? That kind of close to figuring things out?" Izzie rolled her eyes. "Please."

"You're right. I'm ridiculously optimistic because I just want it to be over." I smacked the chair with one hand. "Nick, Audrey, Frank, and Rita. Oh, and maybe if we include those last two, we should add all of the protesters as suspects."

"And Melissa." Willow wiggled her nose and offered an impish grin.

"No, not Melissa." I pointed to each of them. "Okay, show of hands. Who thinks Nick is the most likely one to murder?" I raised mine, but I was alone. "Fine. What about Audrey?"

Both Willow and Izzie's hands shot up.

I had to admit everything we knew about Audrey made the possibility of her guilt strong. Even the scented mask with the lipstick smudge was incriminating. Though I hadn't any evidence to confirm it was hers, putting that together with all the other pieces sure made me lean that way. It was time to let them know about the mask. "Guys, there's something I haven't told you." I related the details and my suspicions.

"Oh, wow. Did you tell Winsell?" Izzie asked.

I shook my head. "I should've, but I can't be certain it's her mask or what it means to the case."

"Isn't that for Winsell and Hunter to decide? You should tell them, Chloe." Izzie patted my arm.

I sighed. "You're right. And I will, as soon as possible. Now, what about Frank as the killer?"

Only Izzie's hand rose.

"You can't vote twice. I said most likely to be the killer," I argued.

"Too close to call. Though if I am forced to choose, I'll go with Frank," Izzie said.

"That leaves Rita. She was bitter about losing the mural job from the start. Even though she's denied vandalizing the mural, that could be her work too. Shows even more of her anger about the situation."

Both Willow and Izzie shook their heads.

"Rita may be a drama queen at times, but I doubt she'd have it in her to commit murder," Izzie said.

"I agree." I stood, grabbed a towel from the rack, and helped Willow clean tables.

"See? We can eliminate one of our suspects. Rita." Willow pumped her fist. "One down, three to go."

"Still, it's kind of strange that she seemed to show up whenever something happened. When Lana took a fall off that broken ladder? You spotted Rita across the park, hiding behind a tree then running away. How about the face she made when medics carried Lana's body?" Izzie shuddered. "Almost like she enjoyed the moment."

I frowned. "Odd how she signed up for our mixed event at the last minute. That made no sense since she's bitter about the mural job. And being found at the mural site when it was vandalized? Plenty to think about."

Willow sighed. "Back to four suspects, I guess."

I looked around the room. The weight of the day's events and this discussion about making no headway in a case that really wasn't our case because it was Winsell's case to solve exhausted me. "Let's finish cleaning the tables and throwing the trash in the bin then go home. I'm too tired to think about solving crimes anymore tonight."

"I'm with you." Izzie eyed the trash can and stuffed the used paper towels and plastic cups inside. "Tomorrow, we'll feel better."

Someone's phone dinged. "Ooo! It's a response from the ad," Willow said. "Let's see what our thief has to say."

"Possible thief. We can't be sure." I cautioned with a pointed stare.

"Right. Okay, so our alleged thief wants to meet." Willow looked up. "Which means he or she hasn't sold it. So, what do you think?"

I nodded at Izzie. "We need a time. Let's say tomorrow evening?"

"After our event." Izzie trailed her tongue across her lip. "How about nine-thirty? The guests will be gone well before that. We'll have enough time to go over our plan."

"Plan? We haven't got a plan. Other than arranging to meet." I frowned.

"And pretending to be the authorities. We decided on that part." Willow glanced at her phone. "I should be the one to go. I'm still new to the area, and unless the seller is a previous paint party guest or a tenant in my apartment complex, I probably won't be recognized."

"Good thinking. I'll come with you and stay in the background in case you need help," I said.

"Let's just hope the tapes are with the camcorder. Otherwise, we won't have anything to prove Nick is the killer." Izzie sighed.

Willow typed out a response, then we all waited in silence until the phone dinged again.

"Well? What's it say?" Izzie peeked over Willow's shoulder.

"They want me to bring cash and be there on time at the corner of Summers Lane and Meadow Drive." Willow shrugged. "Do you know the area?"

"Yep. It's by a trailer park. Sort of rundown but safe as far as crime goes. We should be fine." I finished wiping the last table and tossed the paper toweling in the trash. This could be the lead to break the case and end the search for Lana's killer, or yet another dead end. Either way, we had to follow through. Like Winsell, the careful detective, would say, leave no stone unturned.

Chapter Twenty

I cuddled with Max in bed for several minutes. I hated to leave the cozy setting, but the agenda I planned for the day couldn't wait. After tossing last night before finally dozing off, I came up with a few ideas. Miles, even though he hadn't made it on our suspect list, must fit somewhere. Either directly or indirectly, his actions could be the one domino that made all the others fall. "My metaphors could use some work. Right?" I ruffled Max's fur before throwing off the covers.

Aunt Constance had made it clear. Trudy didn't want to talk about the amphitheater zoning drama. However, that didn't mean no one else in the department would be willing to dish some information. I'd heard a rumor from Millie. She knew plenty of folks from Mayville, some of whom worked in zoning. They liked to stop by the diner for dinner or lunch occasionally. I intended to follow up on one particular lady. Millie claimed this woman loved to talk shop and had voiced her dislike of Miles Terrell quite a few times.

I picked up Max and lowered him to the floor. "First, breakfast. Bagel for me and kibble for you. Maybe a scrambled egg. We can share. Sound good?"

Max wagged his tail and pawed the air as he barked.

I laughed. "You men are easy to please. A tasty meal always puts you in a pleasant mood. Let's go."

"Hey! Morning, sleepy girl. Get enough z's?" Izzie licked jam off of her finger.

I eyed her from styled head to pump-healed toe. "Where are you going all dressed to kill?"

"I'm not. Just trying on different outfits to see which I'd like to wear to the casino event. You do remember it's tomorrow evening, don't you?" Her brows peaked.

"I've been trying not to, but yeah, I remember." I popped a strawberry in my mouth to keep from saying more. No doubt, I wanted to go to the May Fling with Hunter. Taking time to buy a dress and spending three or four hours at the charity event instead of working to find Lana's killer was what I hated.

After pouring kibble into Max's bowl, I spread cream cheese on my bagel. The scrambled eggs were keeping warm in a covered pan on the stove. I scooped a spoonful to put on my plate.

"Well, we're going dress shopping sometime today because I don't like anything in my wardrobe, and you have one dress, a black one that's better suited for a funeral." Izzie covered the fruit bowl before I could take another strawberry. "Agreed?"

"Of course. How about eleven? I have work to get to ASAP." I smacked her hand lightly, which she removed. I picked out a few more berries and placed them on my plate.

"No, you don't. The shop is closed this morning." Izzie narrowed her eyes. "It's about the case, isn't it?"

"I'm calling someone at Chautauqua Zoning and Planning. I want to find out more about that zoning snafu with Miles."

"Hmm. I thought Trudy—"

"She's not who I'll be speaking with. Don't worry. I'll let you know what I find out, if anything. See you later for dress shopping." I wiggled my fingers and carried my plate out of the kitchen with Max trotting behind me.

Scarfing down my breakfast, I left a few pieces of egg on the plate and set it on the floor for Max to finish. A glance at my watch showed a quarter after nine. Not too early to call, I decided. I'd saved the office number Aunt Constance had given me. Dialing, I leaned back against the bed headboard to wait.

"Chautauqua Zoning and Planning, Ben speaking. How can I help you?"

"Hi Ben. I'm Chloe Abbington. I was hoping to speak with Evelyn

Winthrop. Is she in this morning?" I crossed my fingers.

"Sure. Let me connect you."

"Evelyn Winthrop. What can I do you for?" Her voice lifted and dropped as if she sang her words.

I grinned at her choice of greetings. "Hi. This is Millie's friend, Chloe Abbington. I believe you came to one of our paint events. At Paint with a View along the lake?"

"Oh! Of course. Such a fun way to pass an evening. My gal pals and I are ready for another round, maybe one day this fall? Things are crazy busy around here right now." She tisk-tisked "Would you listen to me? I'll stop gabbing. I'm sure you called for a reason."

"Yes. I did. I was hoping you could tell me about the trouble brewing with the amphitheater? I heard Miles Terrell had to fight to keep it in Whisper Cove. Such a shame."

Evelyn snorted. "As if. He could fall in a bucket of poo and come out smelling like the sweetest rose every single time. And that's what he did. More than once. Of course, I shouldn't say anything, but that man doesn't follow the rules. He thrives on breaking them. Enjoys it, too."

"Is that so? What exactly did he do to keep the amphitheater?"

"I shouldn't say, but the numbers don't add up. It's like Santa delivered his gifts early to our department. Don't get me wrong. We sure can use the money. What makes me mad, though, is how the proposal submitted several months earlier to put a playground and walking trail in your park was kicked to the curb, all because of Miles Terrell and his scheming. That poor man was heartbroken. But you didn't hear it from me."

"You lost me. Who is a poor man? Miles?"

"Oh, good grief, no, not him. I'm talking about the one who made the playground proposal. Such a dear heart. And brave, too. He fought hard to change the minds of zoning committee members, submitted formal complaints about corners that Miles took, even implied there were bribes and payoffs involved. Poor Frank tried so hard. Butted heads with Miles several times in the process. I have a truckload of admiration for Frank. His ideas are worthy of everyone's praise."

"Wait. Are you talking about Frank Benworthy?" My eyes widened.

"Yes. My poor Frank. He's gone through a lot. His B&B business will suffer. I tried stopping by to console him, but he's such a busy man. It may not be nice to say, but I believe Miles Terrell should get what's coming to him. One way or another."

"I'm sure he will. Thanks, Evelyn."

I tossed my phone on the bed and stared at Max. "Can you believe it? Frank Benworthy. He told me about his troubles with Miles, but not the deal with zoning. Why?" I paced the room, replaying my last conversation with him. *I only thought of myself. I worried they'd blame me for her murder.* He told me that's why he didn't come forward to confess he'd been at the park that night. Could that be the reason he hadn't mentioned the issue with zoning? How he'd been the one to lodge complaints with zoning against Miles? And how Miles had ruined his proposal for a playground? I couldn't imagine more valid reasons to want revenge. I slumped my shoulders and sat on the edge of my bed. Any argument I'd had to defend Frank was fading quickly.

Gloria's was crammed wall to wall with customers. I groaned. Every female in the Chautauqua Lake area must be shopping for dresses to show off at tomorrow evening's May Fling. Why hadn't I taken the time the other day when I was here to grab one off the rack? I'd have been in and out of Gloria's within twenty minutes. Eying Izzie who carried a half dozen gowns to the dressing room, I sank in my chair. This trip would take hours.

I scrolled through my phone, searching for the ad Willow had found on Marketplace. Sometimes, the way people wrote gave clues about their background. Choice of words, punctuation, spelling, or misspellings. At least that's what I'd read in *Crime Doesn't Pay,* an ezine I'd stumbled on.

"Hey! You haven't tried on any dresses? Seriously, Chloe. The May Fling is tomorrow. Do you want to go or not?" Izzie let out an exasperated and dramatic sigh.

"It's not that. I'm anxious about this case, and if we—" My phone rang to interrupt. "Hold on." I glanced at the screen. Thank goodness. "Hi, Willow. What's going on?"

"Everything. And way too fast. The seller messaged to say we have to push up the meeting time to one. That's less than an hour from now. What do we do?"

"We meet at one. That's what." I smiled at Izzie. "I'm sorry, but I have to go. Willow says the seller wants to meet at one."

Izzie swatted my arm. "Don't look so happy. I'll stay here and finish shopping while you go play detective. Be careful." She hugged me, then returned to the dressing room.

I hurried out the door but skidded to a stop on the front stoop. The same green Toyota SUV from the other day slowed down as it drove in front of the shop.

Pulling over to the curb, the driver got out and marched from the car to the top step, inches from me. Her eyes glared, full of enough anger to burn a hole through me. Barely five feet tall, maybe middle-aged, with red hair cut short.

I stepped back as if those eyes could really shoot fire.

"You." She stabbed a finger at me. "You stay away from my Frank. He's spoken for and doesn't need the likes of you coming on to him. Consider this a warning." At once, she spun around and marched back to her car.

"Well, that was certainly interesting." I leaned against the hand railing and remained on the top step, deep in thought. Though I would've never come up with this explanation as to why she tailed me the other day, it made sense. She, whoever the woman was, had a thing for Frank and believed I had visited the B&B for personal reasons, like romantic ones. I curled my hand around the railing and took the stairs to the sidewalk. Suddenly, I froze. I knew something about her voice sounded familiar. I opened my phone and went to the zoning website. Under staff, there was her photograph. "Evelyn Winthrop. Well, what do you know about that?" I laughed. Frank had an admirer. I wondered if he was aware? I hurried to my car and slid into the driver's seat. "Better watch out, Frank. She's coming for you." I laughed some more and merged into the far left turn lane.

Reaching the trailer park, I bolted across the open lawn area. I hid behind a large tree and peered around the side of the trunk. Willow stood about a hundred yards away. She extended her arm with something clutched in her hand. I assumed it was the fake badge I'd given her, which I dug out of a box filled with Halloween costumes and accessories. She was showing it to a stocky figure of a man dressed in faded jeans and a sweatshirt. Our seller. In the next second, he handed her a rather large black bag.

I came from behind the tree as Willow jogged in my direction. "You did it. You persuaded him to give you the camcorder."

"The badge did the talking. Thanks to you." She wiped her brow, then lifted the bag. "Nick's initials are on the bottom corner. So now we know it's his. Oh, and once I told our seller the camcorder was part of a murder investigation, he begged me not to press charges. Turns out he didn't steal it. He found the bag and camera in a dumpster near the trailer park. Says it's one of his spots to search for valuables he can sell for cash."

"In a dumpster? Well, he sure hit the motherlode until you came along, that is. I'm guessing the money wasn't necessary?" I took the bag from her and slung the strap over my shoulder. She looked ready to pass out. "You okay?"

"Yeah, I was in such a hurry, I forgot to eat breakfast and have my morning caffeine boost." She avoided my gaze and walked to the street.

"Okay. Well, let's take a look." I patted the bag. "How about we sit in my car? I have a rather cold but almost full cup of coffee left over from breakfast. You're welcome to it."

"Thanks. That should help." Willow slid into the passenger seat and took the coffee in hand. "The guy's name is Chuck. He didn't offer his last name, and I didn't push."

I unzipped the end pocket of the bag. "Hmm. We probably won't need to contact him again. We have this." I searched through the first pocket but came up empty. I moved on to the other side. Nothing in that one, either.

"Chuck did mention another person called about the camcorder. A man."

I left my hand resting on top of the bag and turned to face her. "Did he give a name? What if the caller was Nick?"

"He didn't say, but Chuck never called him back because he thought the sale with us was a done deal." Willow emptied the coffee cup and set it in the cupholder. "Much better."

"Makes sense." I unzipped the top of the bag and lifted out the camcorder. "So far, we have nothing. If I don't find a tape inside…" I pressed the button, and the compartment snapped open. I held the camcorder facing Willow. "Guess we're out of luck."

"Great." Willow slouched in her seat.

"Why wouldn't there be tapes? An efficient cameraman keeps at least one or two handy. Especially loaded inside the compartment, so he's ready to film. Right?" I reasoned aloud.

"There's only one obvious explanation. Whoever stole the camera kept the tapes. But why?"

"Something tells me that's a key detail. If only we can find out who took them." I set the camcorder inside the bag and placed it on the backseat. A sudden thought made me cringe. What if one of the tapes had Lana's murder recorded? That certainly would be a reason to hide or destroy it.

"In the meantime, we should give the stolen goods to Winsell or Hunter." Willow pointed. "And you know I'm right. We can't keep this."

I pressed the start button, and the engine hummed. "Without the tapes, we don't need it anyway."

I gave plenty of thought to the camcorder and the interested buyer, who called Chuck. As I turned into the parking lot, I'd made a decision. We hurried to the shop. When I threw open the door, Izzie stood in front of two dresses hanging on wall hooks meant for canvas paintings.

She turned and clasped her hands. "What do you think? The blue one's for you. Pink for me."

"Nice. Thanks. Look, I have an idea. What if we get Chuck to call the guy who wanted the camcorder and make arrangements to meet later this evening? Maybe Chuck can entice him to come by saying there are tapes included. What do you think? If Nick is the caller, this would show how desperate he is to get the merchandise back. We could catch him in the act, put him off guard, and pressure him to tell us what's on those tapes." I took a breath.

Izzie anchored a fist to her hip. "Seriously? All you have to say is nice and thanks?"

I rolled my eyes and walked to the dress, giving it a more thorough look. "It's beautiful, Izzie. I never could've chosen one so perfect. Thank you, and I love you." I nudged her shoulder.

She sniffed. "Well, that's more like it, and you're welcome." With a wide grin, she added, "Besides, you know I love shopping. Now, back to your suggestion. It sounds dangerous. Why not tell Hunter your idea and get him to make the arrangement?"

"I don't know." I lowered my bottom lip to pout. "How about it would be a fun and exciting thing to do?"

Willow raised her arm. "I'm all in for some fun and excitement."

Izzie shifted her gaze back and forth. "I can see I'm overruled, which means I'm coming with you. Safety in numbers."

Mother Nature blessed us with a spectacular sunset, even though the cool evening required guests to wear lightweight jackets or sweaters. Better yet, a colorful sailboat remained still on the lake, floating in full view with the orange and purple sky in the background, as if its owner had planned to be part of the canvas scene. Our theme, Sunsets on Chautauqua, was perfect.

While Izzie wrapped up the event with a greeting to give thanks and the hope that everyone had an enjoyable evening, Willow and I began clean up, carrying equipment back to the shop. We had less than an hour to get to the trailer park. I was determined not to miss this one-time opportunity. Who knew what would happen? A lot of maybes were in play. Maybe Nick would be the one to show up. Maybe we'd corner him and demand answers. Maybe he'd tell us the truth. I very much doubted the last one had a chance of happening.

As I carried in the last chair, Hunter popped in to visit. Happy to see him but not about the timing, I forced a smile and enthusiasm in my voice. The last thing I needed was to give any hint of what we had planned. Plus, I wasn't ready to hand over the camcorder or explain how we have it. Especially the part about meeting alone with some shady character named Chuck. If we got the results we hoped for this evening, that news might ease any anger or reproachful lecture. "Hey, Detective. What brings you by? Miss me much?"

Hunter leaned down to kiss me. "I always miss you when we're not together." He straightened and waved to the chairs. "Have a minute?"

"This sounds serious. Everything okay?" I eased into a chair while he sat next to me. If he was delivering bad news, this was even worse timing. I needed my game face and full focus on the meeting with Chuck.

"Good news for you, actually. I spoke to the granddaughter of the woman in Jamestown. She admitted to telling her boyfriend about her grandmother's car, even letting him know where the key was hidden, in case he wanted to take a ride. The choices teens make really baffle me."

"They are teens, still learning. Come on, Hunter. It hasn't been that many years since we were teenagers ourselves."

"Speak for yourself. I was an excellent student and never got in trouble."

"According to Izzie, you were awkward and geeky. I imagine the very thought of doing something rebellious made you shake in your Reebok pumps." I teased him with a wink.

"Nice." He laughed. "I never wore those, but the rest was totally true. Anyway, I tracked down the boyfriend and got him to spill the story by telling him we have the traffic cam video and a clear shot of his face in the driver's seat."

I wagged a finger. "Way to use those detective skills, Barrett. Tell the kid a stretch of the truth just to get a confession. My how the geeky teen has changed."

He smacked his lips. "Yes, I have. The boy wanted to impress his friend by taking him on a joyride. He says the friend bumped him in the shoulder, trying to get his attention and check out some good-looking girl walking by. That move caused him to swerve and almost hit you. Not the lamest excuse I've heard, but I still lectured him how someone could've been seriously hurt. He'll have to go before a judge on charges of stealing a car. As for charging him with reckless driving and almost hitting a pedestrian, you'd have to attend the hearing and give a witness account. You up for that?"

I shrugged. "Sure, but don't be surprised if I suggest leniency. His story sounds kind of pathetic. Did you know the part of the brain that uses rational thinking—I think it's called the prefrontal cortex—doesn't fully develop until after the teen years? All those impulsive decisions and acts make sense, when you take that into consideration."

He chuckled. "Okay, Doctor Neuroscience. I'll let you know when he's scheduled for court."

I checked my watch. "I have to ask. Has Winsell said anything to you about Frank?" I held back what I'd learned from Evelyn. After all, that was public information. I was sure Winsell already knew of Frank's park proposal and the filed complaints about the amphitheater.

Hunter stood. "Frank did come to the precinct and talk to Winsell. All I know is that he confessed to being in the park the night Lana was murdered. His story matched what you told me."

He stroked his chin. "Still, Winsell asked me to check with people who might be able to verify when exactly he returned to the B&B that evening, or maybe anyone who noticed him in the park. Besides you, of course."

I gripped the chair. "Of course. In other words, Winsell doesn't want to accept I'm telling the truth."

"No." He laid a hand on my shoulder. "As I said before, he's meticulous with his cases. Checking, rechecking, and triple checking. It's exhausting working with the guy, but his record for solving cases accurately is near ninety-nine percent."

"What about the other one percent?" I twisted my mouth. "Hmm?"

"Nobody gets one hundred percent." He tweaked my nose.

"And the other suspects? Nick, Audrey, Rita. Is he doing the triple-check on them, too?"

Hunter sighed. "In time. Cases aren't solved in a day, Chloe."

"Or in two weeks, it seems. Okay, I'm through asking questions. I have cleanup to help with." I walked him to the door. "Thanks for letting me know how things turned out with the grandmother's car. She should really hide that key somewhere else, and putting a bolt lock on the garage door wouldn't hurt."

"Damn that prefrontal cortex. Right?" He winked. "I'll call you tomorrow afternoon to discuss the charity event and when to pick you up." He glanced up at the wall behind me. "Blue is your color. Goes well with that gorgeous black hair." He tugged at one tendril and kissed my cheek before leaving.

"Swoon."

I turned to find Izzie in the storage room doorway with one hand over her heart and eyelids fluttering. "Whatever. We need to hurry. We've got twenty minutes before showtime."

"You didn't tell him about the mask." She clucked her tongue.

I snapped my fingers. "All that swooning distracted me." I *was* distracted, but not by the so-called swooning. Winsell might suspect I'm not telling him the truth or holding back evidence. As for the latter, he'd be right. I'd talk to Hunter tomorrow and spill what I knew about the mask.

By nine, dusk had fallen into total darkness. Izzie, Willow, and I hovered close together behind a trailer. I moaned, watching Chuck pace back and forth in front of the row of trailers. He stood out underneath the yellow glow of a nearby lamppost.

"If he doesn't stop, whoever shows up will get suspicious," I whispered.

"He must be nervous. In his line of work, he probably meets all sorts of thugs, some with guns." Izzie's eyes widened.

"Yeah, that must be the reason." I met Willow's gaze, and we both smiled.

"Look! Someone's coming." Willow jabbed my arm.

To the far left, a tall figure stepped away from the shadowy cover of an oak tree. He paused, as if waiting. Taking something from his pocket, he lifted his arm and pointed.

"Holy wow! Is that a gun in his hand?" Izzie screamed.

I gasped as the man turned to look our way. "It's Nick." I took off, sprinting across the open area. I could never catch up, but I had to try. With any luck, he'd trip on a tree root or rock. I wasn't sure what I'd do if that happened. I was no match for his size.

After I reached the grove of trees surrounding the far end of the trailer park, I bent over to grab my knees and take several deep breaths. My heart pounded, and my head grew dizzy. I was not cut out for track, not sprints, dashes, or any other kind of race that involved this much exertion.

"Wow. You run faster than I remembered from high school." Izzie's words spilled out, then she paused, holding up one hand. "I think I'll stick to yoga classes. No wonder I don't buy a gym membership."

"Guys. Chuck is passed out on the ground," Willow said as she approached. Raising the object she held in her hand, she added, "Flashlight. Not a gun."

"It looked like a gun," Izzie mumbled.

"Guess it doesn't matter. We didn't get the proof we wanted." Willow led the way over to Chuck, who was now standing on his feet.

"True. At least we know the buyer is Nick. I'd bet those tapes are what he's after," I said.

"Are you sure? I mean, it is dark out. What about Frank? The guy ran fast, faster than we could." Izzie handed me a water bottle. "Always come prepared."

I thanked her and took a couple of swigs. "I'm ninety-nine percent sure it was Nick. And why be so determined to pin this on Frank? Besides, why would he want the camcorder? I doubt he even knows about it."

"That's true. However, I'm not ruling him out as the killer." Izzie lifted her chin. "You should give Hunter a call. The camcorder might be a good lead."

"Right." We'd done what we could. While I got on the phone to make that call, Willow asked Chuck if he was all right. She also told him whenever she had anything to unload, like furniture or appliances, she'd let him have first dibs. He seemed to like her idea because the smile on his face spread ear to ear.

"Hi, Hunter. If you have a minute, I've got news for you."

Chapter Twenty-One

The conversation hadn't gone as badly as anticipated. Hunter swept over the news about the mask with a grunt and focused his attention on our nighttime rendezvous. His speech about needing protection in dangerous situations didn't sound angry or too judgmental. He knew me well, and trying to keep me in a safe bubble would never work. He questioned how sure I was that Nick had been the one who came to the trailer park. I'll admit to feeling a bit offended, but he was right to ask. Winsell would expect that assurance. We ended the conversation with an agreed-upon time for him to pick up the camcorder.

I examined the lilac cuts we'd picked a couple of weeks ago and hung them in the basement to dry. "These look ready. What about the yellow trout lilies?" I turned.

Izzie stepped on the stool and lightly fingered the blossoms. "Yep. These will work, and so will all the phlox. I'm excited to use these in next Monday's event. Willow sure has great ideas."

Willow had talked about a craft activity she'd used with children when she worked in New York. That's when she suggested that rather than painting them we should use actual dried flowers and glue them to canvases. We finally decided to have the guests paint colorful vases with a window in the background, then add the dried flower sprigs. We'd named the event Burst of Spring.

I folded the ladder and placed it against the wall. "Yes, she does have wonderful ideas."

"Why so glum? We made some great progress last night," Izzie said.

"Did we? To me, it feels like being stuck on page one of a mystery novel. Not one of those suspects stands out. All of them have motives, but where's that gotten us?" I climbed the basement stairs.

Izzie stepped close behind me. "Well, I'm not sure, but we've certainly been busy trying."

"That we have." I closed the door after she passed by me.

"I know it sounds like I'm flip-flopping my opinion, but Rita can't be the killer."

I frowned. "Why the change of heart?"

"True enough, she's shown guilt by acting the way she does, but why would she knowingly do that if she was the killer? Wouldn't the killer keep a low profile and stay out of sight? At least not be anywhere near the crime scenes."

"I agree. Rita is bold and overly curious, but also smart." I snapped my fingers. "Smart enough to keep a close eye on the investigation. If you're guilty, you keep one step ahead and be ready to bolt."

"Ooh. That's some clever reasoning."

"Which brings us back to four suspects." I sighed. "See? Page one. That's where we are."

"Let's put this conversation on hold and talk about the charity event. Did you find a pair of shoes to go with the dress? How about jewelry? I have a sapphire necklace and earrings that are a perfect match." Her face beamed to compliment her cheery tone.

I caved and joined in. "Maybe you can go through my closet with me and choose a pair? I don't have any dress shoes, other than the black pumps, but I left behind several pairs of shoes in my closet when I moved to New York. Maybe there are ones that fit the occasion. You're much better than I am at fashion." I led the way toward the front hall.

"Sure! You know I'd love to." She squealed.

I chuckled. "Calm down, Fashionista." Relief washed over me. She was right. Too much thought about this case was stressful and not productive.

The doorbell rang as we reached the upstairs floor. "Ugh. Sorry, Izzie. That's got to be Hunter. He's early, but I'll be quick to hand over the camcorder and keep the conversation short."

Izzie waved. "Nope. You take your time. I will have fun all by myself picking out shoes."

"Thanks. Though I shouldn't be too long. We need to leave for the shop within the hour." I called out, but she'd already disappeared into my bedroom with Max scurrying after. I shrugged, took the stairs two at a time, and hit the floor in seconds.

"Good morning." Hunter stood on the porch with a flower in his hand. "For you."

"Sweet. From Mom's flower bed?" I sniffed the lavender sprig to hide the smile.

"Hey. It's the gesture that counts." He stepped inside.

"Yes, it is. Thank you." I planted a kiss on his cheek, set the flower on the foyer table, then picked up the camcorder bag. "One bag, one camera, and no tapes included."

He curled his fingers around the strap. "Winsell was impressed when I told him the story last night. That impressed *me*. I fully expected him to spout off a list of rules to follow in a proper investigation, most of which you avoided."

"He was talking to you, not me. Secondhand news is not nearly as effective. I'm sure he'll get to that lecture when we meet. Did he mention what he plans to tell Nick?" I bit down on my thumbnail. If only I could be the fly on the wall listening to that conversation.

"Story to be continued." He shrugged. "So, what time should I be here this evening? Are the four of us riding over together?"

"Yep. Izzie will obviously be late getting ready, but I'd say around seven would work."

"I'll see you then." He pointed behind him. "I should go. I have a few more people to question. Verifying Frank's alibi isn't as easy as it should be. He told Winsell he went straight back to the B&B after leaving the park, which sets the time to a quarter 'til nine or thereabouts. The idea of tracking down former guests and talking to all the B&B employees will take a while."

"I bet. Keep me posted. I'd love to hear how Nick reacts when he learns his tapes are still missing."

I hurried upstairs and found Izzie sitting on my bed, staring down at several pairs of my shoes. She'd sorted and lined them up according to color and heel height. I burst out laughing. "Only you."

At my insistence, we made a quick decision on the shoes, then drove to the shop. The day was dry, with a few gray clouds that hinted at rain, but nothing in the forecast called for bad weather. I'd take along my umbrella this evening, just in case.

I stepped into the shop just as Willow said goodbye and ended a call. "Hey. You're here early." I caught the frown wrinkling her forehead. "Is everything okay? Please tell me that wasn't your parents on the phone." From the stories Willow had told us, I knew how controlling they could be, despite the fact she'd signed papers to disclaim any rights to the family fortune. It seemed cutting the financial umbilical cord didn't help.

"Not them. Chuck. He told me the buyer contacted him. His text message said, and I quote, "Forget the sale. Dump the camcorder. Police are looking.""

"Hmm. I bet Nick got the call from Winsell. That could've put him on alert."

Willow swiveled a chair around and sat, resting her chin on the back. "Whatever Nick's feeling, Chuck sure is spooked. After last night, thinking his life might end with a bullet to the head, I don't blame him one bit."

"Yeah, me yelling the man had a gun didn't help." Izzie lifted her shoulders and smiled apologetically.

"The point is Nick had to be the one we saw last night. I'm sure Winsell has asked him to come to the station, maybe hinted at finding the camcorder," I said. "I'll give Hunter a call later and see what he knows."

"Do you think all of us should be worried like Chuck is? I mean, if Nick recognized us and he is Lana's killer, what would stop him from trying to take a shot at us?" Izzie clenched her bag before placing it on the counter.

"No, I doubt he'd do that. Too many bodies to bury." I dropped my jaw and covered my chest with one hand. "What? Too soon?"

Izzie scowled. "Not funny, now or ever. Suit yourself. I'm keeping my eyes open at all times. He could turn up when we least expect it."

"Fine. Now let's—" I snapped my mouth shut as Rita walked into the shop.

Talk about coincidence; I was about to suggest going over what we knew about Rita.

"Morning, ladies!" She punctuated her enthusiasm with a wide smile. "I'm here to get my canvas of the mural and amphitheater. So, take it out of that window display, please. I'm packing up to leave town soon."

"Huh. Okay. Do you need a canvas bag to store it in? We have a few in the storage room," I said while leaning across the window ledge to grab hold of her painting.

"Really? You aren't going to ask why I'm leaving town?" She rested one hand on her hip. "I'll tell you anyway. I got a full-time gig in Buffalo! It's huge news, and I'm beyond excited." Her voice shrilled.

I jerked at the high-pitched sound, and the remaining window display items toppled like dominos.

"Of course, Lou isn't happy. I told him if he insists on keeping our house, Buffalo is only a ninety-minute drive. I could come home on weekends and holidays." She lifted her chin. "I can't turn down the offer. I just can't." Her chest heaved.

"What exactly is the job you can't turn down?" Izzie handed her a canvas bag.

"Oh, I can't divulge too many details, but it's a business and involves mural painting." She slipped her canvas inside the bag. In seconds, she stepped to the exit, but before pushing the door open, she turned to wink. "Watch for me on the local news in the next few days. You'll get the full scoop then."

With that surprising announcement, she left. The chimes tinkled as the door shut, making the only sound in the room. We remained quiet, with me in my own thoughts. Izzie and Willow probably were digesting Rita's news, too.

"What a strange coincidence," Izzie said.

"Strange and suspicious." I couldn't avoid drawing the conclusion. It shouted loud enough in my head to make me go deaf. As an obvious suspect, leaving right now, before Lana's murder was solved, absolutely seemed suspicious. Yet, her story sounded legit. There was only one way to find out. We'd have to watch the local news. Or maybe we shouldn't wait. Just in case,

I picked up my phone to call Hunter.

"Who are you calling? Shouldn't we be discussing this? Rita might be a criminal, and she's getting away, going who knows where because somebody on the run wouldn't tell you where they were really going, would they?" Izzie gasped, running out of air from that lengthy, non-stop comment.

"Hunter. I'll see if he has time to track down Rita before she leaves town." I waited to hear him pick up, but got his voicemail greeting instead. "Drat." I left a message and ended the call.

The rest of the morning passed by quickly. We cleaned the place and reorganized the shelves in the storage room. By noon, I was ready for a break. When my phone rang, I grinned. "It's Hunter," I announced before heading out the back exit for some privacy.

"Hey, your message sounded urgent. What's up?"

The noisy chatter in the background told me he wasn't alone. "I'll make it quick. Sounds like you're busy."

"Not really. I had to stop by to pick up a lunch order for a couple of us in the office. I have plenty of time to talk."

"Good. It's about a visit we got this morning. Rita had some news that's concerning." I relayed the details.

"I'll head to her house as soon as I take this food back to the office. Let's hope she hasn't left already."

"Thanks. While I have you on the phone, do you know if Winsell informed Nick about the camcorder? The reason I ask is because we heard from Chuck. He got a message from the buyer." I gave him that information, too.

"I attended the meeting with Winsell to question Nick, who, I might add, was acting nervous at first. His eyes were twitching, and he stammered when he talked. But his behavior changed after Winsell told him we were keeping the camcorder until the case is solved. He flipped out. I mean, he totally lost it, demanded to know what his camera had to do with Lana's murder case. I gotta say, Winsell's strategy worked. He kept calm and said he was referring to the stolen merchandise case, not the murder."

"I don't understand. Are you saying Winsell was intentionally vague about which case in order to get Nick's reaction?" I paced back and forth in the small area behind the shop.

"That and by waiting until near the end of the conversation to mention there were no tapes found with the camcorder. Nick looked ready to pass out or explode, but then he didn't. He stood up and asked if we were finished. He couldn't seem to get out of the building fast enough. Definitely signs of a troubled man."

"One with a guilty conscience, if you ask me. So, what happens now?"

"Winsell is putting a tail on him until we have this case figured out. Hey, I'm approaching the Morgan's house. Let me call you back after I check on this."

It only took a few minutes when my phone rang again. "So, what did she say?"

"*She* didn't say anything because *she* wasn't there. Her husband claims he hasn't seen her since early this morning, which he insisted isn't like her. Not exactly the news we want to hear, is it? Besides that, he told me they argued a lot lately, but wouldn't tell me about what."

"Great. She could be all the way to Canada by now." I gripped the phone. Would this case ever be solved? I was beginning to have serious doubts. What puzzled me was why keep Lou in the dark? Rita had already talked to him about her job. I guessed that was the topic of their arguments. Unless she lied to us, fabricated the whole story as a cover up for what she really had planned.

"You don't believe her story about the job either, do you? I'm thinking the same. After my conversation with the husband, he agreed to my idea of putting out a BOLO to track her down. He claims she won't like it, but he doesn't care. He just wants to know she's safe."

The afternoon passed by slowly. Very few customers stopped in, mostly to grab copies of our summer events schedule. I reasoned that people were visiting dress shops, hair salons, and anything else having to do with the May Fling. Mom had told us this year's contributions for the charity auction set a record. Shop owners and residents were feeling extremely generous, I imagined.

"Maybe we should close up earlier than five. Business is dead, and it's not worth us staying when we could be getting ready for this evening. What do you think, Chloe?" Izzie sorted and stacked the paint samplers for the umpteenth time.

I smiled. "Well, since you asked, partner, I say yes, we should close early."

"Then it's settled. Willow, would you help me carry these boxes to the back?" Izzie shifted a couple of them in her arms.

"I'll add up the sales and close out the register," I said as the front door opened. "Or maybe not quite yet."

Penny took a few wobbly steps to enter, stopped, and leaned against the counter. With a flickering smile, she blew a stray wisp of blonde hair out of her eye.

I grabbed a water from the minifridge and handed it to her. "You look put out, Penny. What's wrong? Anything we can help you with?"

She held up her hand while downing half the bottle. Screwing the cap back on, she set the container on the counter. "I have been over every square inch of Whisper Cove, talking to any warm body I could find. And do you know what I have to show for it?" She drew a circle with her finger. "A big fat nothing. That's what. This reporter stuff is exhausting."

I gestured for her to sit down. "I'd have to agree. Exhausting and frustrating. That's turning out to be our experience investigating."

"The only thing I am sure of is that the killer is either Audrey or Frank. Or maybe Rita, but she's a bit goofy to commit murder, in my opinion." She tapped the counter.

"Oh? What about Nick?" Izzie came from the back and sat next to me.

Penny shook her head. "Off my list. I read the news about Nick becoming the head of Poling Industries. After a lot of financial woes that could've sunk the business, he managed to gather enough funding to keep it running. Anyway, I made up my mind that he wouldn't dare commit a murder only to end up behind bars for the next twenty to thirty years. Too much at stake and a whole lot of money to lose control of. He has a younger brother who'd be next in line. Rumor is he's a spending fool."

I frowned. "Wait. When did this happen? I never heard anything said about it."

"It was in the financial section a couple of weeks ago. I came across it the other day when I was searching for info about him. Seems the story was carried in major papers all over the country, including *The Buffalo News*."

My mind raced. The family business was in trouble, and Nick somehow found the money to save it. What if the money he used was what he'd stolen from Lana? Did she find out and confront him about it? She must've been livid, so angry that the argument turned physical. Two weeks ago meant she could've read or heard about it right before she was murdered. Maybe she threatened to go to the press and tell them about his criminal actions. That would destroy his family's reputation. Would Nick have been desperate enough to make sure Lana never got the chance to speak out? I shuddered at the thought.

I turned for a quick glance at Izzie. Her expression mirrored mine. We both knew what this news could mean.

"Thanks for the water, but I should be going. I won't stop until I figure out this story. See you ladies at the casino later." She stopped before reaching the door. "Almost forgot. Could you pass this along to Audrey since you'll probably see her before I do." She reached in her pocket and pulled out a small bottle. "It's the lavender oil she wanted. Poor thing has migraines that won't quit. At least the lavender helps some." She set the bottle on the counter, then turned. "As they say, reporters never sleep!"

My breath caught as I glanced at Willow whose eyes widened. Were we so focused on Nick that I'd ignored all the clues pointing to Audrey? The mask with red lipstick and lavender scent, her signature on the mural in bold red color, and the handcloth—how could I dismiss those? All because I decided Nick was the most-likely-to-kill suspect. I shook my head. This case couldn't get more complicated.

Chapter Twenty-Two

The Whisper Cove Casino displayed an array of colors decorated to celebrate spring. Sprigs of lavender, lilies, and tulips placed in vases provided centerpieces on tables while the walls and ceiling were filled with shiny appliqués and paper mâché streamers. The music set played by the band had been carefully chosen by the amphitheater's new music program director in a way to connect the May Fling event to the upcoming grand opening theme. Notes and lyrics from "Here Comes the Sun" by the Beatles streamed throughout the stereo speakers.

I linked my arm with Hunter's as we walked across the floor. Izzie and Brody followed close behind us. I tugged at the sleeve of my dress and winced at the tight fit.

"Are you all right?" Hunter asked.

"Yeah." I drew out the word, which sounded like a moan. "This dress is itchy. Thank goodness I insisted on wearing my sneakers." I stared at the more comfortable footwear.

His brow curled. "You must've had a fun time convincing Izzie. I bet she called them a fashion disaster."

"They match the blue dress. Besides, when I'm right, I'm right. Fashion sense or not, she didn't have a chance to win." I grinned.

He tugged at my hair. "My nature girl. Wouldn't want you to be any other way."

"Oh yeah? Well, tonight, you get the whole package." I teased with a wink and twirled around.

"As long as we spend the evening together, I don't care what you wear."

He squeezed my shoulder. "Let's dance. I think a slow song is coming up."

He was right. The soft tune of Ed Sheeran's "Perfect" shifted the mood to romantic. I rested my head against his chest as we stepped in time to the beat. From the side, I spotted Audrey and Tate talking. They looked happy, most likely because the mural was finished and payday would come soon. I imagined they were anxious to leave town. Unless Winsell came up with significant evidence, he had no reason to stop them. That concerned me. At least they'd showed up for the charity event despite all that had happened. "Have you heard any more news about Rita?"

"It's only been a few hours, Chloe. Give the authorities time. They'll find her."

"How about Nick? Any word about the tail put on him?" The dance was supposed to be a relaxing break, but I couldn't stop thinking about the case.

"No, and I thought you weren't going to talk about this tonight?" He raised my chin with the tip of one finger. "Chloe, let's enjoy a few hours of fun, okay?"

I groaned. "I'm trying. All these thoughts keep rolling through my mind, and I can't seem to stop them."

"Take it from me; you need to find ways to shut down those thoughts. If I didn't, I'd have quit this line of work." He pulled me close again.

My gaze shifted to the front entrance. I stifled a gasp. Winsell appeared in the doorway. His head moved back and forth as if he scanned the room to find someone. I tensed, hoping his eyes wouldn't fix on me. In seconds, he walked over to stand with Nick. From his gestures and Nick's expression, I suspected the conversation was serious. I leaned back. "I could really use a drink. How about you?"

"Sure. While I'm at it, I'll get us some chips for the gambling table," he said. Motioning to Brody to join him, the two of them headed across the floor.

Izzie hurried to my side. "Do you see Winsell and Nick? They seem pretty intense."

"Look. Winsell's on the move. Who's next on his list, I wonder?"

"Not you, I hope." She nudged my arm.

My gaze followed him as he maneuvered through the crowd of guests and around tables. He stopped to take one of the glasses of punch and drank it down. "He doesn't act like he's in any hurry. Maybe he's not here for business."

"Forget him." Izzie pointed. "Look who's anxious to leave the casino. Do you think it's because she spotted Winsell?"

I followed her finger to where Audrey stood before turning to pass through the doorway leading outside. From her vantage point, Audrey wouldn't have been able to see Winsell clearly. "Maybe, but those huge potted plants kind of block her view of the other side of the room. I think we should focus—" Before I could finish, Izzie took a quick path toward the back exit which led to the lake, the same direction Audrey had taken. "Dammit, Izzie. Really not smart." I griped under my breath.

With only seconds to react, I grabbed the sleeve of the person close by. "Hi, if a tall, handsome man with brown hair and eyes asks you where his date is, please tell him I'll be somewhere out back by the lake." I didn't wait for a response. The puzzled look of the woman didn't give me much hope the message would reach Hunter.

As I struggled to move through the crowd and dancing couples, Winsell spotted me. I slowed my pace and nodded with a smile. I couldn't decide whether his presence would be needed. After all, Audrey might have gone outside for some fresh air, and the situation was totally innocent.

I scanned the room for Nick, who had disappeared. My gut told me that wasn't a good sign. Now, both he and Audrey were MIA. My gaze shifted sideways, and I clutched my throat. The stranger from the council meeting who'd approached Audrey entered the room. Though he hadn't worn the hat this time, I recognized the stocky build. The graying hair hinted he was much older than Audrey. Could he be her father? Maybe he begged her to return home to France, and that pressure upset her.

"Excuse me." The stranger smiled as he stood in front of me.

I wasn't sure how to react. "Do we know each other?"

"*Mais non.* Audrey is my friend. I don't suppose you've seen her this evening?"

His accent was thick, but he managed to speak English perfectly. The smile wavered a bit, and his eyes expressed concern. Risky or not, I made a snap decision. I pointed to the rear exit. "She left a few minutes ago. I'm worried, so I plan to follow. Maybe you'd like to join me?"

I clutched my dress on the sides and hurried my pace, maneuvering around every obstacle to reach the door. "Bet you wish you'd worn sneakers, Izzie Abbington," I whispered. Weaving around a server carrying an appetizer tray, I cleared the way to reach outside.

"I'm Chloe, by the way." We were half way down the slope leading to the lakeshore.

"Glad to meet you, Chloe. I am Émile Trousseau." His voice grew breathless. "May I ask why we are running? Please tell me." He grabbed my arm to pull us to a stop. "I demand to know what has happened to my fiancée."

My jaw dropped. I didn't know what to make of that news, but obviously, Émile was truly worried. He was staring at me with wild eyes. "Fiancée?"

"*Oui*. I am. I *was* a professor at the university. We met there."

I looked over his shoulder to watch Izzie running down the path and Audrey only yards ahead. How anyone could move that fast in those heels, I couldn't imagine.

"Chloe? Why are we running?"

My attention snapped back. I grabbed his hand and pulled, pursuing Izzie and Audrey once more. "There was a murder, and I think Audrey might be involved, or at least she knows something about it." I paused speaking for a second to mull over what he'd told me, and to catch my breath. "Why were you two arguing at the town meeting?"

He nearly tripped over a clump of dirt in his path. Stopping for a second to regain his balance, he straightened his shoulders before we moved on. "I warned her she should go to the police. The truth is always best, and she was so very upset when we spoke."

I set my jaw and kept my gaze straight ahead. The problem was killers avoided telling the truth. I had to wonder, did Audrey confide in him? However, this wasn't exactly a great time to ask. Plus, he wouldn't take it so well if I came out and called his fiancée a killer.

A scream pierced the silence, but it sounded rather faint. I guessed whoever made it was farther down the shoreline and near the amphitheater. I picked up speed until I spotted Izzie. She stood yards away from Audrey. I stiffened. They weren't alone. I recognized the tall, athletic frame of Nick.

"Come on. We need to move faster." I tugged on his sleeve but then sprinted to reach Izzie, leaving Émile behind. I was more concerned about Izzie's safety, and Audrey's. I skidded to a stop when I got a clearer picture. Maybe I should've thought about Nick's safety too.

Audrey waved a gun at him. "Don't you dare come closer. I swear. One more step, and I'll shoot." She wiped the snot off her lips. "You ruined me. All those accusations? That's right. I know." She wiggled the gun. "You've been trying to frame me, feeding that detective lies so he'd think I killed Lana."

"We have to do something." Izzie rasped and squeezed my arm.

I inched closer to the side where Audrey stood. "Audrey, why don't you put the gun down?" I spoke as calmly and softly as I could. "Nobody needs to get hurt."

She swung around and pointed the gun at me. Her eyes were filled with panic, like a cornered animal ready to attack anyone who tried to catch it. In an instant, she blinked. Tears overflowed, and as if it had grown too heavy, she lowered the gun slightly.

Nick took that moment to step closer. He extended one arm, palm facing down. "She's right, Audrey. No one needs to get hurt. Hasn't there been enough of that? Lana's dead. I loved her too."

"What is going on?" Émile stepped alongside me, out of breath. "Audrey?"

Audrey whimpered and shook her head. "No, Émile. Why did you come?" The gun dropped to her side.

Nick took several more steps, now only feet from Audrey. "We need to stop this."

Audrey's expression suddenly hardened. She narrowed her eyes and glared, pointing the gun once more. "I won't go to jail for something I didn't do. I cared for Lana like a sister. You had no right." She heaved a sigh. "No right to take her from me."

CHAPTER TWENTY-TWO

He took another step. "Audrey, please."

"No!" She leveled the gun at him. "She was kind and generous. She gave you everything, and you took and took and never really cared. She loved you, Nick. Why would you kill someone who loved you?"

Voices shouted in the direction of the casino. I turned to glimpse Hunter, Winsell, and Brody running toward us.

A loud grumble sounded from my side. All at once, Émile pushed past me and charged at Nick. In seconds, he tackled him to the ground. "You are a coward. *Tu es mort, le diable.*"

"What did he say?" Izzie whispered.

"Something about a devil and dying. My French is a little rusty." I prayed Hunter, Winsell, and Brody would get here quickly. Izzie and I were not equipped to tackle two men or Audrey, who still held on to that gun.

"Émile!" Audrey shouted. She aimed the gun at Nick. "I'll shoot."

Émile was no match for Nick's strength. As if his anger had erupted, Nick sat on top of Émile, his hands wrapped tightly around his neck.

"Stop! You're hurting him," Audrey cried. "I'll give you the tapes. I promise. Just please stop."

"The tapes?" Izzie and I shared a look. Audrey had stolen them. Did she know what Nick was hiding? She must've found something serious enough. Otherwise, she wouldn't have kept them.

Running steps pounded down the hill. Both Hunter and Brody tackled Nick, releasing his stranglehold around Émile, who now gasped for air and clutched his throat.

Audrey rushed to embrace him in a tight hold while kissing every inch of his face and neck. "You crazy man. What were you thinking?" She sputtered her words and strained to keep from crying.

"Nick Poling, you are under arrest for the murder of Lana Easton." Detective Winsell continued to read him his Miranda rights while placing him in handcuffs.

"I didn't murder her. I swear. I loved Lana with all my heart." Nick cried out as one of Winsell's team members led him to a waiting cruiser.

"Are you okay? Nothing broken or bruised?" Hunter checked me from head to toe then pulled me close with arms wrapped tightly around me. "Not cool. Running off like that," he whispered. The warm breath tickled my neck.

"It was kind of cool." I leaned back and smiled. "Chloe Abbington, artist by day, sleuth by night. She catches her man, or woman, no matter what."

He tweaked my nose. "Nope. You don't get to scare me like that. You could've been—Oh, what the heck." He kissed me hard.

Winsell strolled over and cleared his throat. "I don't mean to interrupt this cozy interlude, but we have a job to do, Detective Barrett."

"Absolutely," Hunter said.

"Tell me, Detective. You who always goes by concrete evidence, what made you determine that Nick was the killer?" I tilted my head. He hadn't heard Audrey's accusation or how she'd kept the tapes that everyone was searching for.

Winsell scratched his chin. "Let me give you a few more words from my experiences. Not everything is connected to an investigation. Take the broken ladder Miss Easton fell off of, for instance. I can't prove someone deliberately tampered with it since I don't have concrete evidence. Or your graffiti bandit. He or she may never be caught. There are always loose ends and things that never get solved."

He sighed. "In this particular case, I hate to admit, the concrete evidence, as you put it, wasn't something I deduced or found. Quite the opposite. Someone who'd been in the park that night, filmed Mr. Poling standing on the lift along with Miss Easton and the moment she fell to her death."

"Someone? Who's the someone?" I raced to think of who the person could be.

"Interesting and very unexpected. A boy from Mayville and his friends came that night to the park. They planned to vandalize the mural, but when they found people there, that scared them away. The boy's father brought him to the precinct to confess. Turns out, the group of teens were the ones who painted over the mural that Sunday morning Rita discovered the damage.

"Let me jump to the punchline. This boy wanted to film their crime and show it to all their friends. However, when he saw what happened to Miss Easton, he kept the video a secret. Afraid of getting in trouble, I imagine. That was until this morning when his father learned the whole story." Winsell sighed. "Teenagers can be a handful. I know. I have three boys."

"But why? I still don't understand why they were so determined to ruin the mural." I shook my head.

"A couple of the boys have fathers who worked during the amphitheater events. They lost their jobs," Winsell explained.

"Convoluted logic and a way to get revenge to defend their dads. It's like you said. Teenagers. Who gets them?" I gave Hunter a peck on the cheek and watched as he and Winsell walked to the parking lot.

"Hey. What was that conversation about?" Izzie approached with her arm wrapped around Brody's waist.

"I'll tell you after we get home." I nodded at Audrey and Émile, who were cuddling with their faces cheek to cheek. "Right now, we should give those two some alone time."

We walked to the car, then rode home. I stared out the window. The night sky filled with stars and a full moon. No doubt, I'd learned a few tips from Winsell about detective work. The importance of thoroughly investigating, never guessing or making assumptions, always going by concrete and verified evidence to prove a case. However, in this instance, his slow, calculated investigating wasn't what solved Lana's murder. Some kid with a cellphone who happened to be in the park at the time, ready to pull some foolish prank, solved it. I leaned back against the headrest and chuckled. Talk about dumb luck.

Chapter Twenty-Three

I placed the bunches of dried flowers on the front table for guests to select. Checking my watch, I grew anxious. Hunter should have arrived ten minutes ago. Not the ideal time to talk about Lana's murder when our class would be painting pretty vases with colorful flowers attached. I had lots of questions for him, and he promised to deliver, this evening. Earlier this morning, he'd told me one piece of information. Audrey had taken the camcorder and dumped it in the trash bin. When Nick had confronted her, she'd denied knowing anything about the equipment or the tapes. There was more to the story, and that's what I was impatient to hear.

I waved to Izzie and waited for her to come closer while keeping my eye on the three guests who'd arrived early.

"What's up?" Izzie asked. She picked a spot of puffy paint off her blouse. "How do I always miss some? Remind me why I agreed to host a children's birthday party? I wish you'd been there. Willow's giddy mood in reminiscing about her days at the children's Paint and Play center. I mean, those kids are sweet, but so loud."

"Listen. When Hunter gets here, would you and Willow take over the event while I talk to him about a few things?"

She smiled. "Love is definitely in the air. Go ahead." She waved the towel in her hand. "I think we can handle it."

The chimes pinged to announce a visitor. I turned. Hunter walked into the shop and waved with a nod at me. I met him halfway and clasped his hand. "To the storage room for some privacy."

I pushed down on his shoulders to sit and pulled up a bench close to him.

"Spill. I want to know everything." I rolled my hand in a continuous circle.

"Hey. Good evening to you too. How's the event going? I had a great day, thank you." His smile crinkled the corners of his eyes.

"I'm sorry. Good evening, and yes the event will go well, which happens to start in five minutes." I tapped my watch.

He leaned forward. "About the tapes. Winsell and I watched enough to see Miles convincing one of the electricians to cut corners. When the electrician bulked, saying that kind of shoddy work could cause a fire, Miles promised to pay him a hefty bonus if he'd go along with the idea. Totally illegal, which he and the electrician will have to answer for."

I wrinkled my nose. "What a slimeball. He's even worse than Frank described him."

"Just wait. Audrey kept the tapes because she'd overheard Nick on a call in his hotel room. He had the speakerphone on, so she caught both sides of the conversation and immediately recognized Miles' voice. Seems Nick blackmailed Miles, claiming he'd turn over the tape he had of him to the police if he didn't come through with the money and make sure Audrey got the job to finish the mural." Hunter pulled out a stick of gum and popped it in his mouth. "As for Audrey, she got scared when Nick threatened her and accused her of stealing the camcorder. So, she dumped it and kept the tapes to protect herself."

"Audrey must have taken the camcorder back to the hotel after she finished helping Lana that evening. Before she could return it to Nick, I bet she overheard the conversation he had with Miles, then decided to check the tapes for herself."

"You guessed right. And I imagine Nick suspected Audrey had the camcorder, but filed the report with us anyway, to cover his tracks."

"Yeah, he did. After Tate asked where his camera was, right where I could hear the conversation, Nick knew what could happen." I chewed on my lip and gave the conversation some serious thought. "Did Nick confess? After you told him about the boy's phone video proving he was with Lana that night, I can't imagine he'd deny it."

"Confessed would be putting it mildly. He cried while blubbering on and on, giving us the entire story. We didn't have to prod or convince him to talk."

"Wow. So, give me details. I need to know what could've been so awful that he killed my friend." My heart ached. With a few deep breaths to calm myself, I let my shoulders relax.

"She wanted to break off their relationship. She confronted him about the embezzling and the recent news she learned about his family business. Nick was desperate. He had a choice to make and only seconds to decide."

I nodded. "He went with telling her the truth."

"Yep. And he said she didn't take it well. In fact, she became even angrier when he admitted to using her money to save his business. He begged her to forgive him. He swore his plan all along was to put the money back into her account and hope she never found out what he'd done." Hunter smacked his leg. "No trust, no honest relationship, never works."

I grew sad, and my stomach churned. To think his words of betrayal were the last thing she heard before falling to her death. I struggled to speak. "Did he push her? When he knew he'd lost her, did he push Lana off the lift?" I pressed a hand against my chin to keep it from quivering.

Hunter's head shifted slowly. "He says it was an accident. Supposedly, he grabbed her arm to stop her from backing away and pleaded for her to listen. That's when she lost her balance and fell off the lift. He swears he tried to hang onto her, which explains the bruises on her arm." He drew his hand down the front of his face. "He left her there, Chloe. Left a dying woman there alone. I can't..." He stopped for a second. "He'll face the judge tomorrow morning."

I stood and reached to put my arms around him. "He'll get what he deserves. What Lana deserves."

We stood this way for a minute or two until I heard Izzie calling for me. "I should go. Stop by the house later, if you have time. Okay?"

"I'll be there." He kissed me on the head. "We have things to discuss."

My brow lifted. "Really, do we? Now, I'm curious."

Izzie called out again.

"Seriously. I'm coming," I shouted. "See you in a few."

Hunter went out the rear exit, and I headed to the front. He'd given me lots to digest, but the best takeaway was knowing Lana's killer had been caught. Though it was bittersweet, she'd have justice. That had to account for something.

I sat on the front porch swing with Izzie, soaking in the pleasant and peacefully quiet evening. With another successful event in the bag, we were already looking forward to the next. Izzie had discovered gyotaku, a Japanese artform, and she'd chatted about it nonstop on the way home. The idea came to her during a visit to the Florida Keys a few years ago.

"I think it would be so cool to do one of these projects this summer. Can you imagine the fun? We take the guests out to fish, then bring the catch back to the shop. Why are you shaking your head?" She frowned.

"You really want to smell up the shop like that? How about we take the event outside? Or we could use those plastic fish replicas and forget the fishing expedition."

"Huh, you're so right!" She pushed off to swing even harder. "Let's decide that part later. Anyway, we'll need to order rice paper and black ink and special brushes. We can watch videos on how it's done."

"I love the idea." I squeezed her hand. Izzie's enthusiasm was infectious.

"You know what else we should love? How about Audrey's and Émile's wedding announcement? I'm so psyched they invited us to the event. Next summer in Paris? The Louvre. The Eiffel Tower. *L'arc de Triomphe*. Did I say that right? And the medieval castles. Bistros to dine on baguettes and drink French coffee. That would be fantastic. Don't you think?" Izzie beamed.

I laughed. "Calm down. We'll go for sure. But that's next year. I'm just glad Audrey and Émile worked things out."

"Ooh, can you believe her news about the videotape she kept?"

"The one with her and Lana arguing that night? Yeah, I understand why she worried how incriminating it would look, but keeping it from the authorities wasn't right."

"Obstruction of justice and all that. Certainly goes to show the desperate measures people will take." Izzie stood.

"Even good people. Besides, she seems to regret what happened. I always thought she hated Lana. Here it turns out she admired and respected her, even defended the way Lana treated her. Go figure." I stared out at the lake as Hunter pulled up.

"Well, Lana did help keep Audrey's family out of the news by paying off the reporters. I'd be grateful if someone helped me in that way. Thank goodness you were wrong about her being the killer."

"Me? Don't you mean us?" I rolled my eyes.

"You were the one who thought the mask meant she was guilty."

"No. I said it could mean something, but turns out it didn't." I glared until she burst out laughing. "Ha. Ha. Funny you."

Izzie walked to the front door when her phone buzzed. "Ha! Would you look at that?" She held out her phone to show me the local news streaming with the clear image of Rita sitting next to someone. She sat back down while we watched part of the interview.

"What do you know? Rita told us the truth. Sounds like a big deal. Custom Wall Décor comes into your home and paints whatever mural you'd like. We should do something like that." Izzie's voice pitched higher.

I wagged a finger. "How about we handle that idea later. Okay?"

"Yeah, you're right. Maybe next month we can discuss it." She tapped her lip.

I stifled a moan. Later always meant sooner to Izzie.

"You two lovebirds enjoy your walk." She winked and entered the house.

"Hey there, handsome detective." I stood on tiptoes to kiss him.

"This detective is off duty and ready to relax." He pulled me close. "You want to take that walk, now?"

"I do." I held his hand as we crossed the lawn and on toward the lake. Moonlight lit the path along the shore. In the distance, I spotted a tall, lean man jogging toward the park. A smile surfaced as I recognized the familiar profile of Frank. "Izzie and I watched the evening news on her phone. Rita was telling the truth. She has a new job in Buffalo selling and painting custom wall murals for residents. Izzie is already getting ideas on how to expand our reach. She never stops." I laughed.

"I heard. Lou Morgan called this morning to tell us. He confessed to knowing Rita had interviewed two or three weeks ago, but that was it."

"Ha. That explains things. Or I think it does."

"Explains what?"

"She was probably getting some tips on painting murals by watching Lana and Audrey at work." I detailed Rita's appearances both the day Lana died and when attending our mixed event. "She always bragged how she was an expert at mural painting, but that could've been all a bluff."

"Could be." He wove his fingers through mine and swung our arms back and forth.

My heart skipped. Such a small gesture filled me with love. "Say! Did you hear the news about Frank? He's taking over the amphitheater as production manager to replace Miles. Seems things are looking up for a lot of people now that Nick has been arrested. I wonder when the trial will—" A finger touched my lips, and Hunter shook his head.

"No shop talk, okay?"

I scrunched my nose. "Sorry."

"I was thinking we should plan a dinner with my mom. She'd like to meet you." He stared straight ahead.

I didn't miss the quick side glance, though. I pressed my lips together and kept a serious face. "Oh? So we're at the meet-my-mom stage of our relationship? I didn't know."

He stopped. His brows knitted together. "Listen, if you don't want to. I mean, if you're not ready. I only suggest it because this seems to be a serious relationship we've got going, and I don't—"

It was my turn to place a finger on his mouth. "*Shhh.* I was kidding. I'd love to meet your mom. Just let me know when." I paused a few beats. "Serious relationship, huh?"

He lifted my chin and slowly leaned down to kiss me. "As serious as it gets."

Acknowledgements

First, I'd like to thank my former agent, Dawn Dowdle, who worked tirelessly and gave my career and this series new life. She shared her enthusiasm and encouragement when I needed it most. She will be missed and always in my heart. To my editor, Shawn Reilly Simmons, and all the staff at Level Best Books, thanks for guiding me through this journey. You all make the journey much less daunting.

A huge thanks to all the artists and their works, especially Ruston Baker, whose wall murals can be found in places all over the world. Also, I'd like to give a special shout-out to Sara Aiello, an artist from Warren, Pennsylvania. She hosts so many creative paint party events, including those with children. Something I'll be featuring in future books. Her work is impressive and inspiring. Of course, I'd be remiss not to mention the setting of this series, inspired by visits to Bemus Point, New York. Picturesque and quaint, with a view of Chautauqua Lake. The town is inviting. The people are friendly. All the perfect characteristics of a cozy mystery town and its people.

Finally, to those in my life—family, friends, and the author community—who have nurtured me in many ways. And to my muse, my furry pal, Max. You are the star of this series and a light in my life.

About the Author

Bailee Abbott is a native Ohioan who spends her days plotting murder and writing mysteries. "She's a member of Sisters in Crime as well as International Thriller Writers and Mystery Writers of America." Bailee lives with her husband and furry friend Max in the quiet suburbs of Green, Ohio. Visits to Bemus Point, a town along the Chautauqua Lake in southwest New York inspired the setting for the Paint By Murder mystery series. Bailee also writes the Sierra Pines B&B mystery series under the name Kathryn Long.

SOCIAL MEDIA HANDLES:
    Twitter: https://twitter.com/BaileeAbbott1
    Facebook Page: https://www.facebook.com/BaileeAbbottBooks
    Goodreads: https://www.goodreads.com/author/show/21094675.Baile
e_Abbott
    Instagram: @baileeabbottbooks

AUTHOR WEBSITE:

https://www.baileeabbott.com

Also by Bailee Abbott

Writing As Bailee Abbott:

Paint By Murder Mysteries
   #1 *A Brush With Murder*
   #2 *Kill Them With Canvas*

Writing As Kathryn Long:

Sierra Pines B&B Mysteries
   #1 *Boarding With Murder*
   #2 *Snowed Under Murder*
   #3 *Blooming With Murder*

Mackenzie Blue Mysteries
   #1 *Buried In Sin*
   #2 *Played By Death*

A Deadly Deed Grows

When I Choose

Dying To Dream